SOLDIER OF SIDON

SOLDIER OF
SIDON

GENE WOLFE

A TOM DOHERTY ASSOCIATES BOOK  TOR® NEW YORK

SOLDIER OF SIDON

Copyright © 2006 by Gene Wolfe

Illustrations by David Grove

A Tor Book
Published by Tom Doherty Associates, LLC
175 Fifth Avenue
New York, NY 10010

www.tor.com

Library of Congress Cataloging-in-Publication Data

Wolfe, Gene.
    Soldier of Sidon / Gene Wolfe.—1st ed.
      p. cm
    "A Tom Doherty Associates book."
    ISBN-13: 978-0-765-31664-6
    ISBN-10: 0-765-31664-1
    1. Latro (Fictitious character)—Fiction. 2. Egypt—History—To 322 B.C.—Fiction.
3. Soldiers—Fiction. I. Title.

PS3573.O52S645 2006
813'.54—dc22

                                2006044619

First Edition: October 2006

Printed in the United States of America

0 9 8 7 6 5 4 3 2 1

To

SIR RICHARD BURTON

THE AETHIOPIANS WERE clothed in the skins of leopards and lions, and had long bows made of the stem of the palm-leaf, not less than four cubits in length. On these they laid short arrows made of reed, and armed at the tip, not with iron, but with a piece of stone, sharpened to a point, of the kind used in engraving seals. They carried likewise spears, the head of which was the sharpened horn of an antelope; and in addition they had knotted clubs. When they went into battle they painted their bodies, half with chalk and half with vermilion.

—HERODOTUS

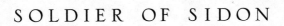

SOLDIER OF SIDON

FOREWORD

SOME YEARS AGO I gave myself the fascinating task of translating two ancient texts in the possession of my friend D.A., scrolls of papyrus discovered in the basement of the British Museum. When I had completed my (admittedly tentative) translation of the second, I declared my work at an end.

A year ago, I received a letter from another friend, the Egyptologist I will call N.D. As is generally known, the ruins of the ancient nation of Nubia now lie almost entirely under the waters of the lake created by the Aswan Dams. Prior to the construction of the dams, strenuous efforts were made to salvage Nubia's archaeological treasures, particularly the famous temple of Isis on the Island of Philae. At that time, the science of underwater archaeology was in its infancy.

It is not so today. Underwater archaeologists, N.D. among them, are probing the depths of the lake and bringing to light many items of interest.

Among these was a sealed vase of post-Pharaonic times. Opened again after two and half millennia, it was found to contain a papyrus scroll written in the Egyptian style with a reed brush, but written not (as was first supposed) in hieratic characters but in archaic Latin. When the first sheets had been translated, N.D. kindly sent a copy of the entire scroll to me.

In translating the whole, I have assumed that the narrator was that of the earlier scrolls. The abundant evidence favoring that assumption will be apparent to every reader. Further, the style is the same, if it can be called that. The narrator (who refers to himself as "L") abbreviates almost every word, creating manifold opportunities for error. He does not punctuate or divide his text into paragraphs, much less chapters. All such divisions are mine. As previously, I have employed the first words of each chapter as its title, and have tried to re-create conversations he summarizes.

The modern reader is cautioned to lay aside all preconceptions concerning ancient Egypt and Nubia. We tend to think the Egyptians morbid, for example, after viewing so many collections of grave goods. It is the opposite of the truth. They loved life, and took loving care of their dead in expectation of a general resurrection.

As the narrator himself was told (as he writes, by a god), the Egypt of the classical period fairly swarmed with divinities. These cannot be organized into a single rational system. Their powers, and importance, varied by place and date, while the priests of each glorified the god they served at the expense of all the rest. Be warned that books purporting to list all the gods of ancient Egypt do not. Be warned also that there is no such thing as THE Book of the Dead. Books of the dead were what today is called a publishing category. Certain elements are common to all; many more depend on which is consulted. Note too that Egypt (which had no more wolves than any other African nation) had a wolf-god, presumably imported at an ancient date from the Near East.

Readers of this third scroll should keep in mind that the Egyptians were famous throughout the Mediterranean world for hard drinking. They seem to have been the first nation to brew beer and the inventors of the beer joint. Beer, the beverage of the Egyptian working class, was drunk from bowls through straws of baked clay. Each drinker was given his straw with his first bowl. When he left, he broke the straw so that it could not be given to another patron. Archaeologists have found millions—literally millions—of these broken straws.

Dancing in taverns and at private parties was segregated by sex. Unmixed wine was drunk at upper- and middle-class parties, which often lasted all night. Egypt produced great quantities of good wine and imported more from Greece. Without the papyrus scrolls that were traded for Greek wine, we would know little or nothing of Homer, Pindar, Sophocles, and scores of other ancient authors. Nor would we have had the first two scrolls written with such desperate clarity by the brain-damaged mercenary who called himself Latro.

Marriage in ancient Egypt was casual in the extreme. Polygamy was common in both the middle and upper classes. A man's chief wife, his *hemet,* was usually, although not always, his first. A queen of Egypt—Nefertiti is a famous example—was the chief wife of the pharaoh. Our puritanical Egyptologists frequently characterize lesser wives as concubines, but this is incorrect; they too were wives (*hebswt*). A man of wealth spoke of his wives, not of his wife and his concubines.

No ceremony, religious or civil, was required for marriage. Marriage contracts were negotiated only when property was involved. Marriage normally required the consent of the bride's parents or her guardians, as well as that of the bride herself. Many girls married at twelve.

The "singing girls" who figure so largely in this scroll are ignored or disguised by most of our writers on ancient Egypt. A famous picture found in a Theban tomb shows a half-dozen richly dressed women singing, clapping, and playing musical instruments while two naked girls, smaller in the picture because they were less important, dance. The books that reproduce it, or more often some part of it, rarely explain it. The well-dressed ladies are guests at a party. The naked dancers are singing girls, hired entertainers.

Another picture, not as widely reproduced as the first, depicts a naked singing girl with her instrument. Long-legged, large-breasted, and slender, this Egyptian miss would have fit neatly into any show in Las Vegas. The cleansing passage of thousands of years has reformed the singing girls; they are called exotic dancers, go-go girls, or strippers now, and have been stripped of their priestly protection. Morality is satisfied.

Slavery in ancient Egypt was legal but rare, perhaps mostly because of the many protections afforded slaves by the law. Aside from galley slaves, such slaves as Egypt had were nearly all servants in upper-class households. If a free man married a slave, their children were slaves; to forestall this, the bride was often freed before marriage.

Many writers on popular Egyptology dwell on Egypt's supposed isolation and peaceful character. These suppositions are erroneous to the point of absurdity. The delta lay open to the Mediterranean and seaborne invasion. The as-yet-unidentified "Sea Peoples" struck by sea and overland (from the east) in the time of Ramses the Third. The date would have been approximately 1176 B.C. To the west, the Libyan nomads were numerous and warlike. To the east, Egypt's immense border beckoned any army with sense enough to follow the coast, as the Persians did—twice.

To the south lay the valiant, half-savage nation we call Nubia. The Nubians conquered all Egypt at one point, giving it an entire dynasty of Black pharaohs that lasted from 780 to 656 B.C. The mysterious Hyksos (although often translated as "shepherd kings," this name probably meant "foreign rulers") had overcome Egypt a thousand years earlier, around 1800 B.C.; their rule endured for 150 years.

Not only was Egypt open to foreign invasions, it was subject to internecine fighting of every kind. When the monarchy was weak, local governors behaved as local governors have elsewhere.

A rational discussion of Egyptian history and military organization requires an understanding of Egyptian geography. Above the delta, Upper Egypt was little more than a river valley stretching south along the Nile for about five hundred miles. Borders are always dangerous, and Upper Egypt was all border. Prudent statesmen draw the borders of nations along seacoasts—or when that is not feasible, down the channels of rivers. Egypt's river was the spine of the nation, not its border.

Small wonder then that Egypt had history's first standing army, for centuries not merely the best but the only standing army in the world. (The gripes so characteristic of infantrymen were first recorded in hieratic script.) This army was a large force organized along startlingly modern lines, with disciplined units similarly equipped. It consisted of two corps, one of infantry and the other of chariots. A third corps might be formed of mercenaries, most often from Nubia, less often from Greece or Libya. In one well-nigh incredible instance there was a fourth corps, of students from the Egyptian equivalent of West Point. The ships of the Egyptian navy were commanded by soldiers, and were considered a part of its army.

It would be easy to fill an entire book with details of Egyptian weapons and military practice. Two very different swords were in use, for example. One, apparently of Egyptian design, was a sharply curved scimitar. The other was long, straight, and double-edged; it seems to have been an importation, probably from Nubia.

Writing of the Sudanese more than two thousand years later, Kipling said,

'E 'asn't got no papers of 'is own,
   'E 'asn't got no medals nor rewards,
So *we* must certify the skill 'e's shown
   In usin' of 'is long, two-'anded swords . . .

After describing these weapons, which are far older than Christianity, modern commentators sometimes theorize that they were copied from swords brought to Egypt by the crusaders. Spears, maces, angled war-clubs like that used by the narrator, daggers, hatchets, and broad-bladed battle-axes were in common use as well. Armor was light, and worn almost exclusively by the soldiers and officers who manned chariots. The Egyptian infantryman rarely had any protection beyond his big shield.

There were two areas in which Egyptian military capability was notably deficient. Although the upper class (which furnished the army with chariot commanders) boasted fine archers, the use of the bow was almost unknown to the middle and working classes. Further, the Egyptians were charioteers, not horsemen as that term is usually understood. Their army needed cavalry and more archers; both these deficiencies were made up by enlisting mercenaries from Nubia whenever Egypt and Nubia were not at war.

To picture Egypt and, particularly, Nubia at the time this scroll was written, the reader must understand that North Africa has been drying up for thousands of years. Twenty thousand years ago, the Sahara was a damp plain dotted with shallow lakes, the home of great herds of hippopotamuses. Rock carvings in the pitiless desert west of the Red Sea show men and dogs hunting giraffes.

The term "Nubia," so often employed by the narrator, is itself interesting. It was only just coming into use in his day, and he may well have introduced it. If so, he presumably picked it up from his Phoenician friends and Latinized it. The original Phoenician probably meant "Land of the Nehasyu." This is the riverine tribe the narrator most often calls the Crocodile People.

The ancient Greeks called Nubia *Aethiopia*—"Land of Burnt Faces." Note that some ancient geographical terms such as Nubia, Aethiopia, Kush, Nysa, and Punt were very vague and meant different things in the mouths of different speakers. Nysa *may* sometimes have referred to the area around Lake Nyasa in Central Africa.

People speak carelessly of Egyptian darkness and the Riddle of the Sphinx. The facts are that the Riddle of the Sphinx is Greek, not Egyptian, and that we know a great deal about ancient Egypt. We understand its language and possess thousands of inscriptions and documents, up to and including love songs and love letters. (Some are charming. In one letter a young man stoutly avers that he would wade a crocodile-infested stream to be with his beloved. In a love song, a young woman yearns "for him to send word to my mother." He may have preferred the stream.)

Nubia, however, is a genuine enigma. At the time this scroll was written, its people did not speak Nubian, but the largely unknown language that we call Merötic. Because they wrote it in Egyptian hieroglyphics as well as in what we call Merötic script, we know how it sounded, the names of some kings, and a few other words. But no more than that. There has been no Nubian Rosetta Stone.

Both the Nehasyu and the Medjay, the principal Nubian tribes, were expert archers and horsemen. Nubian kings paid enormous prices for fine horses from Arabia Felix. (Fortunate Arabia—Arabia, too, was better watered in those days.) Favorite horses might be buried with great ceremony in elaborate tombs.

The Medjay, the narrator's Lion People, were nomads who drove their cattle and horses wherever the grass was long. Employed originally to fend off raiding parties from Libya, their duties were soon enlarged. By late Pharaonic times they were Egypt's police. Many Nubian mercenaries married Egyptians and settled in Egypt.

Allow me to note in closing that the ancient Egyptians, who invented and discovered so many things, never had a coinage of their own. The gold pieces with which the Phoenician captain fees the priest of Hathor, and no doubt most of the other coins mentioned in this scroll, are those of the occupying Persian Empire.

PART I

I

RA'HOTEP SAYS

I AM TO write everything that takes place on this scroll, as concisely as I can. I will try. I must read this every morning, too. Muslak will tell me. I must have Myt-ser'eu tell me also. Let me begin with the first things I remember.

We left the ship and searched for an inn, ate and drank there, and slept in the same room. It was crowded and some of us returned to the ship to sleep, although I did not.

I woke when the others did, awakened, I think, by their footsteps. We ate again, and Muslak told me his name and that he is the captain of our ship. "We're in Kemet, Lewqys, with a cargo of hides. This was where you wanted to go."

I said, "I have been trying to remember my name. Thank you."

"You couldn't remember it?"

I shook my head.

"That's bad. Your memory comes and goes. Now it seems like it's gone. Know why we're here?"

I said, "To sell the hides, I suppose."

"But what about you? Why are you here?"

I had thought myself one of his ship's crew. Clearly I was not, so I shook my head again.

"That settles it. I'm taking you to a healer. They have the best healers in the world right here, and you're going to see one." He rose and motioned to me, and I followed him.

We spoke about healers with the innkeeper and set off for the House of Life, near which they are found. Here I should say that this bustling city is called Sais.

It is of great interest. First, because it seems so strange. Second, because I feel that I have seen such a place long ago. It is familiar, in other words, yet seems very foreign.

The houses of the poor are thatched mud huts, so small that most of the things other peoples do in their houses must be done outside. They have no windows. Only a few are painted.

The houses of richer folk are very different and are gaily painted, most often green, blue, or both. Some are of mud brick, though their paint deceived me until we had walked some distance. Some are wood. Some are of mud brick at the bottom, with wood higher up. All are surrounded by walls that prevented me from seeing what was in their courtyards. Often these walls are yellow or ocher, though a few are orange or red. At first I thought there were windows on the second level alone. Then I recalled the room in which we had slept, how high it was. I think these rooms are like that. The doors of the houses are small and low, the windows small and near the ceiling. It must be because the sun is so hot here.

Before I write of the healers, I should say that all these houses have flat roofs, and that some of the houses really are of two levels, both lofty. There are gardens on the flat roofs. I have seen many flowers there, and even some palms. These must be planted in tubs. There are also triangular sails, or perhaps tents, always two and always back-to-back. The sailcloth is as bright as the houses. I wanted to ask Muslak what they were, but was afraid he did not know and did not want to embarrass him.

The first healer we spoke with was a tall, lean man, as many men are here.

"This fellow," Muslak said, indicating me, "is a mercenary officer who has served the Great King. He's a good man and a fine fighter, but he cannot remember his name. Every morning we must tell him who he is and where he is, and why he is here."

The healer rubbed his jaw. "Why is he?"

(I should write that this was not said in my own tongue, in which I write it, but in the speech of Kemet, which Muslak knows much better than I.)

"He saved me from slavery," Muslak explained. "The price he asked was to be returned to his home in Luhitu."

"You did as he wished?"

"I did, and the next time that we put in there I looked him up to see how he was doing. I hoped he had his memory back and would remember me. He was as bad as ever, but he had written 'Riverland' above his door. I talked to his wife, and she said it was to tell him he must go there again to find out what had happened to him. I asked some other people what it meant, and it is their name for your country."

"Ours is the Black Land," the first healer said. (*Kemet* is *black* in their speech.)

"I know. But other people have other names for it. Anyway, I told him we would go there to trade, and he was welcome to sail with us if he wanted to. His wife wanted to come along, too. I told her it was impossible—a ship has to have special arrangements for women, and we didn't have them. She said she would come anyway. I told her she would be in a lot of danger. You understand."

The first healer nodded.

"Somebody would lift her skirt, then kill her so she couldn't tell Lewqys. Because Lewqys would kill him sure. He's a terror with that crooked sword. When I was to be sold, they had two men guarding us, and he killed them both before they could draw breath."

"His wife is not with you?"

Muslak shook his head. "He came down to my ship in the harbor when we were nearly loaded, but he came alone. I think he must have written his law on her as soon as I left. But what's wrong with him? That's the point. Why can't he remember?"

"I was not merely inquisitive," the first healer explained. "A wife often knows things a man's friends do not. I hoped to question her." He clapped his hands. "I want to consult a colleague of mine."

"You think we're all rich," Muslak said. "Let me tell you that it isn't so, and until I can sell my cargo I'll have very little."

A boy came, and the first healer told him to bring Ra'hotep.

While we waited, the first healer talked with me, asking my name. I gave it, and he asked how I knew it. I explained that Muslak had told me.

"Would your wife call you so?"

"I don't know," I said. "I did not remember that I had a wife until now."

"When we are born, we do not know how to talk. You remember how to talk, clearly."

I nodded.

"Also how to use your sword, from what your friend says."

I said that I did not know whether I knew or not, but it seemed plain how such a sword must be used.

"Just so. May I look at it?"

I drew my sword and offered it to him hilt-first.

"There is a word written here," he said, "but it is not in the true

Thoth-inspired writing. I cannot read it. Can you?"

"Falcata," I said. "It's the name of my sword."

"How do you know that?"

I said I had read it on the blade this morning, which was a lie.

"If he were in the grip of a xu, he would not have handed me his sword," the first healer told Muslak. (I think this word must mean *daemon* in their tongue.) "Also, he speaks sensibly, and those who are in the grip of a xu never speak sensibly for long. Has he anything to gain by shamming?"

"Nothing," Muslak declared, "and he couldn't have deceived me for more than a day. Besides, he pretends to remember sometimes. He wouldn't do that if he were faking."

The first healer smiled. "So, Lewqys, you lie to us, do you?"

I said, "I suppose I do. All men lie at times, it seems to me."

"Oh, really? I would have said not. Who has lied to you recently?"

"I don't know."

While we spoke, the second healer entered. He greeted the first politely and took a stool.

"This foreign man forgets everything," the first healer explained. "His friend the ship-master has brought him to me. The disorder is of long standing."

Ra'hotep nodded, not looking at the first healer but very intently at me. He is shorter than Muslak, and perhaps twenty years older.

Muslak said, "Lewqys is a mercenary. He owns a farm in his own country. His relatives work it for him while he is away."

Ra'hotep nodded again in the manner of one who had reached a decision. "Was he like this when you met him for the first time?"

Muslak shook his head.

"Tell me of your first meeting."

"We were upriver. We'd sold our cargo and were looking for something else—papyrus at a good price, cotton cloth, or whatever.

He had found out that the satrap had sent troops to the Great King, not his own troops from Parsa, but Nubians and your people. He had a hundred men and tried to get the satrap to hire them too. He wouldn't—he'd already sent the Great King what he'd asked for. I told Lewqys he'd have no trouble in Byblos—that's my own city. They'd be snapped up there, and good money. He said he'd go, but he didn't have enough to hire my ship. He'd have to march overland."

"And did you, Latro?"

He was clearly speaking to me. I asked if that was also my name.

"It's the name I was given by your comrades when I saw you with the Great King's army. It took me a moment to recall it, but I'm sure that was it. Did you march overland? It's difficult."

"I don't know."

"You clearly reached this man's country in some fashion. When I treated you, it was said you were one of Sidon's soldiers." Ra'hotep turned to the first healer. "He is somewhat improved, but not greatly. Have you anything to suggest?"

They spoke of herbs and potions for some while. I could not write all of it here if I wished to. Ra'hotep said that he had tried to drive out a xu and thought there was none. The first healer tried, but achieved nothing. He gave me medicine to take each day.

This is important. Set is master of the bad xu. He is the god of the South. There is a temple far to the south where a successful appeal to him might be made. Muslak says he does not know it.

He paid the first healer. Ra'hotep gave me this scroll, some reed pens, and a cake of ink; but he would take nothing, saying he had been of no help. I offered him my sword, saying truly that I had nothing else. He said I was the soldier, not he. He would not take it. I must talk with him further whenever the opportunity arises, and make him a gift when I can.

Muslak and I walked back to our ship. Muslak said we would go to the temple of Hathor tonight, as we did. "She's a helpful goddess," he told me, "and she may be able to help you. We're right here, and what's the use of not trying?"

I said, "None, of course."

"Right. Besides, I want to hire a singing girl, and that's where you get them."

I asked whether he meant to give a dinner for someone.

He laughed. "I want a wife for the voyage upriver. Now you're going to say I wouldn't take your wife when she wanted to go with you."

I said I recalled his telling the physician about it.

"It was the truth. It's one thing to take a singing girl upriver, something else to take a decent woman across the Great Sea. If one of my crew gets to my singing girl, it won't matter much. I'll punish him and that will be that. Besides, we won't sleep on the ship. I'll have her on shore in a room to myself."

Merchants were waiting to view the hides in our hold, portly, serious men with many rings and oiled skin. At Muslak's order, sailors carried up three and four hides of each kind. They were of fine quality. The merchants went down into the hold, chose others, and carried them up to view in the sunlight, which was then so bright as to be almost blinding. I helped, and these hides too were fine. Several made offers which merely amused Muslak.

He explained to them that he can get much a better price in the great cities to the south. The merchants here in Sais will offer only the lowest prices, thinking that he will wish to sell what he has and get another cargo quickly.

Some time after we ate, a soldier of Parsa arrived with a letter for Muslak. I studied this soldier, for it seems I have been a soldier of Great King's just as he is. He was of medium height, bearded, and appeared strong. He had a bowcase, a light ax with a long haft, and a dagger. He wore more clothing than most people do here.

Muslak scowled at first when he read the letter, then smiled. When he had finished, he read it again before he rolled it up and put it into his chest.

The three of us found a scribe, and from what Muslak said I learned that the letter had been from the satrap of Kemet. Muslak told him that his ship was large and sound and his crew strong, and declared that he would obey at once. The soldier left with Muslak's letter, although I would have liked to speak more with him.

"You'll see thousands like that, Lewqys. We're going to the White Wall, the biggest fortress in the whole country."

"To see the satrap?"

Muslak nodded. "To see Prince Achaemenes himself. He has a job for us."

I asked whether this Achaemenes would pay us, for I wish to earn money.

"He says he'll reward us handsomely." Muslak fingered his beard. "He must be one of the richest men in the world."

There were more merchants, but the heat made me sleepy. I found a shady spot under a tree in the courtyard of our inn and slept.

2

IN THE EVENING

MUSLAK WOKE ME to go to the temple. He asked what I remembered, and I told him everything.

"That's good. You'll have forgotten most of it tomorrow, I'm afraid, but you may remember telling me now. Here, carry this."

It was a ram skin dyed red, very fine. "We'll have to give the goddess a nice present," Muslak explained, "and that can be sold for a good bit more than I'm willing to give."

The priest smiled when I held it up, and accepted it graciously; he is a tranquil man of middle height and middle years, with a shaven head. I took advantage of the moment to ask about Hathor, explaining that I was a stranger to his country and knew only that she was a great goddess here.

He nodded solemnly. "I would rather try to teach you, young man, than those who feel that they already know more than enough, as I must so often do in the House of Life. First let me assure you that no mortal ever knows enough, much less more than enough. You have seen her image?"

I shook my head.

"Then come with me. We will go into the forecourt."

It is a vast building, and the columns that support the lintel are larger than the houses of the poor and as tall as trees. Lamps flickered within, lonely dots of yellow light in the gloom. Beyond them, the broad doors of the inner temple were half closed. Through the opening I glimpsed the image of the goddess.

That, too, is huge, taller than any of the tall private houses we had seen. Its dress is rich, and it gleams with many gems. In form, it is a woman with the head of a cow.

"Hathor was wet nurse to Osiris," the priest explained. "We give animal heads to many of our gods to illustrate their honor and authority. You foreigners are frequently puzzled by it, wishing your gods to be like yourselves. Hathor is not like us, but a mighty divinity. It is Hathor who feeds the dead and governs love and the family. . . ."

I heard no more. A horned woman taller than any man had stepped from behind the image of the goddess. As she strode toward us, it seemed that some other held a lamp behind her, so that her whole form was outlined with light, although her smiling face was shadowed. "You go into danger, foreign man," she told me. "Do you wish my help? You may have it at a price."

I wanted to kneel but found I could not. My body was still standing next to Muslak. "I need your help very much, Great Goddess, but I have nothing to give but my sword."

"You will have other uses for that. You are strong and a warrior, a man who has much love to give, and protection to give to those you love. Will you give those things, if I help you?"

"Very willingly," I said.

"That is well. I am going to send my kitten to you. You must love and safeguard her for my sake. Will you?"

"With my life, Great Goddess. Where is it?"

"Here. She will come to you and rub herself against you. When she does, you must accept her as your own."

The goddess was gone as though she had never been. The priest was saying, "There are seven Hathors along the river, and all are Hathor. When they meet, they decree. Whatever they decree must come to pass, no matter what gods may do or men may say."

I asked, "If they were to decree that I was to remember as other men do, would it happen?"

The priest nodded, his face more solemn than ever. "Whatever they decree must come to pass, as I told you."

"I've nothing to offer," I said; then recalling what the goddess herself had told me only a moment before, I added, "beyond love and protection."

"You have prayers to offer, young man. Those alone may be sufficient. As for love, it is hers. Therefore those who love have her favor. Not all that passes for love is true love, however. Do you understand?"

I nodded.

"As for protection, many families require it. Protect them, protect children particularly, and you will gain her favor. Rich gifts from the rich are very well, but the things the goddess most desires are things anyone can give."

Muslak asked, "Will you pray for Lewqys here, Holy Man?"

"I will."

"And for me and our ship?"

"I will do that also, Crimson Man."

Muslak cleared his throat. "That's good. Now I'd like to hire a singing girl to go to Mennufer with me. The satrap wants my help."

"In which case," the priest said carefully, "you must provide it."

"That's right." Muslak cleared his throat again. "Now as I understand it, I can pay a flat fee and get a girl for the trip. Is that the way you do it here?"

The priest nodded. "For a long journey up the river, if you choose, and if you will return here at journey's end."

"Absolutely. I'll be going back to my own city after I've helped Prince Achaemenes."

"Then there is no difficulty. You must treat your singing girl well every day that she is in your company, you understand. Share your food and so on. You may beat her, but not beyond reason and not so as to endanger her life. She is entitled to leave you if your provisions for her are worse than those you provide for yourself."

Muslak nodded.

"When you return her, you will owe no more, since you must pay the full fee in advance. It is customary, however, to make some gift to her if you have been pleased."

"I will," Muslak said. "Something nice. I should have quite a bit of money when I've done what your satrap wants."

"He is not our satrap, Crimson Man." The priest frowned.

Muslak shrugged. "He's not ours either, the way you mean. But we've got to do what he says. So do you."

"You wish to hear the singing girls?"

Muslak nodded.

"First I must see the color of your gold."

Muslak shook a few coins from his burse into his hand and displayed them.

"One of those," the priest said, and pointed.

"A daric? That's too much!"

"You are accustomed to bargaining," the priest told him, "and will bargain much better than I. I will not bargain at all. One of those, and I must hold it first and pass on it."

"You yourself told us there are six other Hathors on the river." Muslak sounded indignant.

The priest smiled. "Go to any. You have my leave."

Muslak turned on his heel and walked away. I followed him very reluctantly, recalling what the goddess had said. When we had nearly reached the entrance to the forecourt, he stopped and turned back. "One daric? That's the price?"

The priest had not moved. "Unless you wish to give her something when you bring her back. That is voluntary."

"All right," Muslak said, "let's see them."

The priest held out his hand.

"After I've had a look at them."

The priest shook his head and continued to extend his hand.

"Suppose I don't like any of them?"

"Your money will be returned," the priest told Muslak. In this and in everything, the priest seemed neither angry nor eager; his eyes showed neither disgust nor fear. I admired him for it.

"All right," Muslak said at last.

The coin changed hands. Smiling, the priest left us and strode to a small gong near one wall. He struck it twice, and returned to us.

"What about you, Lewqys?" Muslak grinned at me. "Want a singing girl?"

I shook my head.

Soon we heard the murmur of voices and the shuffle of bare feet on the stone pavement. Five young women joined us. All were comely, with shapely legs and high breasts. All wore black wigs, as all but the poorest women do in this land. Two bore instruments.

The priest asked Muslak if he wished to hear them sing.

Muslak nodded and pointed.

"They will all sing," the priest said, "then you can quickly choose her whose voice you think sweetest." He signaled to the women, and they sang at once. I could catch only a few words of their song, but their girlish voices were lively and merry. Those who held instruments played them with a will.

"Her," Muslak said.

35

"With the lute?"

He hesitated. "No, the one next to her."

The priest gestured. "Come, Neht-nefret."

She came forward smiling and took Muslak's hand.

"This trader is going to Mennufer on his own ship," the priest explained. "When his business there has been completed, he will return here. You will be his wife until you return."

Neht-nefret said softly, "I understand, Holy One." She is indeed tall for a woman, but no taller than some others.

The woman with the lute, shorter it might be by twice the width of my thumb, came forward too, taking my arm and rubbing her soft flank against mine.

"That trader does not wish a wife," the priest said severely.

"He's a soldier, not a trader like me," Muslak explained. "He's from Sidon." He turned to me. "Lewqys, you said you didn't want one."

"I want a handsome husband," the young woman with the lute declared, "and I would like to visit Mennufer, and all the grand places along the river." She feigned to be speaking to Muslak, but watched me slyly from the corners of her kohl-rimmed eyes. All the perfumes of a garden filled my nostrils.

The priest shook his head, a little sadly as it seemed to me. "You must go back, Myt-ser'eu."

I was trying to grasp the meaning of her name when I caught sight of the clasp on her headband. It was the face of a cat.

"She wants to go because I'm going," Neht-nefret told Muslak. "We're friends. You can have two of us, if you like. I won't mind."

The priest nodded. "You may, for another such coin as the first."

"But not this one," I said. "I want this one for myself. Give this holy man another daric, Muslak."

Myt-ser'eu giggled.

Muslak did, saying he owed me far more than that.

3

———

IN THE SHADE OF THE SAIL

WE ARE WARM, although not unpleasantly so. Myt-ser'eu fans me with a palm-frond fan. It cools her as well, or so she says, and waves away insects. Here I write, as Muslak has explained I must. He says a healer gave me this scroll and my cake of ink. My pen is a frayed reed. I dip it in the river and find it difficult to write as small as I wish.

Myt-ser'eu laughs at my letters and offers to show how her people write. Neht-nefret says she writes better. She will show me, not Myt-ser'eu. I will not let either have my pen, although this scroll is so long. I will write on both sides. Who can say where I can find another?

Muslak has sold all the hides in our hold. It took most of the morning. As soon as the money had been paid, we put out. This river is the Pre. Myt-ser'eu says there are three big rivers through this land, and many smaller ones. The Pre is the largest. She shows three fingers. This River Pre is the first. They come together farther south to make the Great River. After that, there is but one. She and Neht-nefret do not name it. It is the river. Muslak calls it the Great River, and says that Hellenes say Neilos or Aegyptos.

The fields to left and right are marvelously fertile. I do not believe I can ever have seen such fertile land. If I had, it would not surprise me as it does. Everything is green, dark and full of life. The crop this year will be bountiful. All these fields are as flat as my hand. Here and there, there are small hills. These have a house or two on them, or a village when they are larger, I suppose because they are less fertile than the fields. People who till the land cannot be rich, but these look well fed and seem busy and content. When we wave, they smile and wave in return.

The river is sea-blue or blue-green. It looks like good water, but Muslak says those who drink of it fall ill. Everyone drinks well water, wine, or something else in this land. I am going to ask the women about this.

THEY SAY WE must not drink from the river at any season, and that it changes color to mark the changes of the year, now blue, now red, now green. We can wash ourselves in river water, but not mingle it with wine to drink. It will be bluer at Mennufer, Neht-nefret says. She has been there, though Myt-ser'eu has not.

Myt-ser'eu wished to know what I had been writing; I read it to her. The houses and villages are built on the hills so they will not be drowned when the river rises. Sometimes it rises very high, and then they are swept away and must be rebuilt. Neht-nefret says it is better to build on red land, but there is no red land here. I said I would make a raft of logs and live on that. She said wood was costly.

―――――

NOW I HAVE seen a raft such as the people here build. It was of reeds. These would rot soon, or so I think. Being on this ship made me think of rowing. I believe I have done that—my hands know the loom of a sweep. I asked Muslak whether we would row when the wind died.

"It won't. The Great River is the best for shipping in the whole world, Lewqys. A north wind blows you up it for most of the year. When you want to go back down, you can furl your sail and let the current do the work."

That is marvelous indeed if it is true. Since we spoke I have seen a big boat rowed. The white oars rose and fell with the chant, so that it seemed to fly. It was gay with paint, the property of a rich man who lounged in the stern, and flew very fast, like a warship. Who could object? Such things fill the bellies of the poor.

Our ship is not like it, though it is painted too. Ours is wider and has a tall mast and a big sail. There are ropes to brace the mast, and others to hold the corners of the sail, which is sewn of many strips. There can be no loom wide enough to weave such a wide sail. When I spoke of this ship to Myt-ser'eu, she explained that the satrap wants it, and us.

"Don't your people build good ships?"

"The best in the world." Myt-ser'eu looked proud. "Our ships are the best, and our sailors the best."

I glanced at Muslak and saw that he smiled. He does not agree, and it seems to me that he must be right. Little skill can be needed to navigate this river, if it is as he says.

"Then why doesn't the satrap use your ships and your sailors?" I asked Myt-ser'eu.

"He doesn't trust us. The Great King treated us terribly in my mother's time. Now he is not here and things are better, but he fears we will rebel against him. Our soldiers are very brave."

I asked Muslak what he thought of them.

"They are," he told me. "Many fought for the Great King, and they're tough fighters—better than my own people are. We're sailors and traders. When we need soldiers, we hire mercenaries."

Looking at this green land, where barley shoots up wherever a seed is thrown, I can see that what Muslak said must be true. Only good fighters could hold it. If the people of Kemet did not make fine soldiers, it would be taken from them.

OUR SHIP PASSES white temples as massive as mountains— mountains white as snow beneath this blinding sun, and sharp and pointed as any sword. Who would have thought human hands could make such things? Neht-nefret says the ancient kings are laid there. The people of Kemet built many temples, Muslak says, and very large ones, of which the mountain-temples are largest of all. If gods wished temples, would they not build them? They build mountains and plant forests instead, and that is what I would do were I a god.

IT IS MUCH later. I am on the roof of our inn, where I write by lamplight. Myt-ser'eu is asleep, but I think I will wake her soon. I have read this scroll, and see that I must write. I will do this first, though I must hold the papyrus very near the lamp to see the letters.

We are staying here for the night, though most of the sailors will sleep on the ship. Muslak and Neht-nefret have a room on the floor below, but my river-wife and I sleep in this roof-bed. We are in a tent of nets, which seems very strange to me. The mosquitoes are evil here, she says, and her people sleep as high up as they can to escape them. The wind that blew us up the Great River blows the mosquitoes away, if they fly too high.

There was music and dancing tonight, which Neht-nefret and Myt-ser'eu wished to join. Muslak agreed to pay, and all four of us had a fine time. Everyone who was not dancing or playing the flute sang and clapped. I did not know the songs, but I clapped with the rest, and quickly picked up the choruses. The young women danced and danced, which was very pretty. Myt-ser'eu was the loveliest, and Neht-nefret had the most jewelry. All eyes were on them, which they greatly enjoyed as anyone could see. Three men played double-flutes while two beat drums. The young women swayed, stepped this way and that, shook rattles, snapped their fingers, and kicked higher than their own heads while we sang and cheered.

We did not drink wine, but "beer." It is a wine made from barley. I cannot imagine how a juice can be pressed from barley, but that is what Myt-ser'eu says and Muslak confirms. Chaff floats upon it, there is a taint of leaven. It is warm with cardamom and too heavy and sweet for my taste, but I drank two bowls because everyone else drank. Sucking up the beer through a tube of thin clay leaves the chaff on the bottom when the bowl is empty. When the evening was over, we played a game in which we broke our clay tubes. He who holds the longest piece wins.

At last the young women tired and the young men danced. It was an easy dance, so I joined it. I was not the best dancer and the rest laughed at my errors, laughter without malice that even a child could bear. I will dance better next time. The flute-players and drummers did not join our dance. All the women sang, most clapped, and Myt-ser'eu played her lute. When everyone was tired we drank more beer and washed in the river. She wears an amulet that protects her from crocodiles.

In what I read today I wondered about the sails I saw on roofs. This inn has such sails, and Myt-ser'eu explained them. There are holes in the roof below for both. One is open on the north-facing side and catches the north wind, directing it into the inn. The other lets the wind stream out again. The first is like the mouthpiece of a flute, the other like the little holes a player fingers. Our inn is the flute. When the wind blows well, as it does tonight, the rooms inside are cool and there are few mosquitoes because the doors and windows are shut. Myt-ser'eu says her people are the wisest in the world. I do not know that, but they are surely very clever.

I was a soldier in a city called Sidon. That is plain from what I read. I wish to go there and speak with those who may remember me. Muslak says that when we leave Kemet we will sail to his own city of Byblos, and that it is near Sidon. It will be easy, he says, for me to reach Sidon from there.

Now I will blow out the lamp and wake my river-wife. There are others sleeping on the roof. I do not think they could watch us even now. When the lamp is out, they will surely be unable to watch us through the nets, which are fine nets for small fish. These a man might see through in sunlight, but the other sleepers will not be able to watch even if they wake. I must remember to be quiet, and to hush Myt-ser'eu, who moans and trembles.

4

NIGHT HAS GONE

I HAVE WATCHED the boat of a god bring the sun, a great and wonderful sight I must set down here so that it shall never be forgotten. He steered the boat that held it. With him were a baboon and a lovely woman who wore a plume in her hair. His head was that of a falcon. When the sun cleared the horizon they were gone, and their boat with them. Perhaps the falcon-god flew away. Perhaps it was only that they and their boat could no longer be seen in the glare of the sun. I would like to ask the woman who slept with me about them, but feel I should tell no one. Some things are too wonderful to be spoken of.

We are in a ship at anchor. I remember lifting the anchor with another man. We threw it over the side, careful not to be caught in its cable. The woman had made a place where she and I could sleep, in the stern too near the captain and another woman. "Come to my bed," she said, and motioned to me in a way I found irresistible. We lay upon a folded sail and covered ourselves snugly with the sail-cloth, for the wind grew cool when the sun was gone. She whispered of love, and we kissed many times. I caressed her and she me, I wondering always whether the others slept; at last I heard them snore. When we were exhausted and ready for sleep, the stars above us shone brighter than any jewels. They seemed close enough to touch, tracing men and strange beasts.

I woke early, sore from sleeping on the folded sail. I stretched and scratched, and looked for something better than river water to drink, but found nothing. Soon, I thought, I would return to the sleeping woman and embrace her again. The east grew bright—I saw the prow of the boat that bears the sun, and watched. Then I saw the falcon-headed man with his steering oar, and the other gods, and knew that I must write of them, as I have.

MYT-SER'EU AND I lounge in the shade. No one works now but the steersman, who must keep our ship turned so that our sail catches the wind. Our sailors talk, argue, lay bets, and wrestle for sport. I could wet my pen with sweat, but it leaves a black mark on my chest.

I have had my head shaved, and that is why I write. Neht-nefret saw me scratching and examined it. I had lice—she showed me several. Myt-ser'eu says I got them in an inn, but I do not recall an inn. She cut my hair as short as she could, and Neht-nefret oiled it and shaved it with her razor. The two of them made a hundred jokes at my expense and laughed merrily, but I could tell they were dismayed by the scar they found there. They guided my fingers to it.

Neht-nefret and Myt-ser'eu shave each other's heads, Neht-nefret said, and said too that I had seen them do it but that I can remember nothing. That is not quite true, yet true enough to sadden me. They wear wigs.

Between kisses, Myt-ser'eu is sewing a headcloth for me such as the men of her people wear. (I know that this is so because I saw one on the riverbank not long ago.) It is simple sewing, a circle large enough for my head at one end, another a little larger at the other.

MY HEADCLOTH IS finished. It protects my shaven head and my neck and ears from the sun. Muslak laughs and says no one will know I am foreign. Neht-nefret insists we do not speak well enough for men of Kemet and teaches us both. We try to speak as she does while Myt-ser'eu giggles. Azibaal and the other sailors say only Muslak is brown enough—I am too red. Both women say brown is better and feign to spurn me.

THREE WARSHIPS ARE passing. They have sails but are rowed as well, and so go very fast. There are bearded men of Parsa on them, and men of Kemet too, long-legged soldiers with spears and enormous shields. We would have died very quickly, I think, if they had attacked us. The women say they would be raped, not killed, and Muslak and I would be chained to benches and made to row. I would not be chained. I would rather fight and die than row until death under the whip.

Those ships are nearly out of sight now, but we still hear their drums beating the rowing-rhythm. There is no singing. Free rowers would sing at the oars, or so it seems to me. The whip steals the song.

Muslak says the ships belonged to the satrap, the brother of the Great King. This satrap wants our ship too, though he has many others. Muslak does not know why.

Before I cease to write, I must write that we sail on the Great River of Kemet; it is because of this river that Kemet is also called

Riverland, I think. Is it a great nation, as Neht-nefret and Myt-ser'eu insist? I do not see how that can be when it is no more than this green valley. I have climbed the mast to look at it, and it is so narrow here that I could see the desert to my right. The valley land is black wherever it is not green—the contrast with the ocher desert beyond could escape no eye. We passed a distant city—its name is On, says Neht-nefret. Myt-ser'eu wished to stop there so she might look into the shops before its market closes, but Muslak refused, saying we must make Mennufer before dark.

Many canals water the land, but the river does not dwindle because of them. This seems strange.

One bank is near, to our right. The other is so distant now that it can scarcely be seen. We sail here because the current is slower, and because Mennufer is on this side. Ships coming down the river hold the middle of the channel; those sailing up, as we are, the sides. There are many palms, tall, graceful trees whose leaves grow only at the top. They sway and sway in the wind and were surely lovely women not long ago. Some jealous goddess turned them to trees.

OUR SHIP IS tied to a pier at Mennufer, but Myt-ser'eu and I share this room and will sleep here. When we docked, Muslak told us he would hurry to the White Wall to tell the satrap we had come. Myt-ser'eu and I said we would see the city. He gave me money for the purpose. I bought Myt-ser'eu a necklace and new sandals, but we still had more than enough to eat at this inn. After eating we returned to the ship; but Muslak was not there, and Neht-nefret said he had not returned. She was angry because he had not taken her to the White Wall—she has never been inside, while Myt-ser'eu has not been to Mennufer before at all. Myt-ser'eu and I returned to the inn and rented this cool and comfortable room, four flights up and next below the roof. Servants brought us water in which to wash and will wash our clothes for us, bringing them in the morning. Our bed is matting stretched on a wooden frame. It seems very poor to me, but Myt-ser'eu says it is better than the one we had at the last inn. I have an oil lamp with a fine, high flame to write by.

The city is noisy and crowded, exciting but tiring, particularly when one goes from shop to shop in the jewelers' quarter. The streets are narrow, and the buildings crowd together like men. The floor on the street is always a shop. There are other things above, and Myt-ser'eu says sometimes these are finer shops for the rich. This inn has a cookshop on the street—it was where we ate—and rooms for rent above. The highest are best and cost most. The walls at the street are very thick, as they must be to support so many levels above them. This keeps the lower levels cool, while the wind and a thick roof cool the upper levels.

Myt-ser'eu wants to buy cosmetics tomorrow. She says that she may only look at them and we may buy nothing, but I am not so young as to believe it. She also says that her own city, called Sais, was the capital of Kemet not long ago. Now the satrap rules from here, and she is glad. She would not wish him and all his foreign soldiers in her city. I am a foreign soldier myself—so I read. Yet Myt-ser'eu left Sais with me. No one can know the heart of a woman.

MYT-SER'EU HAS NO new cosmetics, but she is good-natured about it. I tell her we will visit the perfumers' quarter when the satrap has spoken to us. This morning we walked about the saddlers' quarter first. Myt-ser'eu insisted I get a bag in which to carry this scroll and my ink, one that would protect them. We found such a bag and bought it after much haggling. We were about to enter the perfumers' quarter when Neht-nefret dashed up. We were to meet Muslak at the gate of the White Wall at once. He had a dozen sailors searching for us too, she said, but only she was wise enough to guess where Myt-ser'eu would take me.

We rented donkeys and rode to the gate of the White Wall, on red land some distance from the city. The donkey boys are to wait for us there. Muslak and Azibaal soon joined us, and we were admitted by the guards. Muslak has a firman.

Before I describe this fortress I should say that only the center of the city we left is noisy and crowded. Beyond it are many houses of two and three floors, fine and large, with walled gardens and more gardens on their roofs. Away from the shops, the streets are wide, traversed by carts and chariots. It would be very pleasant, I think, to live in one of those houses. There is no city wall. None at all.

Muslak wished us to remain where the soldiers had told us to wait. I was eager to see the fortress and left anyway, promising to return soon. I climbed to the top of the outer wall, walked along it some distance, spoke with the soldiers I met there, and so on. The best quarter of the city lay at my left hand and the fortress at my right. There can be few such views in all the world.

I was slower in returning than I had wished because I became lost, but the rest were waiting still when I returned. Myt-ser'eu had the bag we had bought for my scroll, so when a young scribe passed I asked him for water to wet my pen. (I had found two wells, both very large, but I had nothing to put water in and did not wish to disobey Muslak again.)

He is a priest, and his name is Thotmaktef. He was friendly and gossiped with us. I showed him my scroll and explained that I could not write as the people do here, but only with the tongue with which I think. He brought me a little pot of water, and had me write my name and other things on a scrap of papyrus. The people of Kemet write in three ways,* all of which he showed me, writing his name in all before he left. There is more to say of him, but I wish to think more upon it before I write it.

Perhaps I should not write of it at all.

---

*These were hieroglyphic, hieratic, and sekh shat or enchorial. They may be compared to printing, cursive, and shorthand.

———————

NO ONE IS permitted to build a house within bowshot of the White Wall. The White Wall itself surprised me when I saw it. It is tall, but I had expected it to be taller. It surprised me a second time when we entered, for it is much thicker than it is high. The temples in the city have thick walls and monstrous pillars, but they are nothing compared with this great fortress. There are rings of defenses, square towers to guard the gates and the corners of the walls, and a dry moat. Archers on the towers would command the wall, should an enemy drive the defenders from it.

The soldiers I spoke with were of Kemet. They said the men of Parsa here are horsemen. These soldiers of Kemet were tall and dark. Many wore headcloths like mine. They had spears and big shields with slots in them to look through. One had a light ax as well. It hung on the back of his shield, held by two loops of rope and prevented from slipping through them by the hook at the end of the haft.

5

SAHUSET SUMMONS US

WE ARE AT the inn once more, though we shared a fine roast goose first with Muslak, Neht-nefret, and Azibaal. I will not have long to write before we go, and there is much to write.

The satrap wanted to see us. He is younger than I expected, with no gray in his stiff, black beard. He has the eyes of a hawk. With him were two others, older men of Parsa and Kemet. These three sat; we stood. When the servant who had come for us had named us to the satrap, he said, "I have need of a stout ship—not a trireme with hundreds of rowers to feed, but a small and handy ship with a bold captain. Are you bold, Muslak?"

"Bold enough to do your will, Great Prince," said Muslak, "whatever it may be."

"Let us hope you speak truth. You Crimson Men are brave sailors, I know. Have you been to the Tin Isles?"

"More than once," Muslak declared.

"I will not ask you to go as far as that." The satrap spoke to Azibaal. "You're one of this man's officers?"

Azibaal nodded. "I am first mate, Great Prince."

"In which case you would swear he was bold, whether he was or not. Are you a bold sailor yourself?"

"I'm not as brave as he is," Azibaal admitted.

Muslak shook his head. "Azibaal's as stout a seaman as you'll find anyplace, Great Prince. As stout as I, and more."

"Let us hope. Two of you have women. One does not." The satrap pointed to Neht-nefret. "Whose woman are you?"

She bowed her head, unable to meet his eyes. "Captain Muslak's, Great Prince."

"And you?" He pointed to Myt-ser'eu.

She stood very straight then, and her eyes were proud. "I am Latro's, Great Prince."

For a brief time the satrap sat silent, and it seemed to me that Myt-ser'eu must not only have felt his gaze but feared his claws. At last she turned her head away.

"Latro is not the name I was given."

"I am of Kemet," poor Myt-ser'eu whispered. "We of Kemet call him Latro." (I asked her about this as we rode back. I have read my scroll to her, and it is there.)

The man of Kemet, who sat at the satrap's left hand, whispered something to him. He is very tall but stooped, with a shaven head, a hook nose, and glittering eyes.

The satrap nodded slowly. To me he said, "You have one name among the Crimson Men, another here."

I nodded, for I had learned as we sat waiting that Myt-ser'eu and Neht-nefret called me Latro, but Muslak and Azibaal Lewqys.

"You must speak aloud to the prince," said the other man of Parsa.

I said loudly, "Yes, Great Prince, it is as you say."

"I once knew a man named Artaÿctes," the satrap said. "He died at the hands of you Hellenes."

I said nothing.

"You do not recognize the name?"

"I don't, Great Prince."

"You are a Hellene and fear that you will be punished for his death. I understand. You will not be, Latro. You have my word. This Artaÿctes had a guard of Hellenes. He called in three and had them fight a man named Latro, who killed them all. Artaÿctes died before he could tell me of it, but certain others did not. You are that man."

I said nothing, for I recall no such incident.

"You do not deny it?"

I said, "I would never contradict you, Great Prince."

The satrap turned to Muslak. "Where did you get him, Captain?"

"In Luhitu, Great Prince. He's an old friend. He wished to go to Kemet, and I offered to carry him here without charge."

"If I send you south, will he go with you?"

"Only if you wish it, Great Prince."

"I do. Take him. I am going to send soldiers with you as well. What do you know of the southern lands, Captain?"

Muslak said, "I have been as far as Wast, Great Prince."

The satrap turned his hawk's eyes on Azibaal. "No farther?"

Azibaal spoke up like a man. "No, Great Prince."

"Very well. Listen to me, all of you. South of this land lies another called Nubia. It is not subject to my brother, but is not at war with us. Once it was subject to Kemet, thus the wise men of Kemet," he nodded toward the tall man, "know much of its history. Some even speak the tongue used there. No one here knows much

of its state today. No one knows anything of Nysa, the wide land
south of Nubia. I govern this land for my brother, and as his satrap
it is my duty to know much of the neighboring lands. I wish to send
you, with your ship and crew, south as far as the Great River runs.
You will find out these things for me, and return here to tell me of
them. Is that plain?"

Muslak bowed. "It is, Great Prince."

The satrap looked toward the smaller man of Parsa, who rose
and gave Muslak a heavy leather burse. He is short, and like many
short men he sits and stands very straight. His scant beard is white.

"There are cataracts," the satrap said. "You will have to carry
your ship around all save the first. It will be difficult, but it cannot
be impossible. You will have to carry the supplies you buy with my
gold around those cataracts as well. Keep that in mind when you
choose them."

Muslak bowed again. "I will, Great Prince."

"It may be possible to hire local people to help you. This man,"
he nodded toward the small man who had given Muslak the burse,
"will see to that. His name is Qanju. He will go with you. He will
have a scribe and three of our soldiers at his command. You, also,
will be at his command."

Muslak said, "We salute him, Great Prince."

"The man on my left is Sahuset, a wise man of Kemet. He too
will go with you." The satrap turned to this Sahuset. "Will you have
a servant, Holy One?"

If I had shut my eyes when Sahuset spoke, I might have thought
it a snake, so cold and cunning was that voice. "No servant who
must be fed, Great Prince."

"That's well."

Once again the satrap spoke to Muslak. "I will also send soldiers
of Kemet with you. How many, you may say. They will be subject to
Qanju just as you and everyone else aboard are. Bear in mind that
you and Qanju will have to feed them, buying food in the places you

pass. Bear in mind also that you will need many men to help you get your ship past the cataracts. How many shall I give you?"

Muslak stroked his chin. "Five, Great Prince."

So it was decided. A servant returned us to the courtyard in which I had written and told us to wait. Soon Thotmaktef returned. Qanju wished to speak with us, he said, and after that we might go. He led us in a new direction, and soon into a sunlit room in which there were many scrolls like mine in wooden racks. Qanju was writing at a table there, but rose and laid aside his stylus when we came; he is no taller than Myt-ser'eu. He welcomed us, invited us to sit, and sat again himself. "I am to be your leader on a journey that is sure to be long and laborious," he said. "Since that is the case, it seems good to me to become better acquainted with you before we set out. I assume that none of you objects to my leadership? The satrap, Prince Achaemenes, has appointed me—I am a scholar, and would never appoint myself to such a position. If anyone objects, this is the time to say so."

Muslak cleared his throat. "I do not object, Noble Qanju. But I most respectfully ask that any orders given my crew be relayed through me."

"Of course." Qanju nodded, smiling. "I'm no seaman, Captain. I'll consult you on every matter concerned with your vessel, and replace you only if I must. Is that all?"

Muslak nodded.

"Anyone else?"

No one spoke. At last I rose. "Noble Qanju, I have come to Kemet to follow the footsteps I left here years before. I know now that I came to this city, and met Muslak here."

Qanju motioned for me to continue.

"If I find those steps, I will follow them," I finished.

"Ah! But what if you do not, Lucius?"

"I will remain with my friend Muslak until I do, if he will allow it."

Muslak said, "I will."

"Will you inform us, if you intend to leave? Bid us goodbye?"

I nodded. "Yes. Certainly."

"That is well. You know where you are, Lucius—that is your name, by the way—and why you are here, because you read your scroll while you waited to speak with the satrap. You will have forgotten tomorrow, unless you read your scroll again."

Myt-ser'eu looked surprised, but I agreed.

"This girl, and your friend, have reminded you of these and other important matters from time to time, serving as the memory you lack. I join their company, and join it gladly. Yes, my dear?"

It was Myt-ser'eu. "I don't think that name you used is in Latro's scroll, Most Noble Qanju."

Smiling, Qanju nodded. "I learned it by occult arts, my dear. Do you believe that?"

Myt-ser'eu bobbed her head, looking frightened. "If you say it, Most Noble Qanju."

"I do not. I merely wished to learn whether you would believe it. The satrap had been given a name for your patron. He confided that name to me. Hearing it, it was no great riddle to unravel the accent of a Crimson Man. It's all quite simple, my dear, as most tricks are."

There was a moment of silence before Neht-nefret asked, "Then you aren't really a seer?"

"Oh, but I am, my dear." Qanju's dark eyes twinkled. "My tribe is the Magi, and we are quite famous for it. Unlike the pretenders to our art, however, we do not lie about it. Do you wish your fortune told?"

Slowly Neht-nefret nodded.

"Then I will do it," Qanju said, "but not now. We will have many idle hours on the captain's ship. There should be ample opportunity."

He cleared his throat. "Now that we are better acquainted, I will say the things I called you here to hear, so that I may get on with my work and you with your lives. First, that I will be in charge of our expedition. There will be no man on our ship who is not answerable to me, and no woman.

"Second, that I'll delegate my authority in certain matters. Captain Muslak will be in charge of our vessel and its crew. And of you, Neht-nefret. Lucius will be in charge of our soldiers, both those of Parsa and those of Kemet. Also of Myt-ser'eu, of course."

I said, "I forget, Noble Qanju, as you said. It seems to me that I'm not a suitable person to put in charge of armed men."

Qanju nodded, still smiling. "Should the charge of this expedition devolve upon you, as it may, you may remove yourself from command, Lucius. Until it does, it shall be as I say."

Azibaal said, "I think you've chosen wisely, Most Noble Qanju."

Qanju smiled and thanked him. "The third thing I wished to tell you is that Thotmaktef here, whom you have already met, is the scribe our satrap mentioned. He will be in charge of Sahuset—the most difficult post of all. I ask all of you, Myt-ser'eu and Neht-nefret particularly, to assist him in every way. Will you do that?"

Everyone nodded.

"That is well. I need not explain, I hope, that the Great King wishes only friendship and peace between the People of Parsa and the People of Riverland. Not everyone is as well-intentioned as he, however."

"I am," Muslak said.

Qanju nodded. "As am I. If we seven quarrel with one another, how can we not quarrel with the Nubians? If we war among ourselves, we are sure to fail."

Neht-nefret looked from me to Muslak. When neither of us spoke she said, "There'll be three soldiers from Parsa and five from my country. If they fight . . ."

"We will be ruined." Qanju's gentle gaze fell upon me. "It will be your task, Lucius, to make sure they do not. You are not of Parsa, nor of Kemet. Thus you will be resented equally by both. Your task will not be easy, but not beyond your ability. Captain, have you questions regarding the supplies you will buy?"

Muslak shrugged. "Ship's stores, and a few things to make us comfortable where there aren't any inns. Are there inns in Nubia, Noble Qanju?"

"A few, but we will go beyond Nubia."

"I know," Muslak said. "Into Nysa, wherever that is."

"As far as the river runs," Qanju whispered.

We were dismissed, all but Thotmaktef. Qanju's voice halted us before we reached the door. "Be wary of Sahuset. He may mean you no harm, but you will be polite to him without friendship, if you are wise."

Now a woman who serves this Sahuset has come for us, and Myt-ser'eu and I will go with her when the moon is down.

First I will write that when Thotmaktef came to us in the court-yard there was a baboon at his side. It was very large, and looked as grave as any man. I do not think the others saw this baboon, but I did. Thotmaktef himself did not see it, or so it seemed to me. I looked away, and after that I no longer saw it.

6

I REMEMBERED

MY WIFE, MY home, my parents—everything I once knew
came rushing back—my service to the Great King and the death of
my friends. I know this because Muslak and Myt-ser'eu have told
me. Now they say that I must write, as I do. This is what I remember now.

We were at this inn. A woman came, a strange and silent woman
whose eyes do not move as other women's do. She spoke to Muslak,
saying that we were to go with her at the setting of the moon. Neht-
nefret was afraid, and Muslak would not go. She spoke to me, the
last time I heard her speak, saying that if I wished to remember I
must come with her. Myt-ser'eu and I said we would both go, but
sleep a little first, for the moon was not yet high.

I wrote. Afterward we went to a room here, barred the door, and made love. It was long and slow and very good, for Myt-ser'eu knows much of love. When it was done, I slept.

I woke. Myt-ser'eu slept beside me, and the silent woman sat upon a stool on the other side. I supposed that Myt-ser'eu had admitted her while I slept. She says she did not.

The silent woman woke Myt-ser'eu and beckoned to us. We followed her; her name is Sabra. She led us very far, through dark streets, to the house of Sahuset. It is a small house in a large garden. I held Sabra's hand and Myt-ser'eu mine; even so, it was hard to keep to the path. There was an animal that watched us, or something that appeared to be an animal. It did not snarl or roar, but I saw its green eyes gleaming like emeralds in the shadows.

Sahuset's door stood wide. Someone I could not see lit a lamp as we entered, and Sahuset entered from another room. That was when he dismissed the silent woman, calling her Sabra. I expected her to leave the room; she did not, but went to a corner and stood motionless there, regarding Sahuset and us with an unseeing stare.

"You cannot remember, Latro. I have asked you to come here that I might help you." Each time that Sahuset uttered a word, one of the crocodiles hanging from his ceiling stirred.

I said that if he could help me see again the days now long past, I would be most grateful.

"I seek your gratitude. I seek the good will of this woman and of all who will be with us in the south, too. But yours I desire most of all. You have been cursed by a god. That is an ill thing, for you. Yet numinous."

Seeing that I did not understand, he added, "To be cursed by a god is to be touched by a god. To be touched by any god is to share divinity in some small measure. When the high priest leaves the sanctuary he strips off his clothing and bathes. Did you know that? His clothing is burned."

I said that I did not. Myt-ser'eu said she did, but I think she lied.

"He does not wish to infect the worshippers with divinity. Were they so infected, what need would they have of priest or temple? I myself am a priest, a priest of the Red God. Do either of you know of the Red God?"

Myt-ser'eu shook her head. I said that since I was a soldier I might be a servant of the Red God.

"The ignorant masses believe the Red God evil," Sahuset taught us, "because he commands the evil xu. If he tells an evil xu to leave a man, that xu must go. They are compelled to obey him in all things." He sighed. "The Red God is the desert god."

Silence filled the crowded room that seemed too big for that small house. In it we said nothing.

"The horse and the river-horse, the pig and the crocodile are sacred to him. He has a great temple in the south—"

"Set!" Myt-ser'eu sounded frightened. "This is Set."

"The Red God has many names." Sahuset spoke as those speak who calm a frightened child. "You may use whatever name you wish. The names of gods do not matter, because no one knows the true name of any god."

"I think we'd better go," Myt-ser'eu told me, and took my arm.

I shook my head.

"You are a man of courage," Sahuset said. "I knew it. None but brave men have value. I have told you that I will earn your gratitude, if I can. You have not asked why I want it."

I said, "Then I ask now. What favor do you wish from me?"

"Only your favor," Sahuset told me, "only that. Suppose that we found a scroll in the south, a yellowing scroll inscribed with long-lost wisdom. Would you keep it for yourself?"

"Yes," I said, "if I could read it."

"If you could not?"

I shrugged.

"Bring it to me, and I will read it for you. Will you do that?"

"Certainly," I said, "if you wish it."

"Or a stone so inscribed? Any such thing?"

I nodded.

"That is all I ask. You will remember your promise to me—or I will remind you of it. Now take your hand from that."

I looked down at my left hand, and saw that it was holding a winged fish, carved of black wood. I had not been conscious of picking it up, but must have taken it to toy with while I spoke. I put it down as Sahuset asked.

"I will require a drop of blood from you," he said, "and a drop of blood from an impure woman."

"I will gladly give you a drop of mine," I told him, "and go into the city to find such a woman for you, if you wish it."

From a drawer Sahuset took a long, straight knife with a thin blade of bronze, the tongue of the crocodile of green stone that formed its grip. "I doubt that will be necessary," he said.

He took my left hand in his and examined all its fingers, looking, as it seemed to me, for the places in which they had touched the fish. At last he pricked the fourth finger, and squeezed drops of blood into a small red bottle.

"And you," he said, motioning to Myt-ser'eu.

She came forward, trembling. He did not search her fingers as he had searched mine, but pricked the palm of her hand, caught her blood in the blood-groove of the blade, and crossing the room to the corner where Sabra stood, presented it to her.

She dabbled her fingers in it and dabbed it on her face, reddening her cheeks with it. That was the last time I saw her move.

When it was done, he poured water into a wide bowl and dropped the red bottle that held my blood into it. From a metal box he took dust the color of old blood, which he sprinkled with great care over the surface of the water.

We waited for a time that seemed long to me. At length the surface was disturbed, as if by a frog or some such creature swimming below it. This persisted for a time, then ceased. Sahuset peered intently at the pattern of floating dust, sighed, stroked his chin, and last picked up the bowl and dashed its contents on the floor. "You have been cursed by a foreign goddess," he said, "a goddess of the north."

Myt-ser'eu inhaled sharply.

"There is little I can do here, but I will do what I can—if you wish it."

"I do," I said. "You spoke of gratitude. You will have mine, if you can do anything to help me."

Sahuset shrugged. "I can give you a xu to fight the curse. He will enter into you. Do you understand? You will be two, a thing that you may not enjoy."

I said, "Do you mean that there will two of me?" (I am not sure I understood all that Sahuset said correctly. I give it here as I understood it.)

Sahuset reached out to tap my forehead. "This is a house, a tomb. One dwells there, and you say 'Me.' Two will dwell there, Me and Xu. You may not like sharing the house in which you have lived alone for so long."

"But he will lift the curse?"

"He will, for as long as he remains with you."

Myt-ser'eu asked, "How long will that be?"

Sahuset shook his head. "Until he is expelled, but how long it will be I cannot say. Nor can I tell you, now, who or what may expel him. He will have to tell me that."

Slowly, Myt-ser'eu nodded.

"Do you wish it, Latro?" (The tails of all the crocodiles moved, as if they swam.)

"Yes," I said, "I wish it."

"Very well. I must prepare." Sahuset turned to go. Already his closely shaven head gleamed with sweat. As he reached the doorway he added, "Wait here. You may sit in this room, but you must not lie in it. Open no chest."

Myt-ser'eu began to look around the room as soon as he had gone. It seemed to me that she was looking for something to steal, so I made her sit down upon a high stool brightly painted with the picture writing of Kemet. I myself went to the woman in the corner and spoke to her. She did not reply. I touched her forehead then, in a place where Myt-ser'eu's blood had not been smeared. It was wax. When I touched her hand, her eyes saw me. It was as if I had awakened her from sleep, though she did not move a muscle. I backed away.

After that Myt-ser'eu and I waited a long time, kissing once or twice but saying little.

When Sahuset returned he laid a finger to his lips, and with a rod of ivory motioned for us to follow. We did, saying nothing. He led the way through several rooms and down a steep winding stair to a dark chamber where the air was cool but without life.

It must have been far underground. The floor had been strewn with black sand, or perhaps with sand mixed with ashes. A tall box shaped like a man stood there. A man's face had been painted at the top, so that it almost seemed the man stood before us, a hard and handsome man who had lost something else before losing life, and told himself many times that the thing lost was not important. This box was painted as the chests and other things had been, though this paint was old and dull. In places, it had fallen away. In some, the wood was cracked.

Sahuset put my hand upon Myt-ser'eu's shoulder and hers on mine, indicating by signs that we were to stand so. Then he drew a circle around us with his ivory rod, he himself standing always on the inside of this circle he drew. Three lamps stood in his circle too, near the edges of it. He drew a triangle whose points were these lamps, and kindled them by tapping each with his rod and muttering words I did not understand and could hardly hear. As he spoke to each, its flame sprang up, yellow and bright. Strange fragrances came and went in that chamber.

After that, we waited again.

Soon it seemed that someone walked in the house above, the footfalls sounding only faintly down the steep stair. I supposed that it was the wax woman, Sabra, who walked there; and perhaps it was. After a time, it came to me that the walker was searching the house, going from room to room in search of someone or something. Someone screamed, but the steps came neither faster nor slower.

Steps sounded on the stair. The flames of the lamps sank, turning green, then blue. Something or someone taller than Sahuset descended the stair. It was not a man but was like a man. It wore a mask of fresh leaves.

Sahuset spoke to it in a tongue I did not know. It answered in the same tongue, uttering three words each time it spoke, neither more nor less.

"The xu will remain in you until the wind that stirs the grain is in your face," Sahuset told me. "Then it must depart." With these words he took my hand, led me to the edge of the circle, and indicated by a gesture that I was to step out of it. I did.

I will not believe this when I read it, but after that I remember little. What I do remember, I set down here. I walked a dark street with a woman I did not know, and talked loudly and very fast. The faces of my father, my mother, and my sister floated around me. I knew our farm again, every meadow and field, and I relived the deaths of my friends. The woman beside me spoke often to me, but I did not heed her, only telling her everything that raced across my mind—a thousand things I have forgotten once more.

At last I recalled Justa and struck the woman. "You're a whore!" I remember shouting it. I drew my sword and would have killed her, but she cowered and I could not strike.

She led me to this inn. I was speaking loudly all the time, but in this tongue, not in hers. Men stared at me and laughed, thinking me drunk. We climbed many steps to the roof, where there were two bright tents and a hundred flowers that lifted lovely faces to the rising sun. She turned me from it. "Look!" she said. "Look, Latro!" I looked and the morning wind was fresh in my face, cooling it, drying my sweat.

"What is it?" I asked in her tongue. "What are you pointing at, Myt-ser'eu?"

"At the Imperishable Ones—the stars of the north. They're almost gone." She kissed me. "And you're mine again!"

7

———

THOTMAKTEF

THE SCRIBE IS here. His master has sent him to assess the readiness of our ship. His master is Qanju. He did not tell me this, but I heard him say it. He himself is of Kemet, and a priest. We spoke of writing. He showed me their picture writing, and explained the way it is read. It may be written in either direction, but the man must face toward the end. The birds face the end also. It may also be written down, but not up. He wrote the satrap's name and enclosed it in a shield.

He said we should take a Nubian with us because such a one would know the country. I had not thought of that. He says there are many Nubians in the army of Kemet. "They are fine archers," he told me. "We have archers as good, but not many."

Neht-nefret whispered, "They are wonderful lovers, Latro. I had one once."

"Yes," Myt-ser'eu said, "foreigners always make the best lovers." She squeezed my hand when she spoke.

"They are good fighters," Thotmaktef declared.

I asked about their tactics.

He laughed and said, "You neglected to tell me that scribes and priests know nothing of war. You are more courteous than my own countrymen."

I said, "What can I know of what you know of war?"

"I know very little, just what I've picked up from Qanju and the other men of Parsa. But they know a great deal."

"Not more than we," Neht-nefret insisted.

"Not *those* tactics," Myt-ser'eu said, and everyone laughed.

I like this young scribe. He is eager to teach, yet very ready to learn. Not many men are like that. I cannot know whether he is brave or not, for Myt-ser'eu says we have not known him long and there has been no fighting. Yet his eyes say he is, and what is better yet, that he does not know it. I would rather have him at my side than most men. Surely his god must favor him! What god would not favor such a priest?

He will tell his master we are ready. Muslak says there will be no need to wait for tide or wind.

I CAST US off and leaped on board. Men on the yard untied the sail. The wind is stronger in the middle of the river, but we keep to the bank where the current is less—though it seems to me that there is hardly any current at all. The river is very wide, so that little is lost to such current as there may be.

There are three archers of Parsa and five spearmen of Kemet with us. All obey me, and none like it. Two quarreled. I knocked both down. They drew daggers, which I took from them. When they got up again I gave them back and told them that if they did not sheath them I would kill them both. They sheathed them. I hurt Uro's spear arm, although I did not intend it.

I inspected them, and set them to work cleaning their gear and sharpening their weapons. Just now I inspected them again and dressed them down for their shortcomings, both individually and as a group. Just now I set them to cleaning and sharpening some more. The captain suggests that we have them sweep the ship and scrub its deck each day, saying that it will become dirty very quickly with so many men on board. I told him we would do that as well.

All the soldiers wish to be my friends, but I am not friendly with any. Myt-ser'eu says that is wise, and I know she is right. She is my river-wife, just as Neht-nefret is Muslak's. Neht-nefret is a pretty woman, taller than Myt-ser'eu and more graceful. But Myt-ser'eu is beautiful and loving. I would not exchange her.

Both are more clever, I think, than Muslak and I might wish; they are great friends, whispering and gossiping.

I HAVE BEEN thinking of the things I must know when I read this again. We are on Muslak's ship. Its name is *Gades*. We are two women and twenty-seven men. Men: Qanju commands, Muslak is captain, Sahuset is a learned man of Kemet, Thotmaktef is a scribe, I command eight soldiers, and the rest are sailors. Women: Neht-nefret and Myt-ser'eu. The first is Muslak's, the second mine. She is four fingers shorter and I think a year or so the younger. Certainly she is younger than I. I think her afraid of all the other men, save perhaps for Qanju and Thotmaktef—very afraid of Sahuset. She stays so close to me when he is near that I am tempted to tell her to go away, but that would be cruel. It would be unwise as well; she remembers much that I forget.

_____

THERE ARE CROCODILES in the water. I saw a big one just now that must be very dangerous. Muslak says we will soon see river-horses. Myt-ser'eu has seen many pictures of them, but never seen them. Neht-nefret says the kings hunted them when this land ruled itself. They cannot really be bigger than this ship, but she says it.

We spoke of pigs. This is because Neht-nefret said they look like pigs on land, though they are so much larger and eat grass like other horses. Muslak said that pigs are good food, which is true, I know. The women were disgusted. No one in Kemet will eat a pig, they said. Sahuset smiled at that, so I knew otherwise.

Muslak also said that the river-horses are good eating, but very dangerous to hunt whether on land or water. I said that fat animals could not be dangerous, no matter how large they were. I said this because I wished to hear more.

"I have never hunted them," Muslak said, "but I know that they wreck big boats and trample men to death. Their jaws are immense, and their bite kills crocodiles. Their hides are thick and tough, and their fat keeps a spear from reaching their vitals."

"Not mine," one of my soldiers declared.

Laughing, Neht-nefret told him, "Tepu will kill you, Amamu." Tepu is the river-horse.

I READ WHAT I had written about this ship to Myt-ser'eu. A sailor joined us to listen. When I stopped reading he said, "There's another woman."

Both of us said there was not.

He shrugged. "I slept on board last night. There was a woman with us. We offered her money, but she refused and went below, and we couldn't find her."

Myt-ser'eu asked, "Who was her protector?"

The sailor only rose and strode away. Myt-ser'eu says he is Az-ibaal. I asked Myt-ser'eu how she knew the woman had a protector.

"Because they would have forced her, of course. When we're back home in Sais, the priests protect us. That's why you have to go to the temple to get us. You don't remember the money you made Muslak give the priest, do you?"

I admitted I did not.

"I knew you didn't. It was a lot, and we don't get any of it. What you give us afterward is all we get—if you make a present of money to me when we part, or buy me jewels while we're together."

"I don't have much money," I said.

"You will have," Myt-ser'eu told me.

THAT WAS EVERYTHING we said then, but I have been thinking about what Azibaal said. There cannot be a third woman on the ship this afternoon. Therefore, she was a woman of the place where we stopped last night. It was very large, so there must have been women there beyond counting. If she came on the ship but would not take money, she must have come to steal. If that is so— and it seems it must be—her protector was another thief. Since she went below, her protector was there stealing. Perhaps he told her to keep the sailors occupied while he stole. I have gone below and looked at everything, but if there is something missing, I do not know what it is.

Besides, Azibaal and the other sailors who stayed on board were there to guard against thieves, and would have seen the man and this woman when they left. Would not many men have taken everything? Would Azibaal and his sailors not have beaten one man or even two or three and driven them off? There is something here that I do not understand. I will stay on the ship myself tonight.

THE BRIGHT MOON we saw has slipped behind the western mountains, leaving the sky filled with innumerable stars; Qanju

71

studies them even now, but I sit where he sat, writing swiftly by the twofold light of his lamps. Much has taken place tonight that I must record.

The village at which we stopped had no inn, only a beer shop. Qanju and Sahuset have tents; I had Aahmes and the other soldiers put them up for them as soon as we landed.

After we had eaten and drunk, I returned to the ship. Myt-ser'eu wished to come with me. I wanted her to stay behind, but she cried. We had drunk beer, and she fell asleep as soon as we sat down. I had persuaded Muslak to let my soldiers guard his ship, some of his men having guarded it the night before; and I had assigned the three from Parsa to do it. Now I questioned them. They had seen no one and heard nothing, so I told them they could go into the village and enjoy themselves. When they had gone, I laid Myt-ser'eu in a more comfortable place (earning a kiss, with sleepy murmurs) and covered her to keep off the insects. I sat up, swatting them from time to time and smearing myself with grease. To tell the truth, I did not expect to see or hear anyone; but I was reasonably sure that the sailor had not told Muslak, and I could not tell him myself without betraying the sailor. Guarding the ship seemed to be the only thing to do.

I had nearly fallen asleep when I heard her step. She emerged from the hold, her gems and gold bracelets gleaming in the clear light of a quarter moon, and walked with graceful, unhurried steps toward the bow.

Rising, I ordered her to stop. She turned her head very far to look back at me, but did not. It was only then that I felt certain she was not Neht-nefret.

I overtook her easily and caught her shoulder. "What are you doing on this ship?"

"I am a passenger," she said.

"I haven't seen you on deck. Were you below all day?"

"Yes."

I waited for her to say more. At last I said, "It must have been very hot and uncomfortable for you down there."

"No." Her voice is low, but quite distinct.

"Now you want to go ashore?"

"Yes." She smiled at me. "I've no quarrel with you, Latro. Stand aside."

By that time I had seen that she was carrying nothing and had no weapon. Also that she was tall, young, and very beautiful. "I can't leave the ship unguarded to take you to the village," I told her, "and if you go alone, you may be attacked."

"I do not fear it."

"That's courageous of you, but I can't let you risk yourself like that. You'll have to stay here with me until someone else comes."

"Someone else is already here," she told me.

As she spoke, I heard the spitting snarl of a cat behind me. I spun about, drawing Falcata.

The cat's eyes blazed brighter far than the moonlight, smoking braziers of cruel green fire. When I took a step toward it, it snarled again, and I saw the gleam of its teeth. I feared, at first, that it might attack Myt-ser'eu—then that it had already, tearing her throat swiftly and silently. I advanced, wishing with all my heart for a torch. It moved to its left. When I moved to counter it, to its right. It was as large as many dogs.

As a bubble bursts in the river, it was gone.

I looked everywhere for it, certain it could not have jumped from the ship without my seeing it. At last it seemed to me that it could only have darted down the hatch and into the hold. There may be men who would have pursued that cat into the pitch dark-ness of the hold, but I am not such a man. (This I learned only a short time ago.) I replaced the hatch cover and tied it down with the rope that had been coiled beside it.

Only then did I look around for the woman who had come out of the hold. She was already well along the path leading to the village. I called to her, but she did not stop or even turn her head. Perhaps I should have run after her, although Qanju says I was right to stay on the ship. In a moment or two the woman had vanished into the night.

He arrived, and his scribe with him, not long after. "I came to study the stars," he said. "Are they not beautiful? They are best seen when the moon is down."

He lay on his back on the deck so as to see them without craning his neck.

"The moon has not set," I said, wishing to tell him what had happened but not knowing how to begin.

"It will be down soon," he told me, "and I will be ready. Even now, one may learn much."

Thotmaktef had seated himself beside him and spread a scroll like this upon his knee, ready to write as his master directed.

"A woman has gone into the village," I told them.

"A village woman?" Qanju asked.

Recalling the way her jewels had gleamed in the moonlight, I said, "No."

"Not your woman—she would not leave you."

"Myt-ser'eu?" I knew she was mine, but I wanted time to think. "She's asleep in the stern."

"Not the captain's woman. We left her behind us, didn't we, Thotmaktef?"

Thotmaktef nodded. "We did, Most Noble Qanju."

"Another woman?"

"Yes," I said.

"You have forgotten her name."

It was not a question, but I said, "No doubt I have."

"Indeed." Qanju sat up, surprising me. "Tell me everything, Lucius."

I did, speaking worse than I write and using too many words.

"This is an important matter," Qanju said when I had finished. "Will you remember everything in the morning?"

"Perhaps I will." Although I know I forget, I cannot be sure how soon I forget, or how much.

"I did not intend to pain you. You appear sober enough to write. Are you?"

"Certainly," I said.

"Good. You speak our tongue badly, making it difficult to judge. Thotmaktef?"

"Yes," Thotmaktef said.

"You are to come with me, Lucius. There are two fine lamps in my tent. You are to write of this incident in your scroll before you forget it. Include every detail. When you have finished, you may return here, if you choose."

I protested, saying that Muslak would be very angry when he learned that his ship had been left unprotected. This I knew to be true.

"It will not be unprotected," Qanju explained. "Thotmaktef will take your place until you return. He is young, strong, and honest. I would trust him with my life."

I offered to lend him my sword, but he declined with thanks.

That is all, and now I will return to the ship and Myt-ser'eu.

No, one thing more. When Qanju and I had traveled some distance up the path from the river, I looked behind me to see whether Thotmaktef had uncovered Myt-ser'eu. He had not, but he was untying the rope with which I had fastened the cover over the hatch.

8

SHADE

A BREEZE AND a lovely woman must be pleasant at all times—
or so it seems to me. Sahuset, the wise man of Kemet, has been
speaking with Myt-ser'eu and me beneath these fragrant trees.
There is nothing my eyes can see here that is not beautiful, save my
own feet. Sometimes Myt-ser'eu speaks. Sometimes she is silent.
That is the best way for a woman.

For anyone.

At times we kiss and laugh. Work is good, I think. No doubt
hard fighting is good sometimes as well. But there are times when
the best thing is to sit as we do, in a place of beauty, watching the
sails upon the blue waters of the Great River. Before Sahuset came,
we washed in the canal.

Myt-ser'eu says I speak her tongue well. I do not think so, yet she insists. I want to learn it, but know (because she tells me) that I forget each morning. Yet she insists that I speak much better than I did when we met.

She chose me, she says, in the temple of Hathor in her city. She says also that it is already written in this scroll; thus I need not write it again. That temple is very far from here.

The temple behind us is that of Sesostris, a different god. He was a king long ago, but has become a god of a thousand years. (The priest told us this.) He built a mountain of white stone here, very beautiful, and his priests have built the other things, the wall, the temple, and many other buildings—a little city, Myt-ser'eu says, and I agree. I would call them of no use; the people of this land do not, and the labor was theirs, not mine.

MYT-SER'EU TELLS ME I must write of the counsel we gave Qanju this morning. She says it because she wishes to know what we said, I know, and will tease me until I have read all that I write to her. Very well.

The sailors had complained to Muslak, and Muslak to Qanju, who summoned Azibaal, Sahuset, Thotmaktef, and me. He made me read from this, all that I had written when I remembered the woman herself. Now I recall only the things I read to the others.

Azibaal told us what the sailors had seen this morning, then what they had seen earlier, because I had mentioned it in my account. The sailors wish to turn back, Azibaal said, and to leave Qanju, Thotmaktef, and Sahuset here. I think they would like to leave my men, the women, and me behind as well; but they know Muslak would not consent to it. Soon they will want to leave Muslak, too—no one said that, but I think it.

"Let us do the other thing," I told Qanju. "There must be many good sailors among the men of Kemet. My men and I will drive these ashore, and you can hire others."

Muslak said, "You'll have to put me ashore too."

"Then I will not do it," I promised him.

"Nor will I," Qanju murmured. "These men have a legitimate complaint. It is our duty to resolve it. You have searched the ship for the woman?"

I nodded.

Muslak said, "So have I—I went with him."

"Without finding her. What of the cat?"

"It's larger than other cats," I said. "I've seen it. I believe I'm the only one here who has."

Thotmaktef said, "We breed cats much larger than any of you foreigners have, and use them to hunt small game." He looked to Sahuset for agreement, but Sahuset did not speak.

Muslak added, "Besides, you've forgotten it, Lewqys. You're just telling us what you wrote down."

"No," I said. "I remember the cat." I held my hands apart to show its size.

"Do you?" Qanju whispered.

Muslak grinned and slapped my back. "You're getting better!"

Sahuset smiled too.

"What of my question, Lucius? What traces of the cat did you find?"

"None," I said.

"The urine of cats has a strong odor. . . ."

"I know," I said. "I did not smell it."

"Neither did I," Muslak declared, "and I would have."

"In that case, the cat is not on the ship, though I feel sure the woman must be."

Thotmaktef looked puzzled. "How can you know that, Most Holy Qanju?"

Qanju spoke to me. "You remember the cat, you said. A large cat with green eyes."

I nodded. "Very large."

"Do you also remember the woman, Lucius?"

I held up my scroll. "Only what I have here. But I remember also that it was you who insisted I write, for which I thank you."

"In which case we may assume that the woman is here."

Qanju turned to speak to Thotmaktef. "The cat vanished while Lucius was looking at it. He says it could not have jumped into the water, and I agree. Cats walk very quietly, but they cannot leap into water quietly. Since this cat was at the back of our vessel, some distance from the riverbank, it could not have sprung to the bank unseen. Having no other explanation, Lucius assumed that it must have gone into the hold. We know it wasn't there."

Slowly, Thotmaktef nodded.

"In which case . . ." Qanju sighed. "Let us call it a ghost. That will make things simpler. The woman is not a ghost, however. Lucius touched her shoulder. Wishing to go to the village—or to our tents, which were near it—she walked up the path, even as we."

"I am blessed," Thotmaktef said, "to hear such wisdom."

"I will bless you further. Lucius forgets the places he has visited and the people he has seen in them. He even forgets Myt-ser'eu. In short, he forgets all the occurrences of common life. He does not forget the cat. Therefore, it does not belong to common life."

Thotmaktef murmured, "Myt-ser'eu," and wrote something on the deck with his finger.

"Interesting," Qanju murmured.

Sahuset nodded, I noticed, although his head scarcely moved. Thotmaktef was seated at Qanju's right, Sahuset at Thotmaktef's right. Sahuset, at least, had read what Thotmaktef wrote.

Muslak turned to Azibaal. "Which one scares them most?"

Azibaal spat. "They both do."

"You're saying that the woman's still in the village," Muslak told Qanju, "but the men say they saw her come back to my ship."

"I am saying nothing of the kind, Captain. I am saying that she is here on your ship and might be found."

"I searched it. So did Lewqys."

Qanju sighed. "You did not know where to look. I do, and may tell you later. If the woman were not accompanied by the cat, your men would not fear her."

Muslak and Azibaal nodded.

"They would offer her money, and if she would not take it, they would take her by force. Thus we need not rid ourselves of her, only of the cat."

I said, "I would protect her."

Azibaal frowned at me. "If she were gone, her cat would be gone too. That's what I think."

"Perhaps, but I doubt it." Qanju turned his head. "You seem eager to speak, Thotmaktef."

"As the Most Noble One wishes. We will soon be in sight of a great temple, the Mortuary Temple of Sesostris."

"A suitable venue?"

"I believe so, Most Noble Qanju."

Qanju smiled. "And what does Sahuset say?"

The wise man of Kemet shrugged.

"The cat must cease manifesting itself on this ship—or so the matter appears to me. Who among you disagrees?"

No one spoke.

"My scribe has suggested a means that may prove effectual. Has anyone some other means to suggest? Learned Sahuset?"

Sahuset shook his head.

"Then let us follow my scribe's suggestion."

That was everything of importance. We tied up in the canal that feeds the sacred lakes. Qanju and Muslak went to the temple and talked with the priests, then with the chief priest. When they returned they said we must wait.

Myt-ser'eu points to words, presses herself close, and tickles me, asking what those words mean. Sahuset frightened her, I think. She would endear herself to me more than ever; that is plain. Women are ever affectionate where there is danger, and there would be less danger if it were not so.

9

WE LINGERED HERE

SAHUSET CAME WHEN we had been lolling here for some
time. He brought cups and a skin of wine, which we shared with
him. I do not like unmixed wine, but I drank a cup of it, slowly, so
as not to offend him. Myt-ser'eu feared his wine was drugged (as
she has told me since) and only feigned to sip until he had drained
his own cup.

"I am the outcast of our ship," Sahuset said. "You need not agree.
I know it, and know you both know it. That is enough."

"Everyone respects you," I told him.

He shook his head. "Everyone fears me, except you, Latro.
When a man is respected, no one wants to plant a dagger in his

back. When he is feared, everyone thinks upon it, and tests the point."

Myt-ser'eu turned down her empty cup and spoke boldly. "I fear you because I remember all that happened when we went to your house. Latro has forgotten those things or he would fear you too."

"In that case, I am glad he has forgotten. I want his friendship, not his fear. I want yours, too, Myt-ser'eu."

"Go to the priests of Hathor. They will find you another. I'm engaged."

Sahuset laughed. "So you are, Myt-ser'eu. Some other time, perhaps. Latro, your little cat is most appealing."

Although there had been an unsettling note in his laugh, I smiled and agreed.

"That is what her name means. Did you know? A cat that is not yet grown."

I shook my head. "I know she wears a cat on her headband."

"Not the cat you saw."

"No," I said. "Certainly not."

"What will you do if these priests tell the Man of Parsa that Myt-ser'eu must be killed to rid our ship of the phantom cat?"

Myt-ser'eu sat up straight. "You didn't tell me about this!"

"It has nothing to do with you," I said, "and I didn't want to frighten you."

"Will they really want to kill me?"

"It doesn't matter. I won't permit it. We'll leave the ship."

Sahuset nodded. "Good. Will your men obey if you tell them not to strike?"

"They will."

"There are three of Parsa and five of my own nation. Our five may side with you. It would please me but not surprise me. The three will surely obey Qanju."

"They will obey me," I insisted.

"I hope we won't get to find out. The priests may say no such thing, though priests are often malicious and meddling. Cats are sacred animals, after all. Did I shock you, Myt-ser'eu?"

If she had been frightened, and I think she had been frightened badly, she had recovered. "They are grasping, too, Sahuset. Grasping and devious. You forgot to mention that."

"So I did, but only because it did not seem to apply. I was a priest myself for some years, and thus I am in a position to know."

"Have they cast you out?" Myt-ser'eu's hand tightened on mine.

"I cast myself out. I wanted knowledge. They wanted gold, as you say, and power. More land. More and more land. Yet I still have friends among the priests at my old temple. Do you believe that, Latro?"

"Certainly," I said, "it seems very probable. I feel that I have friends far away too, and though I do not remember them, I would like to find them."

"I may be able to help with it. I mean to take you to my old temple when we reach it and prove the truth of my assertion. Meanwhile, I wanted to warn you, as I have, and remind you I'm a friend—hers as well as yours."

We thanked him.

"Qanju did not know the meaning of Myt-ser'eu's name until his scribe traced it on the deck for him at our meeting. So it seemed, at least. He does now, and we may be sure he will tell the priests here that a woman of that name is on board."

"You called yourself an outcast," I said, "though you say the priests at your temple did not cast you out."

"So I am. I am of Kemet, but a southerner. I was born—it doesn't matter. Here in the north, my own people consider me foreign. We of Kemet have little tolerance for foreigners, the Nine Bows who have brought us only war and rapine, century after century."

I said that I would try to bring none.

"Oh, particular individuals can be well-intentioned, and even useful. But as a class . . ." Sahuset raised his shoulders and let them fall. "Now we are occupied by a foreign power. The satrap governs us mercifully and with justice—governs us better than most of our own pharaohs did, in my judgment, but he is resented just the same, and his countrymen are resented still more."

"And I with them. That's what you're saying."

"Among other things, yes. As for me, the satrap finds me useful, and rewards me for my services. I am a wise man of Kemet." Sahuset laughed again. "We're not the only ones who find foreigners useful at times, you see. As for me, I take his gold. I'm hated for that by men who would grovel for it, were it offered to them."

Myt-ser'eu surprised me then by saying, "I'm as much an outcast as you are. No, as much as you and Latro together."

"'Marry a maid from your own village.'" Sahuset smiled. "Isn't that how the poem goes? 'Have nothing to do with the strange woman.' That's in it someplace too."

"I'm sure it is." Myt-ser'eu turned to me. "I might as well tell you—I don't think I ever have. Once a woman leaves her neighborhood in Sais, she is marked. It doesn't matter if she comes back later and lives there again. She's still marked. I was driven out." Her eyes filled with tears. "By my mother, my sister, and my brothers. That doesn't matter either. I'm still marked. There are men who'll marry a strange woman, but not many."

I hugged her, and Sahuset refilled her cup.

"What she says is true of villages and every city in this land," he told me. "What I've said is true as well. On our ship I'm the greater outcast. Surely you've seen that."

I said, "I noticed that you never spoke during the meeting. The rest of us did, and even Azibaal talked a lot. But you did not."

"Correct. I would have told them the truth if they had asked for it. Yet I knew how the truth would be received, and thought it better not to voice it unless I was asked to."

"Then speak this truth to me," I said, "I ask for it now."

"Very well. But first—our ship is in my country, but neither its captain nor its crew are of my country. It is commanded by a Man of Parsa. A good man, and a wise one by his lights, but a foreigner. The only countryman of mine who has any authority at all has sided with the People from Parsa much more firmly than I have. He governs me for them, or tries. As for the rest—five foot soldiers and two women. Half the men on board would take Myt-ser'eu or the other woman by force, and throw her to the crocodiles afterward. They know that, and if you don't you should."

"I do," I said. "What about the truth you were too wise to voice in our meeting?"

"As you wish. First, that the woman who cannot be found is at least as uncanny as the cat they fear. Second, that the cat is not hers, since it did not accompany her to the village. Third, that neither has done the least harm, but trying to rid the ship of them is likely to do a great deal."

I said that the same thought had occurred to me.

"Then tell them. They will certainly take it better from you than they would from me. I earn a modest living, Latro, chiefly by telling fortunes and driving out xu who have possessed a particular house—less commonly, a particular person. When someone comes to me wanting a xu driven out, I ask what harm the xu has done. Most often the answer is none; when it is, I tell my client frankly that it would be prudent to leave well enough alone. When a xu occupies a place—or a person, for that matter—others rarely try to occupy it as well. No one tries to move into a house that is already inhabited."

"I understand," I said. "Do they take your advice?"

Sahuset lifted his shoulders and let them fall as before. "Do I appear well fed?"

"No," I said.

He laughed. "Remind me never to debate you. But you're wrong. I'm not starving, and I would starve if they did. I expel the harmless spirit for a modest fee—and charge a great deal more for the worse one who finds the first's house empty."

"Could you drive out the cat?"

"Perhaps." Sahuset turned away to gaze out over the river.

"Would you? If Qanju ordered it?"

He shook his head.

"Why not?"

"You are a soldier. Would you accept an order from someone who knew far less of the military art than you do?"

Now it was my turn to watch the sails and the wheeling riverbirds. "It would depend on what it was," I said at last.

"Just so." Sahuset held out his wine skin. "More? You, Myt-ser'eu?"

She accepted a second cup; when he had filled it, he poured another for himself. "I have offered my wine and my friendship. You are both afraid I'll ask some service for them. I will not, but will gladly do one for you if you ask. Do you? Either of you?"

Myt-ser'eu said, "Would you want money if I asked you to tell my fortune?"

Sahuset shook his head.

"Then please, would you?"

"Certainly." From the pouch at his belt he took four gold sticks, none of which were quite straight. "I should have my wand for this," he said—and it was there, a rod of carved ivory, though I had not noticed it before. He laid the gold sticks on the grass, each a corner of a rough square, then traced a circle about them with his wand. Closing his eyes, he looked toward the sky. For a time so long that I grew sleepy his lips moved, though I could not hear what they said.

At last he picked up the sticks, shook them in his hands, and flung them toward Myt-ser'eu. They landed in the circle, as well as I could judge, and he bent above them. "Much sorrow soon," he said, "but joy not long after it."

"That's good," she said.

He nodded absently. "You will travel to strange lands, and will be in danger there. You will return to your native place—and leave it again. Hathor favors you. That's all I can read here."

"That's what I've always wanted," Myt-ser'eu said, "to get away from my family and see strange places and meet new people like Latro. Hathor must be very kind."

"She is. Latro?"

I shook my head.

"Please?" Myt-ser'eu's hand tried to squeeze my thigh. "For me? Just this once?"

I shook my head again. "I'm a soldier, as he said. I'll die on some battlefield, and knowing that I know as much as he can find out."

"But you might not, and we're together, so if we learn about you we'll learn more about me."

I shrugged.

Taking it for consent, Sahuset scooped up his gold sticks and flung them at me. For an instant it seemed they had stuck my face; they had not, and fell in the circle as before. One lay upon another there.

Sahuset leaned over them. I heard his indrawn breath, but he did not speak. He rose, walked toward the temple wall, then returned to us and studied his gold sticks again from a different angle.

"What is it?" Myt-ser'eu asked.

"You are frightened," he said. "So am I." He picked up his sticks slowly, one by one, tossed them straight up into the air, and studied them as before.

"Tell us!"

"Latro? This is ill news, I'm afraid. If you demand it, I'll tell you. I advise you not to."

"I would rather hear bad news," I said, "than know myself a coward."

"Very well. Death is near you. Very near. Myt-ser'eu and I may save you, but we may not. We will try, of course. Certainly I will. Will you, Myt-ser'eu?"

She nodded, and I felt her hand tremble. I said, "How near is it?"

Sahuset bit his lip. "Before sunrise tomorrow. You may be confident of that. If you see the sun rise, you are out of danger. Beyond the proximity of your peril, there is no certainty. Be careful this evening. Be very careful tonight, and recall always that death may be kinder than Hathor. That is all I can tell you."

He left. I opened the leather case that holds this scroll, and Myt-ser'eu fetched water from the canal for me. She said that fortunes told are sometimes wrong, which I know is true. I said that it would be hard to think of a place where danger threatened less than here, which is true too. We made jokes and kissed, and soon her tears dried.

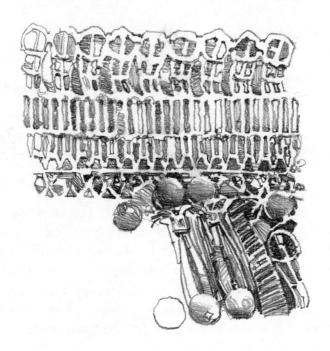

10

WE ARE ONE

DEATH DID NOT seem strange then. I will write it all, though I may think I went mad when I read it in days not yet come. I forget, as the captain told me. And the woman, and the seer. The healer said it was best to remember nothing, but Uraeus tells me that I must remember or wander lost until I die once more.

I flew to this ship. I cannot say how I knew where it was—I flew at the word of the man who gave me the serpent from his crown, and it was before me. I knew I must go there. My body lay in the bow, screened with sailcloth. "Lucius," the seer whispered over it. "Lucius, do you hear me?"

Then I knew that the thin man had returned already, and I must return too. I did, and it was like walking into a cave to rejoin friends. The small man came too, and I sat up. The sailcloth would not let me see whether the dark man had come as well. I took it down, and he had not. I bent to comfort the woman who wept, and quickly he was there. Uraeus is with us too.

Here is what happened.

A man wearing a strange crown came from the direction of the temple. "Get up," he told me, "you must come with me." There was no threat or anger in his voice, but I knew that he must be obeyed. I rose and felt myself pulling others behind me as I rose. I drew the man whose hand I clasped, he another, and so on. I was also drawn by the man whose hand clasped mine. I rose, and we were four.

"Come with me." The crowned man beckoned with a stalk of papyrus. "I am Sesostris."

We did as we were bid, but looked behind us. A fifth man was being rolled into a cloth while women wailed.

One was dark. One was thin. One was small, but shone like a star. All were I, and so was I. Our body was I as well.

"Who are we?" the small I asked Sesostris.

At this, the thin I said, "I am Lucius."

We pressed forward. "Who are we?"

Sesostris pointed to the one I am. "You are Ba." To the small shining one. "You are Ka." To the dark one. "You are Shade." To the thin one. "You are Name."

"I am Lucius," the thin one declared again.

To this Sesostris nodded. "You are."

"Are we dead?" we asked.

"He is," Sesostris told us. "You are not. You came from another land with him who is dead, and have never been taught. If I teach you now, will you learn of me?"

"Yes," we said, "teach us!"

"A man is of five parts," Sesostris told us. He held up his hand, its fingers wide. "A woman or a child, the same. They are Body, Name, Shade, Ba, and Ka. At death, Body sleeps. You will be judged by gods. If you are a found worthy, you will wait in the Field of Reeds until the day when all shall be reunited. If unworthy, devoured."

We nodded one by one, first the small shining one, last I. I said, "There are many gods here."

"There are more than you suppose, more gods than men, by far. Do you fear they will all judge you?"

"I do not fear," I said.

"You need not. Forty-two will judge you, with Osiris to preside."

The gate of the temple wall stood before us. We walked through it, though it was shut. Within were the temple, not large but fine in the way of Kemet, and other buildings.

"What are these places?" we asked.

"That is the House of Life." Sesostris gestured with his stalk of papyrus. "That is the House of Priests. Some are storehouses. Many are thought empty."

"They are not?" Shade said.

Sesostris shook his head, and the cobra on his crown hissed.

"You are Sesostris," Name said. "What is the serpent's name?"

Sesostris smiled. "In a thousand years I have not been asked that question. His name is Uraeus."

We walked, and he taught again. "I was king," he said. "Dying, I was judged worthy and became a god. So you will become at last, if you too are judged worthy. You will dwell in the Field of Reeds until you are needed or invoked. Then you will return to this world of the living, unseen save by those you would have see you."

"All of us?" we asked. "Do we all become gods, who die?"

"Only those deemed worthy. The rest are devoured by Ammut."

As soon as he spoke her name Ammut waddled beside us, huge and stinking. Her head is like a crocodile's, though it is not a crocodile's. Her body is that of a fat woman with misshapen feet, though it is not a fat woman's. "Did you ask whether I would eat you all?" She simpered. "Yes. All of you, if the heart is heavy."

"Better to be devoured by you than to fare in the Deadland," said the small and shining I.

"Here is the Deadland," Ammut told him, and smote her great belly.

We passed through the temple. The figure in the holy of holies was old, the man who walked with me young.

"It is too dark here," the I called Shade said; but his voice was weak and far.

Inside the mountain-tomb it was darker still until Sesostris kindled his light. Then we saw everything, stairs that led only to other stairs, chapels in the rock where no priest sacrificed. The riches of his burial chamber would take more men to tell of than man this ship. From it a stair led down and down through stone until it reached the chamber where the court sat. Sesostris walked before us to show the way, Ammut after us, slow and laboring, panting and slavering.

"You stand before your judges," the bleeding man said. He was the chief judge of that court, a handsome man sorely wounded. He wore a white crown with two plumes. "We shall question you, and you will answer us honestly. You cannot do otherwise."

We nodded. "We cannot." We knew as we spoke that it was true.

"I am Strider of Annu," said a god. "Have you done iniquity?"

"I have not!" We all said this.

"I am Burning of Kher-aba," announced another. "Have you robbed by violence?"

"I have not!" we said.

"I am Fenti of Khemennu," declared a third. "Have you broken the nose?"

"Yes, as a boxer," we said.

"I am Am-khaibitu of Qereret," said a fourth. "Have you stolen?"

"Yes," we said, "we took the Horses of the Sun, doing the bidding of the Lady of the Beasts." This theft has left my mind now, yet I must have known it then.

"I am Neha-hra of Restau," murmured a fifth. "Have you slain man or woman?"

"Many men," we said, "for I was a soldier."

"I am the Double Lion-God," roared a sixth. "Have you given short measure?"

"To none!" we said.

"I am Burning Eye of Sekhem." This seventh god spoke in stately tones. "Have you sworn falsely?"

"Never!" we said.

"I am Flame," hissed an eighth. "Have you stolen from Ptah?"

"Never!" we said.

"I am Set-qesu of Suten-henen," whispered a ninth. "Surely—surely you have lied."

"Never to you, Set-qesu," we said.

"I am Khemi of the Hidden Place," a tenth god told us. "Have you carried off goods by force?"

"We have looted the goods of some we slew," we said.

"I am Brightflame of Mennufer," crowed an eleventh. "Have you uttered words of evil?"

"Never have I cursed anyone!" we said.

"I am Hra-f-ha-f of the Caverns of the Deep," said a god who had no face. "Have you carried off food by force?"

"I have," we said.

"I am Qerti of the Underworld," intoned the sepulchral voice of a thirteenth god. "Have you acted to deceive?"

"Often," we said. At this Ammut edged nearer us.

"I am Firefoot of the Night," shouted a fourteenth god. "Have you raged?"

"Yes," we said.

"I am Shining-teeth of Ta-she." The fifteenth god grinned as he addressed us. "Have you invaded a foreign land?"

"I have," we said.

"I am the Eater of Blood. . . ." So sighed a sixteenth, whose voice was like the wind. "I am he who comes forth from the tomb. Tell me, have you slain the Beasts of Ptah?"

"Yes," we said, "I have slain them."

"I am the Eater of Entrails." The seventeenth licked his lips. "Have you laid waste to plowed land?"

"That also I have done," we said.

"I am Lord of Maat," trumpeted an eighteenth god. "Answer me! Have you pried into the affairs of others to do them hurt?"

"Never!" we said.

"I am Themeni of Bast," mewed the nineteenth. "Have you slandered man or woman?"

"Never!" we said.

"I am Anti of Annu," growled the twentieth. "You have raged, and I know it. Was it without cause?"

"Never!" we said.

"Tututef of Ati am I." The voice of the twenty-first god was an insinuating whisper. "Have you sodomized a child?"

"Never!" we said.

"I am Uamemti of the slaughterhouse." The twenty-second studied us coldly. "Have you poisoned waters?"

"Never!" we said.

"I am the Seer of the House of Amsu. How often have you lain with the wife of another?"

"Never!" we said.

"I am H-her-seru of Nehatu," quavered the twenty-fourth. "Have you made men afraid?"

"Often," we confessed.

"Have you been hot of mouth?" asked Neb-Sekhem, who comest forth from Lake Kaui.

"I have," we said.

"I am Seshet-kheru of Urit," affirmed the twenty-sixth. "Have you been deaf to words of right and truth?"

"More than once," we admitted.

"I am he of Lake Heqat," squalled an infant god. "Have you made others weep?"

"I have," we said.

"I am Kenemti of Kenemet," boasted the twenty-eighth. "Have you blasphemed Ptah?"

"Never!" we said.

"I am An-hetep of Sau," whimpered the twenty-ninth god. "Have you acted with violence?"

"Often," we confessed.

"He was a soldier," said the bleeding man. "We might forgive him that."

"I am Ser-kheru of Unsi." The thirtieth god shrugged. "Have you acted without thought?"

"Too often," we said.

"I am Neb-hrau of Netchefet," cackled the thirty-first god. "Have you taken vengeance on any god?"

"I have willed it," we said, "upon a goddess."

"I am Serekhi of Uthent," lisped the thirty-second god. "Have you multiplied speech?"

"No," we said.

"I am Neb-abui of Sauti," said the thirty-third god levelly. "How many men have you defrauded?"

"None," we said.

"I am Nefer-Tem of Mennufer," thundered the thirty-fourth god. "Have you cursed Pharaoh?"

"I have not," we said.

"I am Tem-sep of Tattu," said the thirty-fifth god, and his voice might have been the chuckling of a brook. "Have you fouled running water?"

"I have slain men whose bodies the river took," we said.

"Beyond that?" inquired Tem-sep.

"Or the sea," we said.

"I am Ari-em-ab of Tebi," the thirty-sixth god told us severely. "Have you boasted?"

"Only in boyhood," we said.

"I am Ahi of Nu," mumbled the thirty-seventh god. "Have you defamed Ptah?"

"Never!" we said.

"I am Uatch-rekhit of the Shrine of Uatch-rekhit," sneered the thirty-eighth god. "Have you acted with insolence?"

"Seldom," we said.

"I am Neheb-nefert, he of the Temple of Neheb-nefert." So saying, the thirty-ninth god stared blindly at a place where we were not. "Have you judged unfairly?"

"No," we said. "Never."

"I am Neheb-kau who comest forth from the Cavern," rumbled the hollow voice of the fortieth god. "Have you augmented your wealth through the property of another?"

"With that other's permission," we said.

"I am Teheser-tep of the Shrine of Teheser-tep," breathed the forty-first god. "Have you cursed that which is Ptah's while you held it?"

"Never!" we said.

"I am An-a-f of Aukert," said the final god. "Have you scorned the god of your own city?"

"Never!" we said again.

"You are not without sin." The bleeding man rose. "But not without merit. Go to the scales."

We did, and he came after us. Sesostris was waiting there with the monster-woman Ammut. A baboon crouched beside them, holding a reed pen and a tablet.

"Will you bless him?" the bleeding man asked Sesostris.

"I will," said Sesostris, and gave us his blessing. It filled us, and we knew then that we had been empty.

"He has been blessed by Sesostris," the bleeding man told the gods who sat in judgment. "Shall he be subjected to the ordeal? Stand."

Five rose. They were the faceless god, the god of the Underworld, the Eater of Blood, the Eater of Entrails, and Neb-hrau.

"Osiris will take your heart for the weighing," Sesostris explained. "Do you see the feather in the other pan?" His hand directed our eyes to the scale.

We did, and said that we did.

"It is Maat, the Law of Ptah," Sesostris told us. "If Maat rises above your heart—"

Ammut said, "I get it and you," and licked her lips.

"But if your heart rises above Maat," Sesostris continued, "it will be returned to you, and I will conduct you to the Field of Reeds."

No sooner had he finished speaking than the man called Osiris motioned for Shade, Name, and Ka to stand aside and thrust his bleeding hand into my chest. For a moment I felt my heart fluttering in his hand like a captured bird.

When it was gone, I was empty of life. I had not known that a man might be emptied like a wine skin, but it is so; I longed to be full once more, and feared I would be cast aside.

Laid upon the scale pan, my heart sank. It had no sooner done so than it rose, higher than the feather by the width of my hand. At once it sank as before, only to rise once more.

"He still lives," the bleeding man declared to all the gods, "and should not be here." Picking up my heart, he returned it to me and spoke further, but so overcome with joy was I that I did not hear him. Only my delight remained.

We were alone in the Hall of Judgment when Sesostris said, "Do you hear me now, Ba?" His voice was kind.

"Yes, Great Sesostris," I replied. "How may I serve you?"

"By doing what you must. But first I tell you this, as Osiris did. His blood has touched your heart. Touching it, it has mingled with your own. It cannot have been more than a drop, but even a drop will have great power. What effect it may have, I cannot say, but you should be aware of it."

I said I would try to remember.

"You will forget. Therefore, I am going to send my servant with you to recall it for you." Sesostris took the cobra from his crown. It was, or seemed, a piece of carved and gilded wood. He held it out, and I took it.

"Hold Uraeus carefully. You must fly far without dropping him."

As Sesostris spoke, Uraeus writhed in my hand like a living serpent. I started to say that I could not fly at all; my wings twitched at the thought of flight, and I knew myself winged.

"Go now," Sesostris told me, "for the rest are on the road."

II

URAEUS

MY SLAVE COMES when I come, and goes when I go. That is what Neht-nefret says. I said that it was Myt-ser'eu who comes with me, and I know that it is true. This is true also: wherever I go, I find Uraeus there.

We spoke to him about it. He said it was his duty to wait upon me; but that when I did not wish him present, I had only to tell him to leave.

"Leave then," I said. "Leave now." And he was gone.

He has not come back. Myt-ser'eu and I talked about it, sitting by ourselves in the shade of the afterdeck. "You were there," I said. "Surely you saw him go."

She shook her head. "He was with us and we spoke to him. You sent him away, and he was not there—but I didn't see him go."

"Men cannot vanish like smoke," I told her, pretending to be angry.

"Smoke cannot vanish like Uraeus."

I admitted that he did not seem like other men.

"Neither do you, my darling." She added that my slave did not look at her as other men do. She thinks his manhood may have been cut away.

I will forget him, if what Muslak says is true. Here I write of him, so that I may know him again if he returns. He is smaller than many women, and stooped. There is no hair on him. None. The healer's head is shaved; but there would be hair there, and on his face as well, if he did not shave it. He has hair beneath his arms just as I do, and eyebrows. Uraeus has none, and is smoother and more supple than any woman. He is humble and never raises his voice, but Muslak and his sailors are afraid of him. So are my soldiers, though they seem bold men. He came to our ship when we were at the tomb of an ancient king of Kemet, the seer says. This seer's name is Qanju. He could not tell me how I came to die, as Myt-ser'eu did, but told me how I was restored to life. I will write now of those things, though only briefly—what the seer said, and what Myt-ser'eu says.

She and I were sitting beneath a tree. We had drunk wine, and I lay down to sleep. She slept too. When she woke, she tried to awaken me and found that I was dead, although I had not been stabbed or strangled.

She ran back to this ship, where two priests were driving out demons. My soldiers carried my body back to the ship, where the healer labored over it, chanting, burning incense, and doing many other things. His name is Sahuset. At last I returned to life and began to write of what had befallen me in death. I know that is here, but I do not want to read it. Not now, and perhaps never. I know that I must die again, and that is more than enough.

WE HAVE SEEN a river-horse, I think the first I have ever seen, for it seemed a new animal to me. It was black. It thrust its huge head from the water and regarded us through tiny eyes. Its mouth was immense, its teeth as long as my hand. I asked Muslak and Neht-nefret about these creatures, but neither knew much, only that river-horses are large and dangerous, and are sometimes hunted. That they are large I knew already, having seen that one; and would it not be a strange and wonderful thing if a beast so large were not dangerous? As for hunting them, I wished to hunt them myself. Any hunter would wish to hunt such an animal. Myt-ser'eu told me that earrings, combs, and the like are made from the teeth, also that a certain goddess takes the form of a river-horse and succors women in labor. One of my soldiers has a shield of river-horse hide, which he showed me. He said it makes the best shields of all, and makes fine whips. His name is Aahmes of Mennufer.

It was not until I asked the healer that I learned more. He seems a most learned man. The river-horses leave the river by night, invade men's fields, and devour their crops, trampling much and eating much. Thus they are hated. They destroy crocodiles, and so are loved and greatly respected. They overturn boats, and so are hated again. Kings and other great men hunt them in fleets of boats with fifty or a hundred hunters. No one ever rides these horses. On this point he warned me. When a man sees them on shore, he thinks they cannot run; but in truth they run very swiftly. That is good to know.

They are seldom seen as far north as this, he said, but as we go farther south, we will see more. I asked him and others to call me whenever they see one.

WE HAVE BEEN wrestling—my men and I. It was good sport, something we should do often. Uro told me I had hurt his arm a few days ago, but it was well again. He said he did not resist me because I am his officer. I said, of course, that if he had resisted I would have killed him, and pretended to recall the incident. He said that though I may be a better swordsman he is a fine wrestler. Aahmes declared that he was a better wrestler than Uro. The Men of Parsa boasted that they were all much better wrestlers than any Men of Kemet. We had matches, wrestling as friends. Baginu beat his first opponent, but Aahmes beat Baginu. I offered to wrestle Aahmes. His friends objected, saying justly that he was tired from his earlier match with Baginu. I said I would wrestle Aahmes and Baginu together, knowing that if they wrestled as one their animosity could not endure. Myt-ser'eu objected and so did they, saying that would be unfair to me. I insisted they do it, and said they might throw me in the water if they could. Myt-ser'eu cried that the crocodiles would devour me. Uraeus whispered to her that no crocodile would harm me. She told me and I agreed, saying I was too tough for jaws like theirs.

We wrestled. Baginu sprang on my back while I was grappling Aahmes, but I threw him off, knocked Aahmes down with him, and threw him into the water.

He is a poor swimmer. Although our ship was sailing no faster than an old man walks, he could not catch up. I dived in, got my arm around his neck, and pulled him near enough the side for his friends to help us up.

When I was back on board, gasping and smelling of the river, I declared that I was exhausted from my long swim and could not continue. Since that was the case, I said, Aahmes was our champion until we wrestled again. Everyone argued against this, saying I was champion. I silenced them all and forced them to accept Aahmes.

Afterward I made Uraeus follow me into the hold so that we

might speak without being overheard by the others. I apologized for sending him away and asked where he had been.

"Down here, master, hunting rats."

I commended him, saying I knew they did great damage.

"You had dismissed me, master. I obeyed, as I always obey. But when the wrestling began, I was afraid it might turn to fighting."

"I will always dismiss you when Myt-ser'eu and I wish to be alone." Because Uraeus looked so despondent at that, I added, "It's no reflection on you. I'd dismiss Aahmes—or anyone—as readily."

"Thank you, master. I will strive not to intrude."

"That's good." I patted his shoulder, which might have been supple leather.

"I am quiet, unobtrusive. Often you do not know that I am with you."

"But ready to serve whenever I need you."

"Exactly, master. Exactly."

Looking at him—at his eyes, particularly—I could not imagine that I would ever have selected such a servant in the slave market. He seems a small man of middle years and looks strong, but his face and silence are forbidding. His eyes are hard and cold. "Where did I buy you?" I asked, adding, "I forget very quickly, as you probably know."

"You did not buy me, master. I was given to you by my old master, Sesostris."

"He must be a good friend indeed," I said, "to part with such a valuable gift. Did I do him some service?"

Uraeus shook his head. He has an odd, swaying way of doing it. "You did him no service, master, but he likes you and has helped you in many ways, of which I was—" He paused, his head cocked to listen. "That was a rat, master. I have marked the place. I will come back for it when you sleep."

From the hatch above someone called, "Is anybody down there? I thought I heard voices."

"Yes," I said loudly. "We are."

"Ah! Lucius—Latro."

Uraeus leaned toward me, his hiss softer than ever. "This is Qanju's scribe, master. Be wary!"

He is young and a hand's breadth below me in height; he has a shaved head and intelligent eyes.

"There you are," he said, and came to join Uraeus and me. "I've been looking for you to congratulate you. Everyone says the wrestling was well worth seeing, and you're the best of all. My master and I had work to do and missed it, but the sailors and the women can never praise you enough."

I did not know how to answer; but Uraeus said, "My master is quick and strong. I only hope he is watchful as well." Clearly that was meant as an added warning to me.

"He is a soldier, of course," the scribe said, "but then they were all soldiers. Some of our sailors said they were sorry, at first, that they had not been invited to take part; but when they saw you wrestle Baginu and Aahmes, they were glad they hadn't been. Would you like to hear all they said?"

I said I would rather we spoke of something else.

"Easily done, because I want to ask a question. Have you been down here long?"

"I haven't," I said, "but Uraeus was down here alone earlier."

"You didn't happen to see the cat, did you? Or the phantom woman?"

I said we had not, and added that I had thought they had been driven out by priests, something Myt-ser'eu had told me earlier.

"So did we." The scribe sat down. "This is a sensitive matter for me, you understand."

I admitted I did not.

"I was the one who suggested we stop at the tomb-temple of Sesostris when the problem first surfaced." The scribe cleared his throat. "I'm a priest myself. You need not remind me of that. But

I'm not skilled in exorcism and own no storied wand. I thought it better to go there and have everything done properly, and my master agreed."

"Qanju?" I asked.

"Yes, of course. As a priest I took part in the exorcism. A small part, but a part. We'd rehearsed exorcism in the House of Life when I was younger, but this was my first experience of the actual rite and I very much hoped that it would be successful."

I said, "But it wasn't." It seemed safe.

"No, it—no. Last night . . . We were ashore. Do you remember that, Lucius?"

I said I did, though I did not.

"I caught a glimpse, more than a glimpse, really, of a—of a cat. An *enormous* cat, you understand. Very, very big. And black. Naturally I wondered."

"All cats are black at night," I said.

"No doubt." The scribe laughed. "No doubt at all. But still . . . Well, I began asking questions, and one of the sailors said he'd seen the woman not long ago. It wasn't Neht-nefret or Myt-ser'eu. He seemed quite certain of it. Another woman of about the same age, quite beautiful, wearing a lot of jewelry."

"He didn't speak to her?"

The scribe shook his head. "He was frightened, I'm sure. Perhaps he was simply frightened of her—I would be, I think. Perhaps he knew the cat would appear to protect her if he threatened her."

I said, "Could he have known that?"

"I don't see why not. The sailors aren't exactly open with me, and one of them might have tried it and not told us."

"You know it," I said, "or you wouldn't have spoken as you did. Did it happen to you?"

The scribe shook his head. "My master told me. I wasn't sure they were linked, the woman and the cat. But he says they are. When he says something like that, he knows. He says the cat is with her, invisible, until she's threatened. It shows itself then so that she can escape."

Uraeus whispered, "It cannot be with her always."

"I suppose not." The scribe shrugged. "There is a man who comes to the White Wall often who has a trained baboon, a big male. It will attack on command, or if it sees its master being attacked. He takes it with him whenever he goes out. But when he's at home it's locked in its cage."

I said, "Not an invisible baboon."

"No. One of the ordinary baboons who worship Ra. You say you haven't seen the cat down here, or the woman?"

"No. Not this time, at least. I suppose I could have been down here earlier, seen them, and forgotten it."

"I doubt it. You saw them both earlier, and described them to Qanju and me. You said the cat was large, half again as large as most cats."

I asked whether I had been afraid of it.

"I don't know. I doubt it. But the cat I saw was much larger than that. It must have been every bit as tall as a greyhound at the shoulder, with a tail as long as my arm." The scribe paused, biting his lips. "Sometimes unsuccessful exorcisms just make things worse. I was taught that in the House of Life, too; I'd almost forgotten it."

He paused to clear his throat. "Where did you get Uraeus, Latro?"

"My friend Sesostris gave him to me," I said.

"I—see. I don't like quizzing you like this, Latro. We've always been friends, and I'd like to stay friends. Do you happen to recall my name?"

Uraeus whispered it behind me, and I said, "You are Holy Thotmaktef."

"Right. I'm sorry to have troubled you." He spoke to my slave. "Uraeus, were you a slave in the temple of Sesostris up to the time we tied up there?"

Uraeus whispered, "Should I answer, master? I do not advise it."

"Yes," I said, "this time."

"I was not," he told the scribe.

"Where were you?"

Uraeus shook his head. There is something eerie about that, as I wrote earlier.

The scribe rose, wiping his palms on his thighs. "Lucius, will you order your slave to answer my questions?"

"No," I said. "Ask them of me, and I'll ask them of him if I choose."

"All right. There may not be many, and I'll ask this one of you. Will you please, as a favor to me, ask him to go over there under the hatch, where the light's better?"

I did.

"Now will you, as another favor, have him raise his chin?"

"Lift your chin," I told Uraeus. "There can be no harm in letting us see your neck."

He did. When I saw how wrinkled his neck was I knew he was older than I had thought.

"I was looking for a scar." The scribe seemed much more relaxed. "There isn't any."

I agreed.

"You said he'd been down here earlier alone, didn't you? Would you ask him whether he saw the cat—a huge black cat—or the woman down here then?"

I turned to Uraeus. "Did you?"

"No, master."

"Neither one?"

"No, master."

"Thank you," the scribe said. "I thank you both. A loyal slave who will hold his tongue is worth a great deal, Lucius. I congratulate you."

We watched the scribe climb the ladder to the deck, and I motioned for Uraeus to sit again. When we were both seated I said, "You understand that a great deal better than I do, I think. Probably better than Myt-ser'eu does, too. Explain it to me."

"No, master. Less than anyone, I fear. I had not heard of the cat until Thotmaktef mentioned it to us."

"But you had heard of the woman."

"Because I did not say I had not, master? No, no one had spoken of her to me. Do you wish to see her?"

"If you can show her to me."

"Then come, master." He led me to a bundle as long as I am high, a box wrapped in canvas and tied with rope. "She is in here, Master."

"Perhaps we shouldn't untie that," I said. "It doesn't belong to us, and there can't be a woman inside."

"I will not untie it, master." Uraeus looked up at me. I doubt that he ever smiles, but there was amusement in his slitted eyes. "Watch. I will show you this woman."

He lifted the lid without difficulty. The wax figure of a beautiful woman lay in the box. "I found this while hunting rats, master. I have an instinct for such things."

I was examining the wax figure. I lifted it, finding that my fingers thought it a real woman of blood and flesh, and laid it back in its box.

"Would you like to hear it speak?"

I shook my head. "I can easily believe that people have been deceived into thinking this wax woman real. Is that what you mean?"

"It is real, master. A real woman shaped of wax. If you change your mind and wish to hear it speak and see it walk, you and I might force the warlock to animate it, I think."

12

<hr>

I WAS AFRAID

"ARE YOU TALKING about our commander, Uraeus?" I returned to the boxes on which we had been sitting. "That little old
man from Parsa?"

"No, master." Uraeus joined me, bringing the lid of the wax
woman's box. "Qanju is a Magi. Holy Sahuset is the warlock. He is a
man of my own nation."

"The healer."

"Sahuset may heal at times, master. I do not know."

"He can make that figure walk and talk? That's the woman the
scribe was talking about?"

"Yes, master. Even by day, perhaps, although those who saw her in Ra's golden light might not be deceived. By night he can, certainly. And in dark places, too, or so I would guess."

"Can you do it?"

To that question, Uraeus shook his head; if I had not been unnerved already, that would have done it.

"You are no common man," I told him. Like so many frightened men, I spoke too loudly.

"There are no common men," he whispered. "Only men others consider so. You yourself are not among those, master."

"I suppose you're right."

"Nor are there common women. Your Myt-ser'eu is no common woman, and neither is Neht-nefret. No more is Sabra."

I asked who Sabra was, and he pointed to the wax figure. "It is a trick known to many, master. The wizard makes an image and causes the image to live for a time. I know you forget many things, but if you have seen a staff carved to resemble a serpent, you may remember it."

"Perhaps I have seen such staffs," I said, "since I feel sure that seeing a staff like that would not surprise me."

"Warlocks have them, master, and anoint them with the blood of serpents. They throw them down, and the wooden serpent lives for a time. I fought such a serpent once." Uraeus does not smile, or so I believe; but he came near it then. "The trick is easily done, and the box that surprised you easier still. Do you not wish to examine this lid?"

I carried it to the sunlight under the hatch; its canvas and ropes had been glued to the wood.

"The ends of these ropes touch the ends of the others, master," Uraeus explained. "The cloth to which they cling has itself been glued to the lid. One must look carefully in Ra's light to see it as it is."

I nodded, mostly to myself. "The healer must have brought this to our ship after dark. It's just a trick."

"They are all tricks, master. None but the gods work miracles."

"I'm surprised the lid didn't fall off while the box was being loaded. Do you know how he kept it on?"

A new voice, low and haunting, said, "You hold the answer."

I turned, and saw the wax woman sitting up in her box.

"Would you like this back?" I asked. I was still frightened, but I showed her the lid. "I suppose it's yours."

"You need not bring it, Latro." She rose. "I will come and get it."

This she did, walking slowly and gracefully, not in the least troubled by the gentle motion of our vessel. Can I ever have been as frightened as I was by the leisurely approach of that beautiful woman? Each fluid step shouted that worse than death may befall a man.

"Look here." She turned over the lid to show its underside. "Don't you have handles like these on the back of your shield?"

I mastered my fear sufficiently to confess that I have no shield.

"Men who flee throw aside their shields and leave them on the battlefield," the wax woman said. "You did not flee when I came to take this."

"Neither did Uraeus," I told her.

"He would not, only slither into some crevice." She smiled. "Do you think him your friend?"

"He's my slave, but I hope he bears me no ill will."

"He is no one's friend, save his master's."

Uraeus surprised me, saying, "This is my master now, Sabra. His is the blood of Osiris."

"What? Your chill ichor warms to him?" The wax woman's laugh was low and soft. "May I sit by you, Latro? There's plenty of room."

I told her she might, rose while she sat, and resumed my seat when she had settled into place. "You are not wax," I said.

"Thank you, kind Latro."

"Your breasts moved as you sat. Wax would not do that."

"My mouth moves when I speak to you. Would wax do that?"

I did not know what to say.

"We've met before, you and I, though you have forgotten me. I came to your inn to guide you and your little singing girl to my master's house."

I said, "That must be why I'm not afraid of you," although I was terribly afraid of her.

Uraeus whispered, "Did your master come here to animate you, Sabra? Can he walk unseen?"

"Oh, sometimes." The wax woman smiled. "No, Serpent of Sesostris, he did not. He would be angry to learn that I walk and speak here."

Uraeus's eyes narrowed. He leaned forward, and it seemed to me his neck grew longer, as a turtle's does. "Who has animated you?"

The wax woman ignored his question. "You do not have your sword tonight, Latro."

"It isn't night," I told her, "and I gave my sword to Myt-ser'eu while I wrestled."

"I pray Great Ra excuse me, though he is no friend of mine. I am accustomed to the night. Possibly you fear that I have some weapon concealed on my person?"

"You may keep it if you do," I told her.

"Thank you. In the same spirit of friendship, you may search me for a dagger." Her hand found mine; it was warm, smooth, and soft. "Wouldn't you like to look under my skirt?"

"No," I said. "By your own account, you belong to Sahuset. He has done me much good."

"He risked your life to make himself great. Shall I tell you?"

"If you wish."

Uraeus whispered, "You speak of what you cannot know."

"Oh, but I do! He told me. Everyone must have someone to boast to." The wax woman's voice was low, dull, and throbbing, but strangely distinct. "Your master boasts to his singing girl, I'm sure.

Sahuset boasts to me, and I to your new master. To whom do you boast, Serpent of Sesostris?"

Uraeus only hissed in reply.

"I do not fear you. Latro will not harm me, and you cannot poison me." The smooth little hand squeezed mine. "He drugged you, Latro. Write that in your scroll when you come to write. The drug often brings death. When it does not, it brings him who takes it near unto death. The breath slows and weakens. Would you feel my breath?"

"Do you breathe?" I asked.

"I must, to speak. Kiss me, and you will feel it."

I shook my head.

"I will tell you more. Then you will send your slave away, giving him no tales to bear to—whom? Your singing girl? She would thank me for saving her so much night labor."

That was untrue, and I knew it.

"You and she sat beneath a tree on the green hillside before a temple. My master came to you with wooden cups and a skin of wine. He gave you cups and filled them. The drug was smeared on the bottom of your cup alone."

I sat in silence, considering what she had said.

"You do not credit me."

I shook myself. "I don't know what to believe. I have to think."

"You are still young, and the strongest man on this ship, yet you lay down to sleep. And died? No sword, no arrow, no fever, not even a cobra's bite. If you will not accept my explanation, how do you explain it?"

"I don't," I said. "Even the gods are not required to explain everything. What is it you want?"

"Your love, to begin."

"It isn't mine to give." I tried to soften my words. "Love can't be handed over like a stone. I owe you friendship, and I'll try to be your friend because you've been mine."

"If you are my friend, will you get me what I want? And need? What I must have?"

Frightened again, I only shrugged.

"Myt-ser'eu's blood. Or Neht-nefret's. It doesn't matter which. But quite a lot of it, not just a few drops."

Uraeus hissed softly. I suppose it was meant as a warning to me, although I did not require it.

"No." I struggled to sound firm. "I won't get anyone's blood for you unless you'll take the blood of beasts."

"Latro, I cannot." Tears trickled from both eyes, streaking her cheeks. "I must have the blood of such women as they. Reconsider, please."

"You spoke of love," I told her. "I love Myt-ser'eu. Neht-nefret is her friend, and my friend Muslak loves her."

"He does not."

"So you say." I shuddered. "No! I won't do it."

"I know all Sahuset's secrets. I can make you great among the xu, and will if only you will get me the blood I need. Myt-ser'eu cannot do that."

I laughed to hide my fear. "My greatness is to begin with betrayal? Will they set up a statue in the forum for that? Well, I suppose they might."

"You'll do it?" She squeezed my hand.

I shook my head. "If betrayal is the price of greatness among the xu, it's too high."

"Then give me back my roof."

I picked up the lid and handed it to her.

"I am a good friend, Latro, but a terrible foe. In days to come you shall learn the truth of that."

Uraeus whispered, "Kill her, master!"

"How do you kill something that isn't alive to begin with?" I asked him. "Burning her would sink us."

"Cut off her head. Now!"

She laughed at him.

"I don't have my sword," I told Uraeus, "and I wouldn't do it if I did. She isn't mine."

"Yet you will be mine someday." Holding the lid above her head, she lowered herself gracefully into her box. Now I write of that, and the other things, because I know I forget. Sometimes it is good to forget and feel no fear. Yet the time may come when I will have to know these things. If Uraeus does not tell me of them, this papyrus will.

13

THE WOLF-HEADED GOD

AP-UAT IS THE god of soldiers. So says Aahmes and all the
soldiers of Kemet. We went to the Magi and explained that we
wished to make offerings to this god at his city, Asyut. He shook his
head. He is under strict orders to make haste, and would not order
our captain to stop there. We protested and he said that we would
be free to make any offering we wished if we tied up there tonight.
We asked for gold, which we might offer or use to buy a suitable offering. He said what gold he has was not his own but the satrap's,
which he could use only for the satrap's purposes.

We went to the captain. He is a Crimson Man, and Myt-ser'eu
says he is Muslak, our friend and Neht-nefret's special friend. He
said we would pass Asyut about noon. My soldiers grumble at this.

I have a little money and would use some of it to buy an offering, but of what use is that if we cannot go to the temple?

I HAVE BEEN speaking with the healer. He asked what was troubling me. "I slept," I said. "Myt-ser'eu says I never sleep by day. She and I were sitting in the shade of the sail. At times we spoke. At others we kissed. At still others we were silent, happy to be in each other's company."

"I understand," he said, and sighed deeply. "You forget, Latro. Because you do, I am going to tell you something. You must tell no one today, and tomorrow it will be gone and others will have to tell you who I am."

"I understand," I said. "I wouldn't have known you for a healer and my friend Sahuset if she had not told me."

"Just as you have Myt-ser'eu, so I have a certain woman. She comes to me when I wake her. We are lovers then, and talk, kiss, and embrace."

I nodded.

"It does not surprise you? It would surprise everyone else on the ship, I think."

"I have Myt-ser'eu," I explained, "and the chief Crimson Man has Neht-nefret. Both are beautiful. Why should you not have a woman also if you wish one?"

"When I do not wake her, my lover sleeps," the healer said, and it seemed to me that he spoke to himself alone, and would say nothing more unless I spoke. Thus I asked whether she slept by day as I had that morning.

"By day and by night." He clasped my shoulder. He is thin, but as tall as I and taller. "And yet, Latro, there was a night not long ago when she woke without my waking her and came to me."

He sighed again. "We were camped on the shore in tents, for there was no inn at the village where we had stopped, only a beer shop. I was in my tent and was thinking that I might return to the ship, carry her to my bed there, and awaken her."

He clapped his hands, loud as a shout. "My door-curtain was thrown back. It was she, and she kissed and embraced me. I was happier that night than I had ever been, and that happiness has been repeated. There is an enchantment, Latro, on this ship, a spell I never wove. Perhaps it is Qanju's. I do not know. What was it you wished to ask me about?"

"My dream," I said. "Myt-ser'eu says I never sleep by day, but I died once by day while I was sitting with her beneath a tree."

The healer nodded to that, so it must be true.

"She thought I had died again and was terribly frightened. She woke me, but I remember my dream, or part of it."

"A frightening dream, from what you say."

"It was. Isn't there a wolf-headed god in this land? You're of it, and the most learned among us, Myt-ser'eu says."

"That god has many names," the healer told me. He recounted some of them.

I said my soldiers called him Ap-uat.

"Then we may call him that, so long as we keep in mind that he is the opener of the ways. When our army marches, Latro, it sends a few men ahead so that it cannot be ambushed."

"An advance guard," I said. "That is always wise."

"These are called the openers of the way. Often they see a wolf-headed man who walks in advance of them. Then they know the way is safe and the army will triumph. For that reason this god was on our pharaoh's standard."

"My men wished to stop at the city of this god," I explained, "so they might sacrifice to him before we reach the wild southern lands. We went to Qanju and explained this, but he would not stop there."

The healer nodded. "I see. Do you believe that this god sent your dream?"

"It seems to me he must. We spoke to Muslak as well. He said that we'd be far south of Ap-uat's city by the time we stopped for the night, perhaps as far as Akhmim."

"Thus you come to me."

I shook my head. "Thus I sat with Myt-ser'eu, and slept. I was in a dark land in which there lay many dead. Slowly, a wolf that was also a man crawled toward me, dragging itself with its hands, which were its forepaws as well."

The healer listened in silence.

"Seeing it crawl, I knew its back was broken. No man and no beast lives long with a broken back. With a man's voice it begged me to slay it, to take its life and end its agony. I—"

The healer raised his hand. "Wait. I have many questions. Did you recognize this man who was a wolf?"

"Yes, I knew who he was in my dream, but I cannot tell you now."

"Yet you knew him then. Was he friend or foe?"

"He had been my enemy," I said. "I knew that, too."

"He came to you begging mercy, nonetheless?"

I raised my shoulders and let them fall as men do. "There was no one else."

"Only you, and the dead."

"I think so."

"Very well. Go on."

"I did as he asked." I showed the healer my sword. "I killed him with this, and quickly, holding his ear while I slashed his throat. When he was dead I saw his man's face." I paused to think and to remember the dark plain of my dream. "After that, Myt-ser'eu woke me, fearing I had died."

The healer took four sticks of crooked gold from his robe, made a square of their corners on the deck before us, and did and said certain things I will not write. These things done, he picked up the gold sticks, speaking a word for each, shook them together, and cast them at my face.

I asked whether they spoke to him when they clattered to the deck. Angry, he motioned me to silence. After a time, he swept them up, shook them as he had before, and cast them again. "You are not telling me everything," he said when he had studied them a second time. "What is it you have not told?"

"I said *girl* as I cut his throat. Only that. I cannot explain it and it seems to me it cannot be of any importance."

"Girl."

I nodded. "Just that. The one word."

"You speak the tongue of Kemet better than most foreigners. Was it in this way that you spoke in your dream?"

"I spoke only one word in my dream. That one."

"Satet?"

"No, another word that meant the same."

"Bent?"

"I don't think it was in this tongue. It meant a tall girl, very young but tall and crowned with blossoms—meant that in my dream, I mean."

The healer looked out over the water. "We must stop at Asyut," he said.

He cast his sticks as before, nodding and humming over them, then cast them again. When he looked up he said, "You must not fear your dream, Latro. Ap-uat favors you. I want you to buy a lamb and take it to his temple. A black lamb, if you can find one."

I objected that the Crimson Man had told me we would not stop for the night where Ap-uat's temple was.

"If we do," the healer asked, "will you do as I have instructed you?"

"Yes," I said. "I will surely do it if I have enough money."

He nodded, as if to himself. "Myt-ser'eu will not have left you much, I imagine. Qanju has a great deal and may give you something if you ask. Wait."

He cast the sticks as before, whistled softly, and cast again.

When he swept them up, he put them into his robe. "Anubis favors you also, as he has long favored me. Now he speaks to you through me. You are to go to the city of the dead. There he will give you more than enough to buy the lamb. You are not afraid of ghosts?"

"Of course I'm afraid of ghosts," I said, "what sane man isn't? But to what city of the dead am I to go? Doesn't every city have a place to inter its dead?"

"He did not say, nor did he say on which night you are to go there. When I spoke of ghosts, I meant only that many men are afraid to enter any city of the dead by night. Will you, knowing that the god commands you?"

"Certainly."

"Is your sword sharp?"

"You handled it," I said.

"I did not examine the edge. Is it?"

"Yes."

"That is well. Anubis wishes you to bring a sharp sword."

I write this while I remember. I have told Uraeus, who says he will go with me. Myt-ser'eu overheard us. She says she will come with me as well.

She says also that this god Anubis who favors me is a very great one, the messenger sent from the Lands of the Dead to the gods, and the messenger whom the gods send to the Lands of the Dead. He oversees the preparation of the body for burial, guards the tomb, and is invoked by everyone. I asked why he should favor me. She could not say, saying only that no one can tell why a god favors one person over another. Perhaps it is because his brother favors me.

Uraeus says we met, this Anubis and I—that he held the scales in which my heart was weighed. I protested that the heart cannot be weighed without killing the man whose heart it is. He conceded it was true, and vanished when I looked away. I wish to ask him more about the weighing of my heart, a thing I have forgotten.

———

A WARSHIP OF many oars has stopped us. Qanju and Muslak have gone to speak with its commander. I feel sure that we will tie up at Asyut after all. I have told the men.

14

THE JACKAL-HEADED GOD CALLED

ANUBIS LED THE grand procession in honor of his brother. Urged by Myt-ser'eu, I had read much in this scroll before we ate this morning. Thus I knew him at once.

We slept on the ship last night, having tried (Myt-ser'eu says) to find an inn without success. The city is thronged with those who have come for the festival. I know now that I ought to have gone to the city of the dead, but by the time Muslak and I faced up to a night on shipboard even I was tired and both women were ready to drop.

"We will have to stay here at Asyut tonight and tomorrow at least," Muslak told me. "My crew is off sightseeing, drinking, dancing, and looking for women now, and it will be that long—if not longer—before we'll be ready to sail again."

Neither Myt-ser'eu nor I had any objection, though I wished we had been able to find an inn so I might enjoy her with decency. As it was, we slept on board, went into the city this morning to watch the bullfighting, and returned to this ship (where we sit now) for a splendid view of the grand procession.

I cannot say whether I have seen bullfighting before; but I think not, for it seemed novel to me. It is a rowdy sport, and for that reason I did not think at first that Myt-ser'eu and Neht-nefret would enjoy it. Soon I learned that they liked it as least as well as I.

It would have been better, I thought, to have had a special place set aside for it, in which the spectators might watch in safety. (I mentioned this to Uraeus, but he would not agree.) As it is, spectators have no protection save the ropes about the horns of the bulls by which their handlers slowed their charges when they tried to toss us.

They were led to the field with ropes through their noses; these were cast aside once the bulls had seen each other and were prepared to fight. Both were large and strong, very fine. Loosed, they charged and charged again, circled, feinted, and indeed made me think of swordsmen who held two swords, something I feel sure I must have seen.

At last the black bull threw down the red and white, and gored him terribly before he could rise. Like bees, the black bull's handlers swarmed over him, and put their rope through his nose once more. Then he was washed and decked with garlands. I am told that he will be kept at the temple until his death, then buried as befits the herald of Ptah.

Besides this, there were races and games of all the kinds befitting soldiers. Muslak and others wished me to wrestle; but Neht-nefret warned me that the crowd would be displeased if a foreigner won, and might well mob me. This was wise, I think. I declined to take part.

This procession is well worth seeing. Richly robed, the images of every god in the city pass us on boats, rowed by their worshippers and attended by their priests. There is great pageantry. Jeweled fans of bright feathers cool these images. Dancers whirl about them. The riverbank is lined with spectators as far as the eye can see, and there are thousands more on boats and ships like ours.

Perhaps I should not write this, but I can expunge it later if I think that best. The image of Anubis was only an image, I would judge of carved and painted wood. So it was with the images of the other gods, until Ap-uat came. He seemed to me no image at all, but a wolf-headed man larger than any man. He looked at me as he passed, and cocked his head as if to ask, "Are you coming?" Had he shown his teeth, I think I might have run like any coward and hidden in the hold.

ANUBIS WISHED ME to meet him in the city of the dead. I had not forgotten that when we tied up here this morning, and indeed have not forgotten it now, though I never saw him. When we were at the quay, I left off whetting my sword and gave Uraeus the long dagger I had borrowed for him from Tybi, telling him where I had gotten it and that it must be returned. It was a fine dagger, double-edged and very sharp. He refused it, saying he did not need it, and gave it to Myt-ser'eu. She thanked him but returned it to Tybi, saying that she would surely lose it.

So it was, with an omen that could scarcely be worse, that we set out. We went to the market to ask the way to the city of the dead. The market was practically empty, though Myt-ser'eu says it was crowded yesterday after the procession.

She looked at jewelry and daggers among the many booths that sold such things; I bought her a small one in what seems to be the style of Kemet—a dagger like a needle, with an eye in its grip.*

---

*These daggers were thus in the shape of an ankh, or Egyptian cross, the hieroglyph for "life"; it presumably meant that the dagger would preserve the life of its owner. A lanyard may have been tied to such daggers so they would not be lost if dropped.

She asked whether we were to go to the city of the dead by day. I had not considered this, but I reclaimed this scroll from Uraeus and read aloud to her all the healer had said and done, and she said we were surely to go by night, since he had asked whether I would be afraid to. Little children, she says, visit the dead by day; but by night all the cities of the dead can be evil places.

"Is it then," I asked, "that the Eater of Blood comes forth from the tomb?" For it seemed to me that I had heard of such a one.

She laughed and said only infants believe such things, but she was frightened, I know. "If I must face the Eater of Blood for you, I want to do it on a full stomach," she told me. "Have you enough left to buy us a good meal?"

I got out my coins, and we decided there was enough to buy simple meals for the three of us; but by the time we had found an uncrowded cookshop that suited Myt-ser'eu, Uraeus was gone. This saved some money, so we got better meals than we had planned, and beer with them. The fried fish and fresh, hot barley cakes were excellent. It was only when we had almost finished that I realized I would not be able to pay for a room that night. I told Myt-ser'eu we would have to return to the ship and sleep there again.

"No, we won't," she told me. "Muslak has a lot of money, and he'll be happy to give you enough for a fine room and more. If you intend to sacrifice today, you'll have to ask him for money anyway, won't you? Enough for a nice black lamb, and they won't be cheap here."

I confessed I had not thought of that.

"Well, you'd better. The way to ask for money is to ask for a lot, take as much as you can get, and come back soon. That's worth knowing, darling, so you'd better write it in your scroll."

"I will," I said. "I'll need to know about it as long as you're with me."

That made her angry. She shouted at me and wept. I tried to comfort her, and when she would not be comforted told her to go back to the ship, saying that I knew now where the city of the dead lay and would go there alone tonight.

"I won't! You're a beast, and you'd think I got mad so I wouldn't have to come with you."

I left the cookshop then, telling her I would punish her if she did not remain there. I had walked far from the market before I realized she was following me. I chased and caught her, and we kissed.

"Aren't I fast runner, Latro?"

"Very fast," I said. "It's those long legs. But you run too fast at first, and so lose a long race."

"Did you think I didn't want to be caught?" She kissed me again and told me I was too big to run as fast as she did. There may be some truth in that, but I know I could outdistance her in a cross-country race; she was breathing hard by the time I caught her.

The city of the dead is on desert land, not as level as it might be, with barren hills beyond it. The sun stood low before us by the time we reached the gates, a sullen crimson. There are streets in the city of the dead, just as in a city of the living. The houses lining these streets are tombs, much smaller than real houses. Most are square; some are of mud brick, some stone. The doors of a few stone tombs are broken.

We walked the streets of the silent city until we had left the last of the newest tombs behind, and there was only red land, and the hills, before us. I told Myt-ser'eu I wished to continue, climb a high hill, and view all Asyut from there. Her feet hurt, but she promised to wait for me.

I did as I had planned. Twilight came before I reached the first sizable hill; even so, the climb was not difficult. I climbed it, and viewed the city from the summit, watching its lights kindle and its shutters close, and seeing the broad and shining serpent of river beyond it, the Great River that everyone says is the biggest in the world. I saw Myt-ser'eu, too, looking small and lonely where she sat on the ground with her back against the wall of the last new tomb.

When I started down, I lost sight of her. I do not believe I saw her again after that; and when at last I reached the city of the dead once more, she was gone. I called her name more than once, and when there was no reply went into it trotting, though I too was tired by then. In the third street (I think it was) I saw a black jackal standing fearlessly in the middle of the street. When it saw that I had seen it, it put down its nose, sniffed something in the street, and fled, vanishing between two tombs. I knelt to examine the place where it had sniffed, thinking that Myt-ser'eu might have dropped some trinket and that it was her scent on whatever she had let fall that had attracted the jackal.

Dark as it was, I could see nothing; but my fingers found a sticky dust and knew it for fresh blood before I ever raised it to my nostrils. I kept quiet then, and listened. For the time of a hundred breaths, I heard only the soft sigh of the night wind. At last there were sounds to my right. Hinges creaked, the voices of men muttered, and something broke and fell.

Soon I found torn cloth.

They had not tied or gagged her, but a big man with a bandage around his chest stood over her with a soldier's bent club. Two other men had broken into a tomb with an iron-shod crow— lantern light shone through its empty doorway.

The big man came for me fast, although he would have been wiser to wait for his friends. He raised his club, but Falcata took his arm before he could strike. He was dead before it fell.

Myt-ser'eu screamed and two more rushed out of the tomb. One snatched up the heavy crow but fled each time I came at him. The other circled, trying to get behind me with his knife. He was well to my left when a dark figure slipped from between two tombs and seized him. It froze the one who held the crow for an instant. I caught its shaft with my left hand, and Falcata took him between neck and shoulder.

When I looked at the man on my left, he lay dead in the street, and Uraeus stood over him wiping his mouth. "The neck is the best place," Uraeus said. "It's over soon when you get the neck."

I admitted it was true, although Falcata had severed the big man with the club to the waist and he had fallen like a stone.

A leather bag we found in the open tomb held jewelry—some of it Myt-ser'eu's—and a few other things. I would have restored them to the tombs from which the men we had killed had taken them, but we had no means of knowing which they were and no way of repairing their broken doors. Myt-ser'eu searched the bodies of the dead men, recovering her dagger and finding a little gold as well as much silver and copper.

"I claim it all!" She showed us a double handful of coins.

"In that case," I told her, "you get nothing from our bag."

"You'll give me a few pretty things, won't you, Latro?"

"Not a single bead," I said. "It's Uraeus's and mine, all of it."

"Pah!" She drew herself up and spat. "Yours, you mean. Uraeus is your slave, even if you won't tell us where you got him."

"We slaves sometimes have some silver," Uraeus hissed. He sounded angry.

"Only if your master permits it," Myt-ser'eu told him haughtily, "but I am his river-wife and a free woman."

"A dead woman, the moment my master will have it so."

"He would never kill me. You wouldn't, would you, darling? Or rob me, either. As for this," she held out the money again, "you know I'd give it you if you needed it. I fought, too. I stabbed the big one. And I—they'd have had to pay three shekels for what they got from me."

In the end we decided to divide everything equally, each of us receiving a third. Uraeus found a pleasant inn near the temple of Ap-uat for Myt-ser'eu and me, and a single daric bought two suppers and a good room at the top, where the air is coolest and purest, and returned silver and coppers to us as well. All this time I was itching to speak to Uraeus alone, but there was no chance of it. He gave me the bag that holds this scroll and fetched one of Myt-ser'eu's bags in which she might stow her share of our loot, then returned to the ship to eat and sleep. He will rejoin us in the morning.

Now she is in bed and teases me about writing so long. But I must tell other things before I sleep. The first is that before we divided what we had won the innkeeper came to ask whether we had heard about the bodies in the city of the dead. Of course I said that I had not, and Myt-ser'eu that there must be countless bodies there to be found by anyone.

"Three men who had been killed tonight," the innkeeper said. "Two with sword cuts too deep for any man alive to give—this is what I was told—and one bitten by a cobra. No one seems to know what happened."

"Nobody but me," Myt-ser'eu told him haughtily, "and any other silly girl you'd never listen to. The third man killed the first two, then he was bitten and died himself."

The innkeeper shook his head. "Didn't you hear me? No man could have made those cuts. They say even an ax couldn't have done it. Besides, he had no sword."

A new customer carried over his bowl of beer. "Tell them about the dog. Go ahead. Spoil their supper."

"It was a jackal, not a dog," the innkeeper told us. "It yipped the way jackals do, and when they got there it had pissed on all three of the bodies. What do you think of that?"

She is getting up. I will remember and write in the morning.

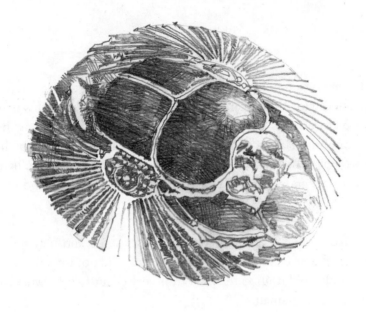

15

THE SCARAB

THE NECKLACE, THE ivory ring, and the silver ring are all very attractive. Myt-ser'eu will try to get me to give them to her, I know. She is trying on the necklace now and admiring herself in the mirror she bought. I may trade them to her or sell them to her cheaply, but I will not trade or sell this scarab. It is a beetle of gold and sea-blue enamel, a beetle with gleaming wings. Last night when I breathed on it by chance its wings seemed to move. That cannot be—they are silver, I think. Yet it seemed to me I saw them move. It is like the ankh, a sign of Khepri. He is the eldest god, she says. The rest are his children, men and women his grandchildren many times removed. The ankh is his because he gives life, the scarab because the morning sun is one of his signs. A bright beetle would not suggest sunrise to me, but I am not of Kemet. Myt-ser'eu says letters are sealed with these scarabs to attest to truth within—this is indeed picture writing here on the belly of mine, and a tiny ankh—and scarabs are laid over the hearts of the dead before their bodies are wrapped. In this way a dead woman is assured that the living wish her life and will attend to whatever omens she may send.

URAEUS SAYS SCARABS are most sacred and may not be killed, and that I should not toy with mine. I did not toy with it just now—only hold it up to the light. It is very beautiful, the work of a great, great craftsman.

Uraeus joined us at the inn. I bought a black lamb, which he and Myt-ser'eu said I must do, and my men and I drove it to the temple of the wolf-headed god. The priest in the leopard skin was pleased and smiled upon us. I hope the god smiled as well.

The wind has returned, a strong north wind that bends every palm and stirs up dust in the red land. Muslak swears we will make Wast by nightfall, but Azibaal doubts we can sail so far in a single day.

QANJU SUMMONED ME. He and Thotmaktef had been working under a sailcloth shade the Crimson Men put up. What they said was important if I am indeed the hero, as they insist. I will write down every word I recall.

"I have neglected you, Lucius," Qanju told me. "We have had no need of your eight, and it appeared to me that you were managing them as well as anyone could. You understand, I'm sure. One attends to the matters that require it, and in doing so one may neglect the matters in which all is well." He smiled as he said these things. He smiles much, the smile of a wise man who adjusts the quarrels of children.

I said that I had not been conscious of his neglect, and that I would have called on him or Thotmaktef if I had required their help.

"Exactly. Now we require yours and call on you. Will you give it?"

Of course I said I would. Myt-ser'eu had told me that the ruler of Kemet had put Qanju in command of everyone on this ship.

Thotmaktef said, "That is well. You forget, I know, but you may not have forgotten this. Has the local god Ap-uat a reason to favor you?"

"Certainly," I said. "I bought a black lamb this morning and offered it for myself and my men, explaining that I was in charge of them and asking that I be given the power of memory others have, and that we might win every fight."

Qanju nodded. "No reason but that?"

I shook my head.

Thotmaktef said, "I have never been to your city, but I have heard that the wolf is honored there."

"No doubt it is," I told him. "The wolf is an animal that should be honored. This Ap-uat is a man with a wolf's head. Pictures of him were shown to us in his temple this morning."

Thotmaktef nodded. "I knew it already, but I saw them too. The big one in which he is shown with Anubis wrapping the mummy of a dead general is very fine."

That surprised me and I said so, adding that I had not seen him there. "I forget," I said, "but not as quickly as that."

"Neither did I see you. Shall I tell him more, Noble Qanju?"

Qanju said he should, smiling as he had before.

"The chief priest of that temple sent a lesser priest to us, asking that the Noble Qanju come to him. This priest did not know what the chief priest wanted. Or perhaps he did, but if he did, he would not reveal it. In any event, the Noble Qanju asked me to return to the temple with him to find out. I myself am a priest, a priest of the temple of Thoth in Mennufer. Perhaps you remember that, Latro?"

I shook my head.

"It is so. I was taken to the chief priest and explained, adding that the Noble Qanju certainly would not come now, as the wind was rising and he was eager to put out. The chief priest then gave me this." Thotmaktef held up a small scroll and coughed apologetically. "It fell from a rack in the House of Life this morning. There are scribes there, as in every House of Life. Perhaps you know. None of them had ever examined it, or so he told me."

I shrugged. "No doubt there are many scrolls there."

"Nothing like as many as we have in Mennufer. He described you, calling you Latro. I explained that you were in command of our soldiers, and that you were a good and a brave man."

Qanju nodded and smiled. "The chief priest then asked Thotmaktef the same question I asked you a moment ago. In reply Thotmaktef relayed to him what Captain Muslak had told him of your city."

"About the wolf standard your armies carry into battle," Thotmaktef said. "Even as Hathor was wet nurse to Osiris, a she-wolf was wet nurse to the brothers who founded your city. When I told the chief priest that, he was satisfied and gave me the scroll. He would have told me what was in it as well, but I was anxious to get back to the ship and promised that the Noble Qanju and I would read it at once."

Qanju said, "As we now have. It contains a prophecy. Anubis is the god of death here. They must have told you that when they showed you the picture Thotmaktef described."

"Myt-ser'eu and Aahmes did," I said.

"A hero of Anubis who had forgotten Anubis would visit the temple, according to the prophecy. He would offer a black lamb."

Qanju waited for me to speak, so I said, "If I'm death's hero I don't know it, but I did indeed offer a black lamb, as I told you."

"This hero is to have the shield of Hemuset," Qanju continued. "The priests at the temple in Asyut, where the prophecy was apparently made, are to inform him of this and tell him how to find it. If you feel this doesn't pertain to you, I won't trouble you with any more of it."

Behind me Uraeus whispered, "My master wishes to hear more." I had not known he had followed me until then.

"Do you, Lucius?"

I nodded. "If you care to tell me, Noble Qanju."

"That is well. Here is what you are to do. You must find the temple beyond the last temple. There you shall find the shield. If I were to speak further, I would be repeating things I myself learned from Thotmaktef only moments ago."

The scribe cleared his throat. He is young, with honest eyes. His head is shaved. He said, "Hemuset is the goddess of fate. She's a minor goddess." He coughed. "By which I mean only that there's no great cult attached to her. When a child is born, she attends its birth, unseen, and decrees the fate of the child. She carries a shield with an arrow on it—in pictures, I mean. It's the way artists show her. Sometimes the shield is small, and she wears it on her head. It symbolizes the protection a man receives from his fate. He can't be killed until he's fated to die, in other words."

Qanju murmured, "Continue."

"The arrow symbolizes his death. Fated to die, he perishes."

Uraeus whispered, "No one sees her shield or her arrow, master."

"I understand," I said.

"If a man meets her," Thotmaktef continued, "and looks at her shield, he sees his entire life reflected there. Or so it's said." He coughed again. "None of this about Hemuset is in the scroll, it's just background. The scroll says Ra will guide you—guide the hero—to the temple beyond the last temple. Whatever that means."

Qanju sighed. "What it actually says is that a scarab will lead you to it. The scarab is a beetle found in this region. It is one of the signs of their sun god."

Now I wonder whether my scarab is meant. I cannot see how it could lead me to anything. But perhaps it will. The gods must know I do not see everything.

"I have said that we require your help," Qanju continued, "and we do. I must ask the obvious question first, however. Do you know yourself to be the hero mentioned in the prophecy?"

"I doubt that I am," I said. "I do not think myself a hero at all."

Behind me, Uraeus whispered, "You have been dead, master. Surely that is meant."

"If I have been dead," I told Qanju, "I have forgotten it."

"You were," Thotmaktef told me.

Qanju smiled. "If not dead, you were near enough to death to deceive me. Sahuset restored you—perhaps only to consciousness. Do you feel gratitude to him?"

"Certainly," I said, "if he saved me from death."

Thotmaktef said, "You should not have told him, Noble Qanju."

"I disagree. Suppose that we had kept it from him. Would he not have reason to distrust us after that?"

"He would forget it."

"He would write it in his scroll, as he writes so much. If he did not, his slave would tell him. What is gained by a lie is only a loss in disguise, Thotmaktef."

"I beg pardon," Thotmaktef said.

"Granted. Lucius, you have a woman with you. Do you know it?"

"Myt-ser'eu? Certainly. She went to the temple of the wolf-god with us."

"That is well. There are three women on this ship. Will you name them, please?"

I shook my head. "I have seen a woman taller than Myt-ser'eu but not as beautiful. She wears much jewelry, but less than Myt-ser'eu. Her right hand bleeds. I don't know her name."

"She cannot be yours," Qanju said.

"I don't want her. I have Myt-ser'eu. We shared a bed in an inn last night. You may have her if you wish."

"That is well." Qanju smiled. "All matters involving women are fraught with difficulty, and when the women are young and handsome, with great difficulty. Thotmaktef, I ask a favor. Will you bring Neht-nefret here?"

16

WITH MUSLAK?

THOTMAKTEF ROSE. "WE'LL have to get him before long, I think."

Behind me, Uraeus whispered, "I will go, if my master wishes."

Qanju shook his head. When Thotmaktef had left us, Qanju stared across the gunwale and fingered his beard. "He is a good young man, Lucius; but he has learned a great deal already and is learning more. Learning often turns good to evil."

I said, "In that case, learning itself must be evil."

"It is not. Everything depends upon what one learns, and the great thing—the thing to learn best—is that learning must serve us. If it does, we continue to serve Ahura Mazda, assuming that we served him when we began to learn. But if we serve learning, we learn too late that the dark god has donned it like a mask. Ah! Here is the beautiful Neht-nefret already. Well done, Thotmaktef. Have you a cushion to offer her?"

"I can sit on the deck like everybody else," the young woman called Neht-nefret said, and seated herself swiftly and gracefully. She has fine eyes, made finer still with kohl, a hard mouth, and a bandaged hand. "Is this about what I think it's about, Noble Qanju?"

He nodded. "Are you and Myt-ser'eu friends, Neht-nefret?"

"You know we are. I'd do anything for her. We're like sisters."

"Would Myt-ser'eu say the same?"

"I'm sure she would."

Qanju spoke to me. "If you would like to speak with Myt-ser'eu privately concerning this, Lucius, you may do so now. We will await your return."

I shook my head.

"Then we may begin. It might be well if Neht-nefret first told you how the three of you met."

Neht-nefret said, "I know you forget, Latro, but you're too smart to believe that women always tell the truth. I'm going to tell you the truth now, just the same. This is all true, and when you leave here you can ask Myt-ser'eu or Muslak, and they'll tell you the same exact thing. Myt-ser'eu and I are singing girls—it means good-looking young women of no family you can hire to entertain at parties. We'll sing or dance, serve drinks, or whatever you want, and we're under the protection of Hathor."

"A great goddess here," Qanju murmured.

I nodded. "She was wet nurse to Osiris." Thotmaktef's eyes flew wide when I said that, although he had told me himself a few minutes before.

"That's right," Neht-nefret said. "Girls like us need her protection more than you might think, so you have to go to the temple of Hathor to hire us, and the priests look after us as much as they can, refuse the money of men of bad character and so on. Try to get us out of trouble when we get into some."

I said, "I think I understand."

"That's good. I hope so. I need protection now, Latro. I think I need it pretty bad, and Noble Qanju agrees. Hathor's priests aren't here and I'm hoping to get it from you and Muslak."

I said that I would certainly protect her if I could.

"Thanks. I was supposed to tell you how we met, and this is how it was. You and Muslak came to Hathor's temple in Sais. That's where we're from, Myt-ser'eu and me."

I nodded.

"He wanted a river-wife and picked me. You said you didn't want one. Then you saw Myt-ser'eu and wanted her. Back then, Muslak was the only friend you had."

"Our captain," Qanju murmured.

"He's still the best friend you've got here, Latro. You may not know it, but he is, and he likes me just like you like Myt-ser'eu. Last night we slept in an inn. Not the one you and her slept in, another one."

I recalled awakening in the inn and nodded.

"It was late and we were both asleep. We'd had quite a bit of beer, and you know afterward. Well, I woke up. I think Hathor must've done it, because there wasn't any reason. I woke up, and a woman with a crooked knife was bending over me. I could see her in the moonlight that got past the shutter, and I saw the shine along the edge and grabbed the blade. Look."

She unwound her bandage. There was a long, fresh cut, not very deep, across her palm; it had been smeared with yellow salve.

"I screamed and Muslak woke up, and the door slammed. He'd barred that door before we went to bed. We talked about it after my hand stopped bleeding. I said I thought he'd barred it, but I'd been sort of—of elevated, you know, so I wasn't sure. He said he most certainly had, he'd had a few bowls but he could drink a lot more than that without getting so drunk he'd go to sleep in a place like that without barring the door. Well, the bar was lying on the floor. We found it and put it back up."

I asked how the woman had gotten in.

Neht-nefret shrugged. "You tell me."

Qanju smiled. "Thotmaktef?"

"I have a theory," Thotmaktef said, "and the Noble Qanju agrees. This woman—others have seen her, if it is the same woman—is often accompanied by a large black cat." He hesitated. "Have you ever seen a leopard, Latro?"

"I don't know. I may have. Certainly I saw the skin of one this morning."

"Yes, I suppose you must have, at the temple of Ap-uat. The chief priest of every temple in our nation wears a leopard skin as his badge of office. Since you've seen that skin and remember it now, you should have some idea of the size of a living leopard. They're far bigger than any ordinary cat, but smaller than a lion."

I nodded.

"This cat is about the same size, but it's black instead of spotted. It could have climbed the outside of the inn. It's mud brick, and I've often seen cats climb mud brick. Inside, it could lift the bar with its teeth."

Neht-nefret looked as skeptical as I felt.

"It could have been trained to do that," Thotmaktef insisted. "We train animals to do things that are far more difficult."

"A baboon would be better," Neht-nefret said. "It would be easier to train, and they have hands."

I agreed and added, "From what Neht-nefret has said, this woman ran when she saw the man she was with—"

"Muslak."

"Was waking up. That would not have been necessary if the cat were her guard."

Neht-nefret said, "Muslak's sword was beside our bed."

"Did you see this cat?" I asked her.

She shook her head.

Thotmaktef said, "A man with a sword might have killed the cat in the wink of an eye. She would not want to lose it. Besides, she may have sent the cat into the corridor to make sure she wasn't interrupted."

I asked whether he and Qanju were certain the woman was on our ship.

Qanju said, "It would appear that she has been with us since we set out, though she is seen only at night."

I suggested that the ship be searched for her. Thotmaktef said that it has been. A moment ago, I asked Uraeus whether I was among the searchers. He says I was not among them this time.

Now I am sitting in the shade to write. We just passed three laden lumber ships; Muslak says they are carrying wood from Triquetra to Wast. May not this woman have her own ship? A ship or boat in which she follows ours? What Uraeus tells me cannot be true.

I HAVE READ what I have written. Here I add that Muslak and I will take care to stay at the same inn tonight. We have agreed on that, and that I am to remain awake and watch.

The scarab is to guide me, but it has no wings now. No doubt they have broken off.

17

THE ALL-BEAST

THE CAT THAT accompanies the woman is terrifying. It
would be easy, now, to pretend that I was not afraid of it; but what
is the use of lying here? If I cannot believe what I myself write, why
write? Besides, fear is a thing that accompanies the thing feared. To
look into the eyes of the panther is to know fear, for any man who
ever walked.

We are in Wast the Thousand-Gated. I told Myt-ser'eu that
there cannot be a thousand gates in the city wall. Such a wall would
be nothing but gates. Neht-nefret said there was no wall—that the
courage of its soldiers was all the defense Kemet had ever required.
Muslak says no one can resist the Great King, and a wall would not
have saved Kemet from his armies.

Later I asked a Hellene we met in the market, because I over-heard him call this city thousand-gated. He said the thousand gates are the gates of its temples, and the gates within them. It may be there are a thousand such gates, or very near that number. Certainly there are many temples here, and Muslak says that all the temples of Kemet have many gated enclosures.

It was already late when we went ashore. We arranged for rooms side by side at the top of this inn and ate a sober supper. Muslak said he would try to sleep, that he must sleep to do his duty as captain, but that he would sleep with his sword at his side, ready to spring up at the least sound. Neht-nefret said she could not sleep; Myt-ser'eu that she would do certain things to keep me awake, and sleep between times. She was less serious than we and tried to cheer us with jokes and smiles. "I'm under a curse," she said. "I must have five bowls of beer and sleep until the sun is high, or lose my beauty." She wants a new wig, and wants me to buy it for her here.

We made love, and I took up my post. I kept the door open by the width of my finger so that I might hear. The corridor was too dark for me to see. Her soft breathing soon told me Myt-ser'eu slept. The innkeeper came with a lamp, showing a new guest to his room and making him comfortable. He left, and I heard the wooden bar drop into its iron fittings. After what seemed to me a long time—I cannot say how long it really was—the light under the door went out. After that, there was a drunken quarrel in the room below, where three or four men, I think strangers to one another, shared a single room. It ceased in time; I found myself more than half asleep upon my stool and had to wake and walk around the room, draw my sword, practice some cuts, and sheath it again, until I no longer yawned.

A gong sounded in the corridor—a small gong, like the striking of a metal cup. It sounded only once, and was not repeated.

It filled me with awe—and fear.

I felt myself in the grip of an evil dream, although I knew I was not sleeping. I stood, drew Falcata again, and picked up the stool. There was no sound at all, none, yet I knew the corridor was not empty. Something waited for me outside.

Opening the door with my foot, I went out. It may be I once did a harder thing—I know I forget, and my friends confirm it. But I cannot believe I have. If opening that door had been any harder, I could not have done it.

The corridor was as black as the soil of this Kemet. At the end, where the stairs began, the gong sounded again. Very soft it was, but I heard it. I went to the stair and down its steps, moving slowly and cautiously, for I could see nothing. A woman, Neht-nefret had said, with a necklace and other jewels. I saw no woman, nor could I imagine any reason for such a woman to ring a little gong. I was frightened. I do not like writing that, but it is the truth. What sort of man, I asked myself, is frightened of a woman? But I knew, I think, that it was not a woman. Even then, I must have known it. There was a sharp odor, half lost in the stench of the stair. I did not know what it was, but it was not such a sweet scent as women delight in.

The floor below was as silent as our own, and darker. I walked the length of its corridor, groping my way with the stool and the blade of my sword.

Twenty or thirty steps brought me to the end. I turned and saw yellow eyes between me and the stair. A voice that snarled warned me to come no nearer.

I did not obey, yet it seemed to me that I walked through water, that the night must end before I reached those glowing eyes.

The scuffle of sandals came and faded away, as someone light of foot mounted the stair. The eyes never moved.

When I had nearly reached them, it snarled. I saw its teeth, fangs like knives that gleamed in the faint light and seemed almost to shine. It was a beast, yet it had spoken like a man, ordering me to come no nearer. I halted, saying, "Beasts can't speak." I did not intend those words, which were forced from me by the eyes and shining teeth.

"Men cannot understand," the panther said.

I had stopped walking. I know that now, but I was not conscious of it then.

"Who are you?"

"You will come to our temple in the south," the panther said, "then you will know me."

Light came to the corridor. Perhaps someone in one of the rooms behind me had lit a lamp or fed a fire so that the light crept from under his door. Perhaps it was only that the moon had risen. I do not know. However the light came, I could see the entire beast then, a great black cat as big as the biggest man.

"Would you oppose me, mortal?" There was death and monstrous cruelty in the question.

"I don't want to," I said, and I have never uttered truer words. "But I must return to the floor above, and you are in my way. If I have to kill you to get there, I will."

"You will try, and you will die."

I said nothing.

It smiled as cats smile. "Aren't you curious about me? Beasts do not speak, you said. I speak. Indeed I might maintain that I am the only beast that does. I explain, and I am the soul of truth."

Someone—I have forgotten who it was—must have told me long ago that gods sometimes take the forms of beasts. Now I found I knew it.

"Would you fight a god?"

I said, "If I must, yes."

"You are a man of the name. I will kill you if it proves necessary, but I would sooner have your friendship. Know that I am a friend to many men, and will be a friend to Man always."

I suppose I nodded.

"Sometimes even to men like you. Listen. My master gave a pet to a worshipper. You know him. Evil men drove that pet away. It returned to my master, mewing numberless complaints. You have a kitten yourself. Conceive it."

I could only think that I was speaking to a god I was about to kill. I took one step, and another, and shook as if awakened from a dream of falling. The tread of sandaled feet sounded again, this time from above.

"I came to investigate," the panther said, "and to help the worshipper if help were needed. Many gods have sought to kill me, and have failed."

The sandaled feet were behind him.

"My master gives him a helpmeet for him." The panther's tail swung to and fro, like the tail of a cat that watches for prey. "Farewell."

At that moment I recalled the stool, which I had brought to use as a shield. I flung it at the panther, but he was no longer there.

The stool clattered on the empty steps. The sandaled feet were already far below. Their quick tread faded. . . . And was gone.

When I returned to this room, Myt-ser'eu was still asleep, in a welter of blood. I cut strips from my headcloth to make a bandage. Neht-nefret heard her sobs and helped, rousing an inn servant, bringing clean rags, and kindling this lamp.

"I dreamed I had the most beautiful bracelet," Myt-ser'eu told us. "It was rubies, and circled my wrist like flame—a bracelet a queen might wear."

Neht-nefret asked, "Did you see who cut you?"

I do not believe Myt-ser'eu heard. Her big, dark eyes were full of dreams. "My sister Sabra asked me to give it to her," she said, "and I did. I gave it gladly."

Neht-nefret bent above her. "Do you *have* a sister? You never talk about her."

"Yes." Myt-ser'eu nodded as the dream left her. "She's older than I am. Her name's Maftet, and I hate her." After that, she wept as before. She is pale and very weak.

It is a clean wound, long, and deeper than I like. Soon I will tell Myt-ser'eu we must change her bandage; I want to look at her wound again by sunlight.

This is enough writing. I must get what sleep I can. Muslak slept the whole time.

WE ARE BACK on the ship. I wanted to take Myt-ser'eu to the healer, but he was still on shore. I took her to Qanju instead, and he and Thotmaktef washed her wound and applied a healing ointment. "This will hold the edges closed," Qanju told her, "provided you do not finger it and do not try to lift any heavy thing. You have lost a great deal of blood."

She promised that she would not, and he made her leave us and lie down in the shade. "You must get the best water you can for her," he told me, "and mix it with wine. Five measures of water to each of wine."

I said that I had no wine.

"You have money, Lucius, and money will always buy wine. Go to the market as soon as it opens. You must get good wine, you understand. Buy from a reputable merchant."

"I'll go with you," Thotmaktef said, "if the Noble Qanju does not object."

"The water must be good, too," Qanju told us, "the purest obtainable."

Then he began to question me about the events of the night. I had read this scroll, and I told him about the chime I had heard, and the cat.

"That was the Dark God," Qanju said; he did not seem afraid.

"We call him Angra Manyu. He has but that one name among us, but many others among other peoples. He is the thing that eats the stars."

I do not believe stars can be eaten, but I did not contradict Qanju.

"We call him Apep," Thotmaktef told me, "and Aaapef. Set, Sut, Sutekh, Setcheh, and many other names."

I asked whether it were not possible to appease this god.

"You would not wish to do so," Qanju said.

The healer returned with a monkey riding his shoulder. This monkey made faces at Myt-ser'eu and me, chattered, whispered to the healer, tried to peer up Myt-ser'eu's thin cotton shift, and did many other things that amused me.

I told the healer how Myt-ser'eu had been hurt, but he did not wish to examine her wound. "If the Noble Qanju has treated it, he will have done all I could do," the healer said. "I will make an amulet for her to keep this from happening again."

He took the little bag Myt-ser'eu wears about her neck; I saw that she was loath to part with it, although she did at my urging. It was given to her by a priest of Hathor.

"What of the Dark God," I said, "the god Noble Qanju calls Angra Manyu?"

"You sit in the sun all day," the healer told me, "in order to be comfortable. Is that not so?"

I said that I did not remember, but that it did not seem likely. Myt-ser'eu said we sit in the shade. The sun here is bright and strong, and even the sailors lounge in the shade when they have no work to do. My soldiers—the five from Kemet—make shades of their big shields.

"In that case," the healer told us, "you must not listen when men speak ill of the Dark God."

I asked whether this god ever appeared as a black cat of great size.

"Ah, you've seen his servant. He often takes that shape. I see him in that shape by night, here on the ship."

I explained that he had kept me from returning to Myt-ser'eu while she was being cut; the healer said it would not happen again, that the amulet he would give her would prevent it.

Myt-ser'eu said, "How was it possible for someone to cut me without waking me? I had drunk only a single bowl. I swear it."

"Her knife is very sharp," the healer said, "and she knows spells that bring deep sleep."

We wanted to know who this woman was. It was clear he knew her. He would not tell us, saying that the time was not ripe and ill fortune would follow if he revealed her name.

"If the panther is a god," I said, "how is it he serves this woman?"

"He is not and does not," the healer told us. "He serves the Dark God, and Sabra serves me."

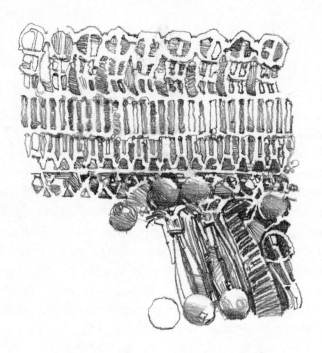

18

THE MONKEY

THE HEALER'S PET wished us farewell as Thotmaktef, Uraeus, and I went to the market to buy wine for Myt-ser'eu. It used both front paws, and it seemed to me the omen was ill. If a man had those eyes, I would at once suppose him a bad one.

Qanju had told us to buy good wine, and to bring Myt-ser'eu only the cleanest and purest water. This is because of the wound she suffered while sleeping in an inn. Now I can recall neither the inn nor the panther, but I know I told Qanju about them. I have read this scroll, and all that I said is written here as well.

When we had left our ship, and indeed the quay and its store-houses, behind us, Thotmaktef assured me that Muslak would not put out without me, and that Qanju would not permit him to put out without us in any case.

After that, the first thing we did ashore was to buy a new head-cloth for me. My head is shaved, I suppose to prevent vermin, and Thotmaktef said people would assume that I was another priest if I did not cover it. My head is large, but a seller of such cloths had his wife sew one to my measure. She was quick, and the cloth is strong cotton with blue stripes. It keeps the sun from my head and shelters my shoulders too. I like it very much and paid for a second for Uraeus, whose bald head might easily be mistaken for a shaved one.

Thotmaktef and I talked of our errand. He pointed out that we would require more water than wine. A single jar of wine would be sufficient, but we should have five of water. We rented a donkey with panniers to carry our jars and bought five large jars for water cheaply and without difficulty. The woman who sold them told us there was a foreign shop not a hundred steps from her stall that sold the best wine in all Kemet, fine vintages straight from Hellas.

We went in and introduced ourselves to the merchant, whose name is Agathocles. "We spoke yesterday," he told me. "You were with a pretty young lady, remember? I told you why we call this polis Thebes of the Thousand Gates. You told me you had only just come to Wast and were traveling south."

I did not remember, but I recalled reading of the encounter in my scroll and said I did.

"I've seen you before that, too." He drummed his chest with his fingers, which seems to be a habit of his when perplexed. "That was why I went up to you and spoke. I wish I could remember where."

"So do I," I said. "My name is Latro. Does that help?"

His eyes opened a trifle wider at my name; but he said, "No. . . . No, it doesn't. There was a Latros at the games one year. So I've heard. I wasn't there, though I would have liked to go. He won the pankration, they said. He was a terrifying fighter."

"Latro is in charge of our troops," Thotmaktef explained. "I know he's a fine wrestler, but he's certainly not a bully."

"Troops?"

"It was thought we might need some fighting men in Wawat."

"I'd say you have at least one good one." Agathocles drummed his chest once more. "Back home . . . I'd almost swear . . . This Latros, the pankrationist, was a freedman of Pausanias's. This isn't the same man?"

Thotmaktef shook his head. "Latro's a soldier of Sidon. You probably know much more about those Crimson ports than I do, but as I understand it, it's a vassal city of the Great King's." (All this was new to me, but I have no doubt it is the truth. I have asked Thotmaktef where he learned so much about me, and he says Muslak told him.)

"That's not you?" Agathocles asked me.

I said it was not, unless the Pausanias he had mentioned was king of Sidon.

"He's a prince of Rope." Agathocles looked at me oddly. "Very famous."

I shrugged, and my slave Uraeus stepped in to explain that we had come to buy wine, and that it must be the best. All this was said in the tongue most men use here.

"That's correct," Thotmaktef told Agathocles, "and we'll buy no jar we haven't tasted."

"Nor would I sell you such a jar," Agathocles declared, "but I must see your money before you taste my wine."

I showed him some of the silver and gold from my pouch.

He smiled and got a jar for us, beautifully painted. "This is the very best I brought back from my last voyage. Grown in Cimon's own estate, on south-facing hillsides. You don't have to believe that, but it's the simple truth and your palate will testify to it. Would you like to taste it?"

We said we would, and he produced tiny cups. It was indeed excellent, warm and fragrant, dry without being sour. We asked the price, which seemed high but not outlandish. Thotmaktef offered to pay that much and a bit more for two jars, and eventually a bargain was struck. I paid.

"We need water, too," Thotmaktef explained. "Not ordinary water, the best and purest water obtainable."

"I know the best well in Kemet," Agathocles assured us. He left his clerk in charge of his shop and took us there himself, telling us truly that we would never find Charthi's house without a guide.

It was a house of many wings and courts some distance from the city, with walled grounds three times the size of most farms. After half a dozen arguments and repeated explanations, the porter went in to speak with some upper servant, leaving the four of us (and the donkey boy) to the beggars who haunted its gate and two savage dogs whose chains let them attack anyone who came too near it.

Admitted at last, Agathocles, Thotmaktef, and I found Charthi lounging in the shade, watching his children play among fountains, flowers, and vines. Agathocles explained that we were strangers sailing south, at which a look passed between them.

"You are welcome in my house," Charthi told us, "and welcome to as much water as will load a dozen donkeys. I've the finest well anywhere, exactly as my friend Agathocles told you. But I could never forgive myself if I did not show you hospitality. You've already sailed far and walked far, and the day is warm. Wouldn't you like to taste my dates and figs, with something better than water in your cups?"

We thanked him, and he led us to a large table in another part of his garden. "You journey to Wawat, my friend tells me," he said when all had been served. "If your errand is confidential, I will take no offense. If it is not, however, I may be able to assist you. Is it something we may speak of?"

"It is not confidential," Thotmaktef told him, "though we do the satrap's bidding. He sends my master, with a ship and nine soldiers, to report upon the south."

"I have met that worthy prince," Charthi said, "and he must know our city well. He has been here several times."

"We must go much farther south," Thotmaktef explained. "Farther than your city and farther even than Wawat."

"Ah! To Yam?"

"And beyond it," Thotmaktef said.

"You are indeed venturesome men, and I well understand why my friend Agathocles brought you to me." There were no smiles now, and for a moment I thought Charthi might weep. "My eldest son, my own dear Kames, has vanished into that land. What do you know of the gold mines?"

Thotmaktef's eyes flew wide at that. Perhaps mine did as well. "Nothing," he said. "Or very little. I know the pharaohs of old had such mines. They are said to be worked out."

"So they are," Charthi whispered. "That is indeed what men say. But are they? Who has seen them?"

"Not I," said Agathocles.

"Nor I. The Hellenes, the men of our friend's country, have advanced the art of mining far beyond anything our forefathers knew. Agathocles, you have silver?"

"Not I, but my city. Athens possesses rich silver mines. There is no land in all the world that does not know and honor the silver owl."

Charthi addressed me. "You are a Hellene yourself, are you not, Latro?"

I shrugged; but when Agathocles addressed me in the Hellene tongue, I answered, finding that I know it better than that of Kemet.

"In my judgment he is not," Agathocles told Charthi. "He is surely no Rope Maker, for he has not the broad alpha of the Silent Country. He speaks more or less like a man of my own city, but I do not believe he was born there."

"Neither do we," Thotmaktef said. "He is a mercenary in the Sidonian service, as I told you. The king of Sidon serves the Great King, thus no Hellene would serve Sidon."

Agathocles smiled and leaned back in his seat. "Don't be too sure of that, Holy Thotmaktef. The Great King will conquer Hellas just as he conquered Kemet. If a mighty empire could not stand against him, do you imagine our quarreling cities can?"

"No," Thotmaktef told him, "but you Hellenes do."

Agathocles shook his head. "Not all of us are such fools. Why not surrender peaceably, I say, as so many places have? Will any of you brand me a traitor for saying what I just did? For trying to save the lives of thousands of my fellow citizens?"

"I will not," Thotmaktef told him.

"Nor will I," said Charthi, "but I want to ask you a plain question, to which I require a plain answer if you wish to be welcomed—as you have often been—to my house. If the mines were to be found again, and proved rich still, would you do your utmost to have the satrap apprised of it?"

"I would, of course," Agathocles replied. "But you're asking the wrong person. Put your question to these three."

"I need not." Charthi removed his headcloth and tossed it to the servant who darted forward to receive it and hand him afresh one. "I bare my head before you and before the Just God. I am revealing everything."

Thotmaktef murmured, "We are honored," and Agathocles and I nodded.

"I have a map. Do all of you know what that is?"

Thotmaktef did and Agathocles did not. I did not know the word and kept silent.

"It is a picture of the ground as a soaring vulture might behold it," Charthi explained, and went to get it.

When he had gone, I said I was surprised that he did not send his servant for it.

"It is hidden, you may be sure." Agathocles spoke to me in the Hellene tongue. Since he has found that I understand it, he does that often. Thotmaktef listened and looked very puzzled, but I believe he understands more than Agathocles thinks.

When Charthi returned, he sent his servants away and unrolled the map. "Here you see the line of the river," he said, "wandering south. This little square marks the city of Nekhen, and this one the southern city of Abu, where Kemet ends."

Agathocles asked the location of Wast, and Charthi explained that it was above the topmost border of the map. "The mines are here," he said, and drew a circle on the map with his forefinger.

"I forget," I said. "It is a fault I have, like a stammer. I regret it but can't correct it. Even so, I would guess that there are kingdoms smaller than the circle you've shown us."

"Much smaller," Agathocles said. "How long would it take me to drive over that, with a chariot and a pair of good horses?"

"Three days or four, I would judge," Charthi said. "That long to drive across, provided you could find water for your horses. Much longer, of course, to explore the whole area exhaustively. A year or more, perhaps."

"It's red land?" Thotmaktef asked.

Charthi shrugged. "I don't know—I've never been there. Some or all of it may be. Some is probably more or less level grazing land. Medjay I've spoken to have said there was a good deal of grass."

"Did they know where the mines were?"

Charthi shrugged again. "They told me they didn't. If you want my honest opinion, the king of the Nehasyu and his ministers know where some of them are and are trying to work them. I doubt they know where all of them are."

Thotmaktef said, "Latro and I thank you for your hospitality and your information. If you'll allow us to fill our jars with your excellent water, we need trouble you no longer."

163

Charthi sighed. "But you won't look for the mines. I don't blame you."

"We will not. We don't have a year to spare, Noble Charthi, or anything like that long. If we come across your noble son, we will aid him in every way commensurate with our mission. But I cannot promise you we will search for him, or the mines."

"No blame accrues to you," Charthi said. "May I ask one favor in return for my water? It is a small favor, and one that will be easy for you."

"In that case we will be delighted to oblige you," Thotmaktef said.

"Then rejoin me here when your jars are full."

This of course we did. Now Agathocles is on board with the second map, the one they say shows the exact locations of more than a dozen mines. He and Thotmaktef are talking with Qanju. He will go with us, as Charthi wished, I am sure.

I mixed wine and water for Myt-ser'eu as Qanju told me. It was excellent water and excellent wine, and she drank a great deal of it and became merry, singing and dancing to her own song. Now she sleeps. I move her so that she is always shaded.

THE MONKEY CAME while I was mixing wine and water for Myt-ser'eu. Just now he was on my shoulder, chattering while he watched me write. When I rolled up my scroll, he whispered, "So, you did not see Master?" I chased him then, and would have stoned him if I could. He is no innocent animal. I fear him.

19

THE HEALER'S GOD

THE GREAT GOD of the South wishes to speak with me. The
healer told me this, and it may be that it is true. We were fencing in
the manner of Kemet with sticks the captain found for us. There
are only four, so no more than two could fence at once.

Aahmes told me of this exercise. It is the way soldiers are
trained in the army of Kemet. A stick is bound to the left forearm.
It is the "shield." The stick in the right hand is the "sword." The
point is forbidden—there is great danger if it is used. I fought each
in turn, beginning with the soldiers of Kemet. They had done it before, and it seemed best to me if Qanju's three from Parsa saw it five
times before they fought. Aahmes wanted to fight last. I took him
last among those of Kemet, but not last of all as he wished.

Myt-ser'eu has a headache. She makes light of it, saying that she always has a headache in the morning. I set Uraeus to mixing wine and water for her, and Neht-nefret to coaxing her to drink it. I let each soldier drink too after he had fought.

When you fight a man with a shield, you try to get him to raise it so as to blind himself. This is much harder in the stick game, which may be good. I am not sure about that.

The men of Kemet fought well, all of them, as soon as they saw I would not strike soft. Uro fought first and nearly beat me. I had thought he would know less than he did, and was striving not to discourage him. He may have been trying not to embarrass me in the same way, and so we played at it for a time. Then he came at me in earnest and nearly won. I hit his head and stretched him on the deck.

And Myt-ser'eu cheered.

I am not sure why it has made me feel so much love for her, perhaps it is because I know how sick she felt. I forget. She and Muslak have told me, and Uraeus confirms it. So does this scroll. I can no longer remember Charthi's walled house and his gardens, which I read about before I began to write; but I have asked the healer, and he says it is only the head that forgets. The head is the seat of reason, the heart the seat of our feelings, pounding when we are moved. My heart will never forget Myt-ser'eu's cheering.

After that I fought the rest one by one. Aahmes was the best, the only one better than Uro. He is taller than I, a great advantage in this game. At last I tripped him, threw him down, and feigned to lop off his head.

The men of Parsa knew far less. They watched my face, not my stick, and my stick punished them for it. We will fence again when their bruises have healed.

The healer watched us just as the captain did. Neither offered to take part. When our fencing was done and we had washed away our sweat, the healer spoke to me privately, saying, "Is there anyone on board you would fear to fight with those sticks?"

I said of course that there was not, that I might be beaten but that no one who fears trivial defeats can ever learn.

"Suppose the swords were real?"

His question gave me pause. At last I said, "My slave Uraeus."

He laughed. "Not many men fear their slaves."

"Not enough, perhaps." I shrugged. "Have I offered to free him?"

"I don't know."

"Then I will tell him he is free today," I said.

"In that case you have," the healer told me. "You are so willing to free him that you will surely have offered him his freedom before."

I said I would ask him, and added that I had learned something new about myself that day.

"Not because I taught you." He shook his head. "All those who teach are hated."

"You mean my soldiers will hate me for teaching them the sword."

"No, that they hated you before it." (I do not credit this.) "I myself teach no one, knowing I would make my students stronger to destroy me. I advise you to follow the same course."

"So you don't teach me."

He smiled and shook his head.

"My men will follow me in battle," I told him. "You'll see."

"Of course they will. They know you're a fine fighter. But where there is no danger, your danger will be from them."

I thanked him for the warning, and said I would tell Uraeus to remind me of it.

"Who will warn you of him?"

I considered that and said, "You will—or Myt-ser'eu."

The healer chuckled, recalling unpleasantly the chattering of his pet. "Next you will say that we will warn you of each other."

"If necessary, I'm sure you will." I turned to go.

He stopped me. "These things were not what I wished to tell

you. The Red One would speak with you. When we met I promised you I would take you to his temple. You will have long forgotten our talk, unless you read it in the scroll you carry."

I confessed that I remembered nothing of it, and asked who the Red One was.

"He has many names."

The healer's monkey dropped from the rigging to his shoulder, but he paid no heed to it or its noise.

"You and I may call him Seth. I am one of his priests."

"He is a god?"

The healer nodded. "The Desert God and the Dark God, the god of night and storm, the son of Heaven's Vault. Tonight, when everyone is asleep, you are to come here, to the bow, to await his coming. If he does not appear before sunrise, he will not come."

It was already evening when the healer said this. We soon put in at this town. I ate with our captain, whose name is Muslak, and his wife, Neht-nefret. Myt-ser'eu drank more beer than Muslak, beer I bought her freely. I lay beside her on the roof of our inn until she slept, then crept away to this ship.

The sailor Muslak had left to watch it soon slept. I waited, sleepy and too full of beer and barley cakes, until a tap on my shoulder made me turn about quickly.

It was a woman, tall and beautiful. She smiled at me, and held up her hands to show that she held no weapon. "I am Sabra, and your friend. Did you leave Myt-ser'eu alone, Latro?"

I nodded.

"Let us hope no evil befalls her. May I ask why you are here?"

I said that the healer had told me to wait here for the Red One.

She laid her hand upon mine, and her hand was cold and hard. "Should he appear, Latro, you must make certain that he is indeed the Red One."

I slept and woke, and slept and woke. Walked the ship from end to end many times, sat, and slept again.

At last I was joined by a man I did not know. He looked tired, and I supposed he wished to sleep. I talked with him for a while even so, for I wished to remain awake and was finding it difficult. I said that he seemed to have had a bad night of it at the inn.

"Oh, I did!" He laughed, laughing at his own misfortune, which made me like him. "I paid to sleep on the roof. A woman woke me—it must have been very late—and offered to lie with me. One of these Riverland women." He extended his hand, palm up. "You know."

I said I did, since he clearly expected it.

"I asked how much, and she said she'd do it for whatever I was willing to give. Like any fool I said all right. Her head was shaved, so she wasn't a low-class woman. She had no wig, which made me wonder." Laughing at his own folly, he shook his head. "I like to think I'm a knowing man. This ought to be a lesson to me.

"I told her to lie down, and lay down beside her, and explained a few things I wanted her to do as well as I could in the barbarous speech of this land. She didn't speak our tongue as well as you do, but she had a few words, the kinds of things they talk about in Tower Hill. So we understood each other well enough.

"Things were starting to get interesting when I looked up and saw another woman with a knife. I couldn't see her face, but the moonlight gleamed on the blade and that was all I needed to know. I yelled, the woman on top of me rolled off, and the other woman slashed at us. She missed me, but she cut the woman who'd been lying with me—caught both hips."

He sighed and fell silent, and I asked what had happened next.

"You won't believe this, but I suppose you'll forget it anyway, so it doesn't matter. This woman wiped her knife on her face." He illustrated the motion, left cheek and right. "Have you ever heard of anybody doing that?"

I said I did not know.

"Well, I haven't, and it wasn't over yet. Some man grabbed this woman and began threatening her. He had a voice like a snake. I was trying to get on my feet, and it scared the life out of me, just hearing him. There was more, too. A lot more that you wouldn't believe."

"I believe everything I've heard so far," I told him, "and I might even know who the man was."

"All right. A lion snarled. That was what it sounded like. I looked around, and there was a man there in a mask, a dog's head or something like that. The cat was with him. It was big, very big, but I don't think it was really a lion. The woman I'd been lying with started having hysterics; and the man who'd been holding the other one, the one with the knife, let her go and prostrated himself." He sighed again.

"What happened after that?" I asked.

He began to speak, fell silent, and at last said, "Have you got any wine, Latros?"

We looked for the jars from which Uraeus had mixed wine for Myt-ser'eu, but those we found were empty.

"I sell wine," he said, "and now that I want some myself there isn't any. I suppose it would take me a week to walk back to my shop."

When I asked where it was, he said it was right off the market. It was late when we landed, so I have not been to the market here.

He asked whether I wanted to lie down and sleep. I said that I did not, that I was hoping someone who had said he would meet me here would come. He said he did not want to sleep either, that he was still afraid to be alone. The woman with the knife had jumped off the roof, he said. The man in the mask had gestured, and she had jumped from the roof, although it was four floors up. Thus we sat talking, though I felt sure the healer's god would not come unless I was alone. This man's name is Agathocles, and he is from Hellas. He is older than Muslak, sought for ways to compliment me, and has a soft voice. I think it will be well not to trust him.

The healer's god did not come, but the healer himself did, his face the mask of sorrow. He went into the hold as if going there to sleep, but soon came up again carrying a box as large as himself. Seeing he meant to take it off the ship, I told him he could not. He said it was his own property and so marked. He showed us the writing, but neither of us could read it. Agathocles wisely said that if it was his, he must know what it contained. He said it was empty, and opened it to show us. He explained that some property of his had been taken ashore, and that he intended to put it in the box so that he could carry everything back to the ship together. We allowed him to take it.

He soon returned carrying a lamp, with which he lighted the way of two other men of Kemet, peasants (as Agathocles told me) since their heads were not shaved. I went into the hold and received the box when they passed it down the hatch, though they would, perhaps, have stolen nothing. Its weight made me wonder about its contents, and although others say I forget quickly I had not forgotten that the healer had removed its lid easily. I did the same, and saw a battered image of wax. Both hands had been broken off, and the face smashed. Then I wanted to ask the healer who had done such a thing, and why; but I did not do so, only replacing the lid and asking him where he wished me to put it. He said that I might leave it where it was and put down his lamp on the lid. I warned him of the danger of fire, and went up on deck again.

Now I shall set down a strange thing. This is the truth, whatever I may think when I read this scroll in the future. The lid of the healer's box has two handles, not on the outside where anyone would expect them to be, but inside. The wax hands grasped these handles.

The sun has risen, and I have written all I know, writing nothing but the truth. I will try to sleep. I have been awake all night.

20

SABRA

THE WOMAN OF wax Sahuset has been shaping in the hold is complete. Thotmaktef and I marveled at his skill. Such figures, he explained, are useful in healing; a woman who hesitates to show a healer the site of her pain may indicate it on the wax figure without shame.

"No doubt you have had such figures before," Thotmaktef remarked, "since you speak confidently of their use."

"I have a fine one at home," Sahuset told him, "and I am sorry now that I left it behind. When I agreed to come, I did not envision treating women on the trip. Now I find that Myt-ser'eu and Neht-nefret occupy me more than all these men."

"Magicians are said to animate figures of wax and wood. I have never seen it done, I confess."

The healer smiled. "Nor will you ever see me do it."

"But could you? If you wished?"

"Am I a magician, Holy Thotmaktef?"

"You are, or so I've been informed."

The healer shrugged. "So are you. That's what the sailors say. You're forever poring over old scrolls—or so I've been informed. I don't doubt that you and Qanju know more magic than anyone else on this ship. Would you like to try to animate her? When I've finished her?"

While they spoke, I was looking at the wax woman whose arm the healer had been shaping. She blinked and looked at me, and smiled, I believe, ever so slightly. I do not know what this may mean.

I HAVE SLEPT through most of the day, the woman who attends me says. Her name is Myt-ser'eu—I just asked her. She is young, hardly more than a girl. I thought her a friend at first, then my slave. She says she is no slave but my wife. I do not believe that I would take as wife a woman of a nation not my own. I cannot recall the name of my own. (Myt-ser'eu says I forget, and that this is to be expected.) Yet I know that I have a nation. It speaks the tongue in which I write, and not the tongue in which she and I speak.

The captain's wife came. She sat and asked whether Myt-ser'eu could sit down. Myt-ser'eu said she preferred to stand, as she was doing at the time. The captain's wife introduced herself with the manner of one who jests, saying her name was Tall Sycamore. When she had gone, I asked Myt-ser'eu what her own name meant. She laughed and teased me until I recalled that it is *kitten*. I find that it is not at all unpleasant to be laughed at by Myt-ser'eu. Or to be teased by her.

Two men of her nation came. The older, a tall, stooped man with a tame monkey, is Sahuset. The younger, as young as any of the soldiers Myt-ser'eu says are mine, Thotmaktef. He told me I had slept long and asked whether I had been awake last night. I said I had been, because I could remember the boat that brought the sun. Sahuset said he had slept a lot too, and that it was normal for those on board to do so. Our captain and crew sailed the ship, which is easy as long as the north wind holds and there is no work to do. He sat and suggested a game that is played with the fingers. I did not know how to play, so he and Myt-ser'eu taught me. Myt-ser'eu did not sit, but reclined on the deck, propped on her elbows. Soon Thotmaktef grew tired of watching and left.

When he had gone, Sahuset said, "You sat up waiting for the Red God, Latro. The Red One has said he wishes to speak with you, and you waited for him. You must wait again tonight."

I promised I would, feeling that it would be a long time before I needed to sleep.

Myt-ser'eu very sensibly asked how I was to know the Red God when I saw him. Sahuset said he took many forms. He might appear as a boar, as a water-horse, or as a crocodile. He named other animals I have forgotten. He described the great statue of the Red God in the temple to which he was once attached, in his city of Miam—a red man with the head of a wild dog.

He stood, yawned, and stretched. "Just smell this air! Isn't it wonderful?"

Myt-ser'eu made a face, but to be polite I said it was.

"The land is rising," Sahuset said. "We near my home. It can't be far to Abu."

The captain overheard him and joined us. He said, "It isn't. I'm hoping to make Abu tonight. It's a wild, foreign sort of place, from what I hear of it." He turned to me, smiling. "I know you don't remember me, Lewqys, but I'm Muslak, the oldest friend you've got."

He is older than I and far from handsome; but when I looked

him in the eye, I knew what he had said was the truth. He and Myt-ser'eu are truly my friends. So too is the tall soldier from Kemet, I think. I do not think the young scribe is a friend to any of us, and although I would like to make a friend of the tall, lean healer, Sahuset, I do not feel I have done so. His cold eyes rest upon me without gladness, and dart away.

"Abu is on the southern frontier of Kemet now," he told our captain, "but Kemet extended a hundred days' travel to the south only a few centuries ago. Many families there are descended from settlers from Wast, just as I am."

Myt-ser'eu asked, "Have you cousins in Wast, Healer?"

He shook his head. "I have no family even in Miam, and certainly none in Wast."

"It's the same with me. My husband Latro's all the family I have these days, and that's only for the trip south and back. What about you, Captain?"

"A wife and three concubines, and seventeen children." He grinned. "Seventeen when I left home. There should be more now."

Myt-ser'eu laughed; she has a pretty laugh, and seems to laugh often. "You could surely spare us a few relatives. Then we'd all have families."

"I might give you a concubine," he told her, "if I had her here."

I said, "But you've a wife here. She was speaking with us not long ago."

"Right. Two wives, seventeen children, and three concubines."

A thickset man as old as the captain joined us. He must have been listening, though I had not been aware of it. He speaks the tongue of Kemet worse even than I. "In that case, one concubine must go to this kind young lady, isn't that right? I'm sure she can make use of her."

"Indeed!" Myt-ser'eu laughed again. "I'll hire her out and live on her wages."

"Women enjoy themselves frequently with other women in my country," the stranger told her, "and Lesbos is famous for it. But, Captain, I wanted to tell you that this learned gentleman is right about the land south of the second cataract. It belonged to the pharaoh. So did the mines, though the king of Nubia claims everything now."

"What kind of mines?" I asked.

"Better not to talk about that," the stranger said.

Sahuset told me, "Gold."

The stranger was chagrined. "I didn't know you knew about it."

"I didn't," Sahuset told him, "but I grew up in Wawat. I know what sort of mines were there."

Myt-ser'eu's eyes were wide. "Is gold cheap there?"

"No," Sahuset said. "The mines are exhausted, and there is no place on all the broad earth where gold is cheap."

WE SPENT THE night on this ship. Myt-ser'eu and I went ashore with the captain and his wife, ate a good dinner with them, and returned here. Myt-ser'eu soon slept, but I stayed awake, looking at the harbor with its many lights and at the city behind it. There is a tower, squat but strong, on an island in the harbor, and a wall separates the harbor district from the city proper. We have not been past it—the gates were closing for the night when we arrived. The captain's helper was on the ship with me. His name is Azibaal. So were Uro of Kemet and Vayu of Parsa, who calls this city Yeb. He says that in the morning I will have to see the sagan, with the captain and another man he named. I did not know who this other man was, but did not wish to display my ignorance.

With us on the ship was my slave. His name is Uraeus. He is of Kemet, a bent, long-necked man of middle years. He had been in the hold, but came up to greet us as soon as we returned. Myt-ser'eu fears him, as I saw, though she would not confess it. Humbly, he asked permission to return to the hold, promising to come at once if I called. I agreed. I suppose he has a bed there.

Later Sahuset the Healer came on board. He wanted to speak to me away from the others, so I sent Uro and Vayu to the stern, where they chatted with Azibaal and the steersman.

"Myt-ser'eu is unfaithful to you," Sahuset told me. "Did you know it?"

I shook my head.

"She lay with Agathocles the other night."

I asked who he was.

"The man of Hellas, the wine merchant."

"The one who speaks of mines?"

"Yes, he. You had gone and she was drunk. She offered herself, and he took her."

I said, "Will he fight me for her?"

Sahuset laughed softly. His laugh is not a good one to hear by night on board a dark ship. "He has not the stomach for it, I'm sure."

I shrugged. "Then she is mine. If he touches her and I see it, there will be trouble."

"I was going to make you an amulet that would guarantee her loyalty."

"She has an amulet already," I said. "It's a bull's head. She says she got it from you."

"How do you know that? You forget everything."

I told him I had seen it around her neck while we ate, and asked what it was for.

"She has not worn it for some days. Last night it would have protected her, but it would not keep her from Agathocles. That was not its purpose."

"Protected her from what?" I asked.

"From me," announced a woman's voice behind me.

I turned to look at her. I had not known she was on the ship with us, and remarked that she had come very quietly.

"We always do."

Sahuset cleared his throat. "Latro, this is Sabra, my wife."

I told them that Myt-ser'eu said she was my wife, and asked if it were true.

"Only as long as you say it." Sabra sounded amused. Her voice makes it hard not to touch her.

"I am here," Sahuset told me, "in the hope that the Red God will visit you as he said. He did not come last night, though you waited for him. I hope that it was because I was not here. If so, he may come tonight."

Sabra said, "I am here for the same reason, though mine is less wordy. I am here because you are, Latro."

"Did I give you leave?" Sahuset sounded angry.

Sabra shook her head. "Not even leave to set foot outside my—compartment? Bedchamber? It gets terribly hot in there, bedchamber or no. I find it much more pleasant up here. With Latro."

"Someone listens," Sahuset told us.

My slave, stooped and smaller than most men, stepped from the darker darkness of a shadow. I saw the moonlight gleam on his bald head. "I was not spying upon you," he told Sahuset. "Only listening for my master's call."

I said, "This is Uraeus. Perhaps you both know him."

"They do, master. What is it you wish?"

I smiled at that. "To remember other men, as other men do."

"I cannot heal you, master. Nor can he who gave me. If we could, we would do it at once. I never forget, however, and I will be your memory whenever you permit it."

I promised I would try to remember that, and declared that he was welcome to remind me of lost memories whenever he thought it wise.

"Then I remind you that this woman is the one you watched Sahuset mold of wax."

I did not believe it, but Sabra laughed softly and said, "Found out so soon! Did you really think me flesh and blood, Latro?"

I said I had, and forbore adding that I still did.

"We lay figures can be animated by magic, as I have often been. Does that amaze you?"

"It surprises me at least," I said, and added that I should have realized she was too beautiful to be a mortal woman.

"Oh, I'm mortal enough. I would burn like a candle."

"As you soon will," Sahuset said, "if you go far on the path you have chosen tonight."

"Would I object, dear?"

Sahuset did not answer.

Sabra took my hand; hers felt soft and sticky. "Most often," she whispered, "the magicians make crocodiles. I myself was such a crocodile once. Magicians have many enemies."

I nodded and said I understood.

"Or they shape serpents to work their will. There is a serpent here, though it is not of that kind."

I said that I would kill it if she would show it to me.

"I would rather you did not. It rids the hold of rats, so it is dear—"

Sahuset interrupted her. "I did not give you life tonight. Who did? Tell me!"

"Why, this handsome soldier, of course. Did you think he had no talents?"

"He has many." Sahuset's words were shaped to hide his anger. "He's a fine swordsman."

"As if you could judge. I wake whenever he is near. He has noticed it, though he's forgotten my lingering glances." She touched me again. "Latro darling, you say Myt-ser'eu is your wife. She's a drunken wanton, as you must know. Suppose—only suppose, Latro darling—that she said she wanted no more to do with you and wished to leave. What would you do?"

"Bid her farewell," I said, "and see that she took nothing that did not belong to her when she left."

"Well spoken! You are a man indeed. May I have another supposition, darling?"

I nodded. "If you wish it."

"Then suppose that she had a certain box, a box given her by you, but a box that both you and she had called hers the whole time she was with you. Would you permit her to take it when she left?"

"Certainly," I said.

Sabra's laugh was music, soft and sweet. "One more. I may have another, I hope? Myt-ser'eu, who has been with you as your wife for all the time I have known you, is a woman of no family. Let us suppose you were minded to take a second wife, as a replacement for her or in addition to her. Which one doesn't matter. Let us further suppose that this second wife, too, was of no family. Would you reject her on that account?"

"No," I said, "not if I loved her."

Uraeus asked, "Do you love Myt-ser'eu, master?" and I assured him that I did.

"He is your slave," Sabra told me. "I will be more than a slave to you. I will anticipate your wishes and leap to obey. I will do everything you ask, no matter how distasteful. You may retain your first wife, and lie with her whenever the desire seizes you. No lightest word nor glance of mine shall reproach you, and should you wish me to fan you both, or do any other such service, I will do it gladly. I ask but one very small service in return, something you can do for me tonight and be done with."

I was curious and asked what it was.

"Cut the cord that holds her amulet, and cast the amulet into the river."

Sahuset sighed. "Shall I explain?"

I said I wished someone would.

"These images must be fed. One feeds them by anointing them with the blood of the thing they represent."

"She sleeps," Sabra hissed. "I swear no harm—"

"Latro?" It was Myt-ser'eu, with Uraeus at her side. "Have you been talking about me?"

I said that Sahuset and I wished to protect her, and had been telling Sabra that she must not harm her.

Myt-ser'eu was asking who Sabra was when a new voice, rich and soft and of the night, interrupted her.

21

BETESHU

THE SPEAKING PANTHER interrupted Myt-ser'eu, as I
have said. I myself was interrupted in writing of it by the scribe of
my commander. We were to wait upon the sagan. I went, but
brought with me the leather case in which I carry this scroll and my
writing materials. Now we sit in the forecourt of his house: Qanju,
Thotmaktef, Sahuset, my friend the captain, and I. I have opportunity to write. We may wait all day, the captain says, and frets, because of it. I do not fret, because I have things of importance to set
down. When I have done it, I will read this.

"Great Seth speaks," Beteshu told us. His voice, which is otherwise deep but soft, stung like a whip when he said it. "Lucius the
Roman has his favor. Sahuset of Miam has his favor. They are to

come to his temple and remain until dawn. Hear the words of the Red God."

Sahuset bowed to the deck. "We hear, and will obey."

Bolder than I would have thought her, Myt-ser'eu whispered, "Latro loves me. What about me?"

"The Red God has not spoken concerning you," Beteshu the Panther told her. His words were black velvet, like his coat. "He saved you. Have you forgotten so soon?"

Sabra said, "He will not have to protect her from me again, Beteshu. You have my word." It was thus that I learned the speaking panther's name.

Beteshu said, "Wax is readily shaped. Shall I remain with you, Holy One?"

"If you will come at my call, that is all I ask," Sahuset told him.

"Then call when you will," Beteshu told him. Rushing waters flow no swifter than he. He sprang from our bow toward the pier. Here occurred a thing so strange that this pen of ragged reed stammers in trying to describe it. I saw him spring for the pier, a great black cat. But at the apex of his leap there was only empty moonlight.

He is an evil thing, Uraeus says. I am less sure, and know that Myt-ser'eu thinks Uraeus evil and Beteshu lovely. "To stroke him would be like stroking you," she said, and kissed me.

Must I describe him? I have no doubt he can change his shape as Sahuset has said. He is not so large as a lion but much larger than a cat. His color is the darkest black. His eyes are burning gold.

Here is all Sahuset said. "I had a familiar, Latro, who took the form of a cat. Qanju leagued with priests of this land to drive him away. I implored the Red God to send another. He did as I had asked and sent Beteshu with him. Beteshu has been a servant of Apep's. The Red God won him and gave him to me. Apep is chief of the bad xu, a terrible enemy and a dangerous friend. Beteshu is very wise, but slow to share his wisdom. At times he appears to be a man, black and taller even than I. His eyes are not changed—that is so for all shape changers, so our sacred knowledge teaches. Man or cat, he is swift to slay."

I said, "Then why do you not order him to kill this Qanju for you?"

"Because I do not wish him to die," Sahuset said, and left me.

MYT-SER'EU AND I are ashore in Abu. We ate in this inn with Muslak, Neht-nefret and Thotmaktef. Myt-ser'eu says the beer is better here than in the inn in which we dined last night, and Neht-nefret that the food is better. We danced and sang and enjoyed ourselves greatly. Myt-ser'eu and I made love and slept for a time. She sleeps still. I slept much while we waited upon the sagan, Muslak said at dinner. I am not sleepy now but thirsty and restless. My head hurts. I would mix wine with the water and drink a great deal of it, but there is no wine here, only bad-smelling water from the well. I write by the first light of the sun in the garden.

The sagan was a man of Parsa with a scarred face. Qanju gave him the letter of a prince. He will give Qanju a letter from the governor to the Nubian king, and send a man with us. The man has not come, nor is the letter prepared; thus we must wait in this city.

Earlier I wrote that the panther called me Lucius the Roman. This is of great importance if it is true. I must ask Sahuset and Muslak. I asked Myt-ser'eu when we returned to the ship. She says that the river we sail empties into the Great Sea, and that Muslak sailed on that sea to bring me to her land. This land is Kemet. I asked whether all the nations of the world were named for colors, as hers is. She says there are only two, and an island named for the rose. She once knew a man from this island. I asked what other land was named for its color. It is the desert, the Red Land. The Red God, she says, is god of that land. She is afraid of him, and she should be. There is no water in the desert and nothing grows there.

It is a land of dust and stones, of sun and wind. I do not know when I was there, yet feel I have been there—and suffered there as well.

This is not so strange as Beteshu the Panther, but it is strange nonetheless, and I should set it down. The landlord lit our way to the chamber we had rented for the night, and left the lamp with us when he bid us good night. (This is the custom.) Myt-ser'eu blew out the lamp before taking off her gown. Later, when I woke, it seemed to me our lamp had been of silver, formed like a dove. I thought it strange that an innkeeper should leave such a valuable lamp with his guests. I rose and examined it with my fingers, and at last carried it to the window to see by moonlight. It was a common lamp of clay. Anyone may buy a score of such lamps in any market for a few coppers. Who visited us, bringing a silver lamp?

At dinner Thotmaktef talked of this city. "Abu is the gateway to the lawless south," he said, "the last civilized town below the first cataract."

Muslak said, "I hear there's a canal."

"There is," Thotmaktef told him, "I believe we will have to pay to use it."

Muslak nodded. "Fee for the city and hire oxen to pull the ship. Qanju will attend to all that."

Myt-ser'eu said, "I saw a woman today as black as my wig."

We had all seen black men, although I did not say so.

"All the people of Kush are as black as your wig," Thotmaktef told her, "and they rule here."

I said, "They are good bowmen—as good as the men of Parsa."

Thotmaktef nodded. "When my nation was in its glory, we enlisted mercenaries from Kush and Nysa by the thousand for that reason. Our own men are as brave as those of any nation, and we are the oldest nation and the best, but—"

Neht-nefret said, "What's this about Nysa? I thought we were going to Yam."

"We are going as far as the river will take us." Thotmaktef smiled. "And it will certainly take us deep into Nysa—my master told all of us that some time ago, and you should have listened. Of course, it may require a year to get there."

(Myt-ser'eu had been holding my hand beneath the table; I felt her grip tighten.)

"You'll drive my wife off," Muslak complained.

"If she's going to interrupt me, I would just as soon drive her off."

"He's angry because you have a river-wife and he doesn't," Neht-nefret told Muslak. "I've seen this kind of thing before."

"Then he'll be angry at Latro and me too," Myt-ser'eu said. "Are you, Thotmaktef? What harm have we done you?"

"None." Thotmaktef smiled again. "No doubt Neht-nefret's right. But I'll offer you both a morsel of good advice. You must learn to be kind, and polite, to those who have money. Suppose Latro were to cast you off because you interrupted him too often. Do you interrupt him?"

Myt-ser'eu shook her head. "Only when we're playing."

"Then you have little to fear. And of course he cannot store up such slights as Muslak can. But suppose he did. You would need another protector, and neither his soldiers nor Muslak's sailors would do. They haven't any money. My master is too old, I think. That leaves Sahuset, the Hellene, and me? Can you think of others?"

Neht-nefret began, "If you—"

Thotmaktef interrupted her. "You might try to join the women of the town, of course. That is to say you might try if we were in a town when your present protector beat you soundly and told you to go. They would stone you, wouldn't they? There are too many such women already in most towns, and too few men who want them."

Myt-ser'eu said very softly, "I would go to the temple of Hathor. So would Neht-nefret."

Thotmaktef nodded. "There may be one here. Certainly you might look. I very much doubt that there are any left south of the cataract."

A stout, middle-aged man whose curling hair is starting to gray had come in. Neht-nefret waved to him. "Join us, Noble Agathocles! There's plenty of room for you."

He brought up a stool, sitting between Neht-nefret and me. "I didn't see you over here," he told me in a new tongue. "You don't mind?"

I spoke in that of Kemet. "You're very welcome here, but you'd better talk like this or the others may think we're plotting."

"They have river-horse meat here," Neht-nefret told him. "Can you imagine? Just like our king used to eat in the old days. We never got that in the delta."

"I've never eaten it," Agathocles said.

"Neither have we, but we all ordered it. It's supposed to be delicious."

Thotmaktef said, "I hope it really is river-horse, and not pork." Looking straight at Neht-nefret he added, "Sahuset eats pork. He told me."

Myt-ser'eu said, "They eat sheep's flesh in that place downriver where the wolf-god was."

"He is Ap-uat," Thotmaktef told her, "and his city is Asyut. They do indeed. They do, but I do not. What about you, Neht-nefret?"

"Certainly not!"

"But pork, of course. You eat pork?"

She shook her head violently.

Agathocles said, "Well, I do. Or I have, back home."

"Ah!" Thotmaktef smiled again. "Sahuset and our new friend here are eliminated, I think. That leaves only me, Neht-nefret."

Muslak nodded. "You'd better be nice to him, and not interrupt. Only not too nice. You know what I mean."

"It sounds like I've stepped into the middle of something," Agathocles muttered.

"It's over now," Muslak told him.

Everyone was quiet after that until a serving girl came with more beer, and Agathocles ordered. Then Myt-ser'eu said, "Sahuset has a wife, really. Latro and I met her last night. I suppose he's forgotten by now."

I had, but had read of her here. I nodded. "Her name's Sabra."

Muslak said, "There's no such woman on my ship."

"I suppose she met us here." Myt-ser'eu looked to me for support.

I said, "She must have known we were coming to this city—no doubt Sahuset told her before he left. Couldn't she have hired a boat?"

Muslak shrugged. "Well, she's welcome to travel with us, if her husband allows it and the Noble Qanju doesn't object."

Thotmaktef said, "What about me, Captain? You're bringing a wife, and so is your friend Latro. Might I have one too?"

Muslak laughed. "Do you expect me to find you a girl?"

"No, indeed. I'll do my own finding."

"Then I don't mind if Qanju doesn't."

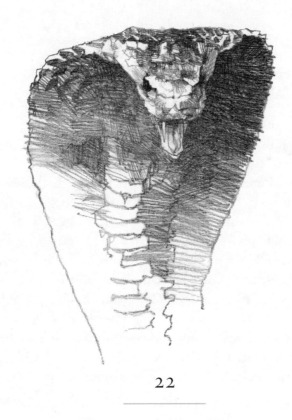

22

WISE COUNSEL

KNOWING SPEECH IS ever worth hearing. Thus, before Myt-ser'eu blew out the lamp, I asked her whether she thought Thotmaktef would really find a woman that night.

She stretched and belched. "I had wonderful time, dancing and everything, but now I wish I hadn't drunk so much beer. If I hadn't, I could tie into you properly, O my lover and protector. Every now and then you can be just unbelievably stupid."

I laughed and said I was glad I had forgotten all the other times.

"Well, I haven't, and I wish I could. Didn't you notice him slipping away as soon as I got out my lute?"

"Of course I did. That's why I asked."

"Well, you might go looking for a girl at this time of night, and you might get knocked on the head for your trouble too. Should I leave on this amulet?"

"Yes," I said, "and if you take it off, I'll put it back on you after you go to sleep."

She yawned and stretched. "Twenty days in the moon you're asleep before I am. No, dearest Latro, that young priest is not the type to sift the alleys after dark. Is it all right if I lie down?"

I said I would prefer it.

"So would I." She removed her wig, hung it on the bedpost, and stretched herself upon the bed. "Let me say all this before we get too excited." She yawned again. "Thotmaktef has his girl. When he left us, he went to see her or went to get her. One or the other. He would never have spoken out the way he did, right in front of Neht-nefret and me, unless he had one. He might—I said might—have asked the captain privately this afternoon. But I doubt it. He—"

"Agathocles and I were there, too."

"Were you? Let me talk. What you said only makes my argument that much stronger. What he did, and you may bet that sword you love so much on it, was ask Qanju. In private, of course. The two of them are always whispering together anyway. Then he went out and picked out his girl at Hathor's temple here. He may have arranged to meet her there tonight, or he might have taken her to a room in another inn. My guess is the first one, since it would have saved him the price of a meal. Then he asked the captain, knowing nobody would make fun of him and the Noble Qanju would back him up."

"You're very clever," I said. "I would not have guessed all that."

"Of course not." Myt-ser'eu belched. "What the Noble Qanju says goes, my tall poppet. I have to keep reminding you of that."

"It certainly does with me," I said. "I know he's my commander."

"If he were to tell the governor here to chop us up for bait, we'd be chopped up for bait. You, me, Neht-nefret, Captain Muslak, everybody. He—well, he's noble and he's from Parsa, and he has the ear of that foreign prince. You've forgotten the prince, but not me. Now kiss me."

MYT-SER'EU WAS STILL sleeping when I returned to our room, so I took a stroll around the city. Porters were bringing all sorts of goods into the market. I was surprised to see how much of the meat was game.

The important point is that I went into the temple of Thoth. A priest I met there said its doors open at dawn every day. I asked him to direct me to the temple of Hathor. There is none in this city. None south of Nekhen, he said. His own god is a man with the head of an ibis.

URAEUS URGES ME to write. This is what just happened. Myt-ser'eu piled her soiled gowns with Neht-nefret's and asked me to have my slave find an honest washerwoman here, whom they would pay when their clothes were returned. I had forgotten that I owned a slave. Myt-ser'eu described him, told me his name, and said he was probably in the hold.

I climbed down the hatch. The hold is dark, silent, and very hot, for there is no wind there; it reeks of bilge water. I called, "Uraeus! Are you here, Uraeus?" He answered at once, but I could not see him and walked aft to look for him. When I had gone as far as one can, I turned to go back and found him bowing behind me. "You're too quiet," I told him.

He agreed. "It is a bad habit of mine, master, and once someone stepped upon me. I beg you not to punish me for it."

"If you've been stepped on, that's punishment enough. I hope it wasn't I who stepped on you." I told him what the women wanted, and asked whether he had been in the city yet.

"Yes, master. You had gone, so I went into the city to get my dinner."

"And drink beer. Had I given you enough for that?"

"More than enough, master, but I do not care for beer. I went only to find food."

"Don't you drink?"

"Water, master. Or milk. I like milk, when I can get it."

I said, "Perhaps you can find some when you've found a woman to do the laundry. Go up on deck, look for Myt-ser'eu, and do as she tells you."

I could not walk past him in the hold; the path through the cargo being very narrow. He went up the ladder first and stepped out onto the deck, where I lost sight of him. I was starting up myself when a voice behind me whispered, "Stay, Lucius. We must speak, you and I."

I turned at once, my hand on the hilt of my sword. I had thought myself alone in the hold.

Toward the prow, two little yellow flames gleamed in the dark. "You will not require that blessed blade. I am your friend Beteshu. Come talk with me. Sit down."

I advanced. The flames were his eyes, but he remained invisible in a darkness they did nothing to illuminate. I asked whether I knew him.

"Oh, yes. We have met before, and we serve the same master."

"The Noble Qanju?" I had read what Myt-ser'eu had said of him not long ago.

"No." He did not laugh but I saw his teeth, whiter than foam. "Great Seth. Do you know that name?"

I said I did not.

"Set? No. I see that you do not know that name either. Sutekh?"

It seemed strange that he could thus read my expression in that darkness, but I only said, "No. Who is he?"

"The Desert God." He paused, and I wished I could have seen his face as well as he saw mine. "Here is a piece of true wisdom for you. Circle it in your scroll so you will read it each time you glance at the place. The true god is the desert god. Do you understand that, Lucius?"

"No," I said. "It seems to me that every god must be a true god. If he is not, he is no god."

"We are both right. Repeat what I told you."

I did.

"You will not recall it. Still you may recall having heard it before when you see it again. You are at the last cataract."

I had thought this the first, having heard the sailors talking.

"This river is born far to the south. Six cataracts stand between it and the sea. This is the last. All is sure and safe below it. There are soldiers of Parsa and Kemet to keep the peace, and the Medjay still function as of old in many places. Above, it is not so. A wise man going south will seek to know his future."

I asked how any man could know it.

"If he cannot see it, he must heed those who can. Set seeks to reveal yours to you. Will you hear him?"

"Gladly," I said.

"That is very well." He laid his arm across my shoulders; it was only then that I realized that he was a larger man than I, though I myself am larger than any of the sailors on this ship.

"Do you object to the company of beautiful women?" he asked me.

I said, "No man objects to it."

"You are wrong. But you do not. Neither do I. Creature of Sahth! Come forth!"

The lid of a long box not far from the open hatch was lifted. The woman who joined us was young and beautiful, and wore a necklace and many rings and bracelets. "You knew I overheard you, cunning Beteshu."

I believe the one who called himself Beteshu must have smiled. "I overheard your breathing."

"I do not breathe," she told him.

"How could I be so mistaken? Will Lucius take you to wife? I know you wish it."

I remembered that Myt-ser'eu had told me she was my wife, and said that I had a wife already and could not support so many women.

"I will not ask for food or beer," the woman declared. "I cannot do heavy work, jewel of my heart, but I can do all else a wife can do, and you will never hear an angry word from me. May I go to Latro, Beteshu?"

"Would you slay your present husband? If I were to say yes?"

"Do you?"

Beteshu did not reply.

"You are as far above me as the stars, Beteshu. Have pity!"

"Do not say such things." Beteshu's voice is as soft as the night wind, but there was an angry snarl in that wind tonight. "Slay your husband and you will be destroyed. Not as my master once destroyed you." He paused and drew breath. "As I destroy." He held out his hand and blew upon it, and red fire shot up from its palm.

I have seen many black men today. Black men unload a ship on the farther side of the pier. Most are dark as tar, but the palms of their hands are not. In the light from that flame I saw this man's hand, and its palm was blacker than charcoal.

The woman returned to the box from which she had emerged without another word, and reaching out of the box picked up its lid and closed it upon herself.

"We were interrupted." Beteshu's voice smiled again. "Do you blame me for that interruption?"

I shook my head. "I do not blame anyone for it."

"That is less than just. You yourself are to blame for it. Your presence stirs her to life. That is why she would be with you always. Did you know?"

I had not, and said so.

"It is true. You see gods and spirits whenever they are near, whether they would be seen or no. There was a time when I had to leap off this ship so that you would no longer see me. You will not recall that time." His hand closed upon the flame, and it was no more.

I laughed as fear makes men laugh.

"You have power over me," Beteshu said. "I have power over you. I could destroy you if I wished, yet I am your friend. You have nothing to fear from me."

"I am a friend," I told him, "to those who are friends to me."

"I must speak about your slave. He is a cobra taken from the crown of a certain one. You must not kill him. He may kill you if you try."

I said, "I will not try. What sort of man kills his own slaves?"

"Every sort of man."

We sat in silence for a time. Now and then, faint voices came through the hatch. Now and then, feet pattered on the deck above our heads. I felt then that we had been sitting so for years, side by side, and might continue so until the Golden Age returned, though the ship rotted around us.

"One man works his slave to death," Beteshu told me. "Another turns drunkard and beats his. You must strike to kill. A slave owns no slaves. Circle that too."

He was gone; and I sat in the stinking hold alone, sweating in the heat. I have told Uraeus what was said, and written the truth at his urging. I must believe it.

23

THE WATER-PATH

THE CANAL AROUND the cataract is long and tedious. So says Kha, the man the governor is sending to the Nubian king. Qanju does not think it so long in truth, only that we will be long there.

Kha came aboard today, soon after the scribe and the scribe's wife. Alala is taller than Kha, slender, young, and silent. Her skin is a ripe olive's. My wife says we have not seen her before. Alala brings with her a baboon, very large but quiet and well behaved. Thotmaktef the scribe is young and two hands below his wife in stature. His shaven head shows that he is a priest. (His wife says of Thoth, but I do not know this god.) Now he smiles much and speaks much, too; but this may be because he has a new wife. I like him and her, but wonder whether I could trust either. Those we like best are not always to be relied upon.

Kha is a man of middle years, thick at the waist. Like Qanju, he has dignity. Although a man of Kemet, he is a sagan. Muslak says this, and explains that these are men whose counsel and probity have earned the governor's ear.

When he came, Qanju was speaking to Thotmaktef and Alala. He invited Kha to join him, but did not send Thotmaktef and Alala away. These four wished to confer unheard, but though this ship is larger than most, it is crowded. I saw that Neht-nefret and Myt-ser'eu were standing nearby, and had little trouble drawing near enough to listen too. Muslak did the same.

Qanju introduced himself and explained that he is our leader and a sagan of the satrap's. Kha bowed and named himself. Qanju introduced his scribe Thotmaktef, and Thotmaktef's wife, and all four sat. Kha asked whether Alala could be trusted in confidential matters. Thotmaktef said she could be trusted absolutely. Kha asked Alala the same question.

"Your first duty is to the governor," Alala said. (She spoke more softly than the men, and Kha cupped his hand behind his head to hear her.) "A wife's first duty is to her husband. Nothing you tell me will be safe from mine."

"What of your friends?" Kha inquired. "Those with whom you are accustomed to share secrets."

"I have no such friends."

"Your sisters then."

"My sisters share no secrets with me," Alala said, "and I share none with them."

Qanju murmured, "Nor are they on our ship."

Kha asked, "Do we sail today?"

"We sail now," Qanju said, "unless there is reason to delay."

Muslak pretended not to hear this, but I saw the look he gave Azibaal.

"My bag is on board," Kha said.

Alala murmured, "So is mine."

They spoke of places for sleeping and eating, but I will not give all that.

"I am to ask King Siaspiqa to show you the gold mines," Kha said. "He may refuse, though I think he will not. Rest assured that any mines he shows you will be exhausted."

"I understand," Qanju said.

"May I ask why you wish to see them?"

"I have with me a Hellene who is familiar with the methods used in the silver mines belonging to his city. We hope that these mines will reveal to him the methods employed in Kemet of old."

"You must not speak so in the presence of King Siaspiqa. These mines are in his land. They are his now."

Qanju nodded. "Your counsel is wise. Neither will I speak of mining methods to King Siaspiqa."

Alala murmured, "Is the Hellene here? Should he not join us?"

"I would have sent for him if he were on this ship," Qanju told her. "He is to meet us above the cataract."

Kha smiled; his smile is very small. "This Hellene is wise to refrain from so lengthy and tedious a journey."

"If you would prefer . . . ?"

Kha shook his head. "I am equally unsuited to walking and the donkey."

Alala whispered to Thotmaktef. "He might be carried in a litter or driven in a chariot. He wishes to know everyone on the vessel before we reach Napata."

Kha had caught her whisper, even as I. He smiled again, and nodded. "You have chosen well, Thotmaktef."

Thotmaktef made him a seated bow. "I have, I know."

"I have reason to hope, however, that we will find King Siaspiqa south of his capital. If the gods so will it, we may enter his presence north of the second cataract."

There was more talk which I will not give here. Qanju called me over and introduced me to Kha; after that he told Kha, "Holy Sahuset is a learned man of Kemet. Perhaps you know him?"

Kha shook his head.

"The satrap sent him to assist me. He speaks the language." Qanju returned to me. "Could you find him for us, Lucius?"

Aahmes, who knew him, said he had gone ashore. I took him with me to search, and we took with us his four soldiers of Kemet. I soon found Sahuset.

When we returned to the ship, Myt-ser'eu and Neht-nefret were talking with Alala. Qanju sent me away, so I joined them.

"My father is a priest of the temple of Thoth," Alala said. "He has often told me I should marry a priest, but none here are suitable. My new husband is a priest of the temple of Thoth in Mennufer. He is young and kind, and suits me very well."

"He is a friend of ours," Myt-ser'eu told her. "Like my own husband, he has the ear of Qanju, and is thus a person of importance. Have you met my husband?"

Alala said she had not, so Myt-ser'eu made me known to her. "Latro is foreign," she explained, "but he speaks our tongue almost as well as you do."

Alala's smile made me like her at once. "You think me foreign, too. I was born here, though my parents came from the south."

I asked whether she was Nubian—of Yam was what I said in the tongue of Kemet.

"We do not speak as you do. There are two peoples. My own, the Medjay, are the Lion People. The old men speak of King Siaspiqa. He is king of the Nehasyu, the Crocodile People."

Neht-nefret said, "In Kemet, Medjay are what we call those who guard royal tombs and bring anyone who breaks the law to the judges."

"They are we," Alala told her. "You pay our warriors to guard your burial places and drive off those who would come to steal and kill."

"Do you speak the tongue of King Siaspiqa?" I asked her.

"Better than I speak this one," she said, and demonstrated, speaking a tongue unknown to me.

"What have you done with your pet?"

"I have no pet." For a moment she looked puzzled. "My mother has a cat. Do you know her?"

I said no more, but before laying aside my brush I should write a thing I have neglected. When I saw Sahuset in the market, I told Aahmes and shouldered my way through the crowd. When we were alone, Aahmes asked how I had recognized Sahuset so quickly when the market was thronged. I explained that Myt-ser'eu had pointed him out to me that morning before he left our ship, and I had seen his pet.

"He has no pet," Aahmes said. This despite the fact that the monkey had ridden Sahuset's shoulder when we brought him to Qanju. I have asked Myt-ser'eu whether I see animals others do not see. She said she could not say what I saw. She looked frightened as she said this.

Uraeus says my memory is among the gods, and will say no more.

WE ARE IN the canal. It is long and winding and has some current, though the water does not rush as it rushes through the cataract. Ten yoke pull our ship along, treading a path beside the water-path. It seems very slow to me, but Myt-ser'eu says we often sailed no faster on the river. I could walk much faster. Myt-ser'eu says I forget, and Uraeus confirms it. Tomorrow I will leave this ship, walk ahead, and see what is to be seen. I have told them to remind me of this.

––––––––––

THIS MORNING MYT-SER'EU told me I had wanted to walk ahead of our vessel before the sun grew hot. She made me promise to take Uraeus with me. Qanju overheard us. He said I might go, but that I must take two soldiers. Thus we set out: Aahmes, Baginu of Parsa, Uraeus, and I.

Here the earth is lifted, thus the cataract. Baginu says that as it rises, the land of Kemet is left behind. He is a horseman, and wished often that we were mounted. It would have been better, he said, if the satrap had sent us on horseback. Perhaps it would, but everything we bring would have had to be loaded on horses or donkeys. There are few horses here, I think, and donkeys would have slowed us greatly. Ships need tar, sailcloth, and sometimes fresh timbers; but ships need not be fed and watered each night and rarely sicken and die.

I STOPPED WRITING to talk with a woman. She spoke of a husband, and Myt-ser'eu says this is Qanju's scribe.

She told me much. "The people of Kemet think themselves very wise," she said, "but they know little of the south. Their forefathers knew more, but they have forgotten." She spoke of spotted deer taller than trees, and showed me one worked in gold to fasten a cloak. They cannot be as tall as she says.

"They speak of the Land of Yam, but there is no Land of Yam, only a memory. They speak of Kush as if Kush were all the southern lands. There is a river-kingdom of that name with very fine horses. Its people are cruel." She pointed south and east.

I said that they could not be cruel to their horses, or they could not have such fine ones. She agreed.

Her people have horses also and herd cattle, following the grass. I do not know what she meant by this, but I did not ask. It is because of their horses and dogs that the satrap pays them to watch the marches of Kemet, and because they are fine trackers.

These things I did not know while we walked up the path the oxen follow. We saw small deer, very pretty and graceful, with spike horns. Baginu wished to shoot one, but I told him to wait until evening, when we would rest and eat. Uraeus drew me aside, saying that Myt-ser'eu might lie with another while we were gone. I asked why he thought this, and he said he thought it because she had made me bring him. I saw the wisdom of this and halted as soon as the sun grew warm. This ship overtook us about midafternoon. Qanju questioned me concerning the village we had seen on the other side of the canal.

24

AGATHOCLES

A HELLENE HAS come to our ship. Myt-ser'eu says he has been with us before. She does not like him and complains that he stares at her. So do the sailors and my soldiers, but Myt-ser'eu remains in our tent now so that this Hellene cannot look at her.

We are camped by a town of mud brick beside the river. Its people are as dark as Alala. I asked whether they had a temple of the Red God, for I have been reading what the man whose hand held fire said. They do not. Alala's hands are black only on the backs; so with these people. I wrote that the hands that held fire were black everywhere.

The Hellene speaks long with Sahuset. I would like to know

what of, but they sit before Sahuset's tent and fall silent when anyone draws near.

I CANNOT WRITE well. I have drunk too much for it. I must
set down what I saw anyway. Myt-ser'eu and I went back to our
tent very late. Without my arm, she would have fallen. A baboon
squatted in front of Sahuset's. It was eating a monkey, eating fast,
cracking and swallowing the bones like a dog. I tried to keep Myt-
ser'eu from seeing it. I write beside our fire.

EVERYTHING WAS READY today, but we did not put out,
conferring instead in the shade of a sail the sailors spread on poles.
Qanju did not want Myt-ser'eu with us, but I have told her something of what was said, and Neht-nefret seems to have told her
everything. Neht-nefret was there because Thotmaktef was in the
village and Alala would not join us without another woman present. Myt-ser'eu was in our tent. The captain called Neht-nefret
over. Alala smiled and they sat side by side.

Agathocles said, "Here is an opportunity for all of us to become
rich and highly honored. Some of you know something of it already.
Sahuset knows everything and is in full agreement with me."

Sahuset nodded.

"Sahuset was sent by the satrap to represent the people of his
nation—most of you know that as well. The Noble Qanju knows as
much as Sahuset. He was sent to represent the satrap himself, as you
also know. He wishes to have counsel from the rest of you before
making his decision, for he is a man of sound judgment."

The captain said, "We'll have nothing to say until we know what
you're talking about."

Agathocles nodded. "I am one of you if you will have me, but the
satrap did not send me. I was sent by my friend Charthi, a man of

the noblest blood of Kemet. His son Kames came here looking for the mines of the pharaohs and never returned. Charthi has promised to reward me if I find him. I'm not hiding it. Without the promise of a rich reward I would not have come."

Neht-nefret said, "Are you offering to share with us? How much?"

Agathocles shook his head. "I am not. I mean to earn it and keep it, but I see the prospect of a richer reward. Most would go to the Noble Qanju, no doubt. That will still leave a great deal for the rest of us. I will claim my share, and not begrudge others who claim theirs. Long ago, the pharaohs had gold mines in the desert west of the Great River. Everyone knows where they were, and many who have traveled to this land have seen them. They had other mines in the east, mines farther from the river. Who has seen those?"

Kha said, "I've heard of them—rumors, at least. They're said to be exhausted as well."

"Said by whom?"

Kha shrugged. "That was what I was told."

Sahuset said, "King Siaspiqa shows exhausted mines—mines near the river—to those who ask about mines. No one in Wawat speaks of those to the east. It is dangerous to do so."

"I do not fear King Siaspiqa," Alala whispered, "but my husband. I will not speak of these things without his permission."

More was said, but nothing of importance until Thotmaktef returned and the matter was explained to him. "Her husband," he said, "stands in awe of the Noble Qanju."

Qanju nodded and smiled, saying, "Ask your wife to tell us," and Thotmaktef did.

"There are places where the warriors of the Nehasyu will not let us graze," Alala said softly. "They are in the rocks. There is little grass there, thus we do not go to war over it. The same warriors buy our cattle." She shrugged.

"Are these the mines?" Kha asked.

She shrugged again. "I do not know what they are, only that there is a temple in one such place. We have other temples, but we cannot offer our bulls at that one. Because we could not, my father was angry and urged our warriors to fight."

"And . . . ?" Qanju smiled encouragingly.

"He was sent north, to Kemet, lest there be war."

"This is worth knowing," Agathocles declared.

Qanju nodded. "Do you know where these places are, Alala?"

She touched the arm of her husband, who encouraged her to speak.

"I do not know," she whispered. Her voice is scarcely louder than a breath. "I was born in Abu, but the older men among the warriors of my people will surely know. So will our priests."

Agathocles said, "While you went slowly up the canal, I went swiftly to Miam and spoke with men with whom I trade. They sent me to other men." He held out his right hand and rubbed its palm with the fingers of the other. "I persuaded them to tell me what they knew, and I found it interesting indeed. I have shared it with the Noble Qanju and Holy Sahuset. At the Noble Qanju's urging, I'm prepared to share it with you as well. I ask no oaths but believe you'll soon see that what I say should go no further." He paused, and waited for someone else to speak.

At length Sahuset said, "It would not go this far, if my advice had been taken."

Qanju shook his head. "I will not justify your presence. You may do it yourself, if you like. To whom do you object?"

"All of them!"

"Then I will answer all your objections," Qanju said. "We have ample time for it. Do you believe Agathocles will keep his information from the Noble Charthi?"

Agathocles said, "I will not. I am here on his behalf."

"Nor would I keep it from the satrap," Qanju told him, "for the same reason. I have his trust and will not abuse it. Suppose that I were to act in a way Muslak found irrational and inexplicable. Would he conceal my acts, if the satrap questioned him?"

Muslak shook his head.

"He would not," Qanju continued, "knowing that the satrap would learn of them from others and punish him, as would be only just. Lucius leads our fighting men. He would obey my orders without explanation. I know that. But he can obey with intelligence only when he understands my reasons for giving them."

Qanju paused, smiling upon us. "You object to everyone save me, Sahuset, and thus to the sagan Kha. He represents the governor of Abu, and has come with us to help us, for the governor obeys the satrap. What reception might we have on our return to Abu if we acted now without informing him? What report might the governor send the satrap?"

Sahuset did not reply.

"Holy Thotmaktef is like a son to me. We share all confidences. Should I die or fall ill, he will act as a good son should, leading in my stead. Am I to keep this from him when I have kept nothing else from him? His wife is of the Medjay and may be of the greatest service to us—but only if she understands what it is we do and why we do it. She wished Neht-nefret present, since the customs of her people require that a married woman alone among men may not speak unless her husband is present. I know Neht-nefret is clever, and our captain declares her a woman of discretion. Whom would you have me send away, Sahuset?"

"I know the tongue," Sahuset said.

Qanju nodded. "So you do, but let us reach the point. Agathocles?"

"My contacts say that gold is coming from a mine in the east. Not much, they say, but some. They also say that a tall young man of Kemet is a slave there, and is being forced to work at the mine. They did not know his name. No one I spoke with has ever spoken to him."

I said, "The man who sent you to find his son must have given you a way to know him when you saw him."

"He didn't have to. I had seen him several times before he left home."

"You'd know him?"

Agathocles nodded. "Unless he's changed a great deal, I would. Besides, I could question him about his father's house, the names of servants and so forth. I know several of them because they've been sent to buy wine from me. He grew up in that house and must know them all." He spread his hands. "It's as plain as day, isn't it? His father sent him to look for the mines and find out if there was still gold to be had. He came as far as Miam and learned where they were. After that, he probably hired someone to guide him there. He was caught."

Neht-nefret said, "They'd kill him, wouldn't they? I would have."

Qanju shook his head. "You are a clever young woman, but you have much to learn. He is the son of an influential foreigner. Such a son is a sword in the hand of whoever holds him."

"Exactly." Agathocles chuckled. "If they kill him, they lose him, and if they bring him to Miam or Meröe, he'll talk about the mines to people who didn't know before. So they keep him at a mine. Let him talk. Everyone he talks to there knows already, and he can do some work."

"They will keep us there as well," Sahuset said, "if we go there as he did. They may arrest us and take us there if they so much as find out we're looking for them. Agathocles told you we were in agreement. That is one of the things we agree on."

"The satrap," Qanju said smoothly, "has sent us that he may learn of the south. We are interested in these mines because they are in the south and thus bear upon our mission.

"Kha, I will have my scribe draft a letter to the satrap, telling him what we have learned thus far, perhaps with some indication of what I plan to do. I will sign and seal it. My scribe will draft another to the governor at Abu. It will say only that he is to take the letter from the bearer and forward it to the satrap. Will you be the bearer? You may, if you wish."

Kha shook his head. "That was not my errand. I will remain with you, Most Noble Qanju, if you will permit it."

"I will, of course. Captain, will you send a reliable man? He need go no farther than Abu, and can rejoin us when he has delivered my letters to the governor."

Muslak nodded. "There's a small boat in our stores. Can I use that?"

"Of course."

"Then he'll get through the canal a lot faster than we did—the current will be with him. I'll send Azibaal. He's completely reliable."

"Good. Send him to me this evening. Both letters should be ready by then."

Qanju smiled as before. "Now I have a problem to lay before you. I will ask everyone's advice, beginning with the youngest. One must do that, I find, if one's younger counselors are not to repeat their elders' wisdom."

He spoke to Alala. "My dear, you are youngest, or so I judge. Here is my problem. A young man of Kemet, one Kames, is said to be held here as a slave, though he is none. He is a subject of the Great King's, and because he is, it is my duty to free him if I can. You are my counselor. How am I to do it?"

Alala spoke so softly we had to lean toward her to hear. "I don't understand. If the mines yield only a little gold, and people willing to tell this man," she gestured toward Agathocles, "know of it already, why does King Siaspiqa bind this Kames?"

Agathocles said, "Surely that's clear. They yield more than a little, and Kames learned of it."

Qanju said, "This Hellene may speak truly, my dear. It may also be that the king is jealous of what gold they yield, though it is but small. Or that he has little use for spies, or some other reason. We cannot know, and so I wish to speak with Kames. And to free him, as I said. How am I to accomplish that end, do you think?"

"By the help of my people, the Lion People," Alala said promptly. "They take the Great King's gold to fight for him and to guard the northern land. They will take it again, overwhelm King Siaspiqa's men, and free this Kames for you."

"It is certainly worth considering," Qanju said, "and I will consider it."

He turned to Neht-nefret. "My dear, you are youngest after the wife of my scribe, I believe. May I have your thoughts?"

Neht-nefret shrugged. "If you wish them. I've never been chary of advice. I don't think we know enough now to come up with a good plan. If I were you, I'd find a handsome young woman and have her get close to the man in charge of one of these mines. She'd soon find out a thousand things you need to know, if she were the right woman for the job. She might even be able to free this Kames herself." Neht-nefret paused and licked her lips. "She'd expect to be well rewarded for what she did. I'm sure you understand."

Qanju nodded, still smiling. "She might say that she had escaped from the Medjay, who had stolen her in the north. Exhausted, she would come limping out of the desert."

Neht-nefret nodded. "I like it. It's simple, and it might work."

"I shall consider it. The Holy Thotmaktef is next, I would say."

"They write here as we do," Thotmaktef said, "having learned the art from us. They'll have a scribe at every mine to write reports and keep track of the gold they gain and the supplies they need— for those purposes, and a hundred others. He won't be there all the time, or I would think not. When he's not there, he'll go to the temple of Thoth in whatever city he reaches. I'd like to talk to the priests in all of them, as we go up the river. This Kames is the son of a rich man. He'll have been well taught in the House of Life in Wast. They won't set him to carrying baskets of rock, not unless they're complete fools."

Qanju nodded. "He may be helping one of their scribes, as you say. Such a scribe may know of him even if he is not. Go to Thoth's temples, as you suggest, and learn all you can. Lucius?"

"You have two problems," I said. "First, you must learn where Kames is. Second, you must free him. They will not sell him for gold. If they were willing to do that they would demand it from his father, who has it and wants him more than anyone."

Agathocles nodded. "That's obvious."

"Thus we must take him by stealth or by force. Have the Medjay good horses?"

Qanju nodded to Alala.

"Yes," she said. "The best. The people of the north buy them to pull their chariots, but our men sit on their backs. My mother has done that also."

I said, "Would you like to learn?"

Alala nodded.

"I have three soldiers of Parsa. They are all good riders, or say they are. I've listened to them talk, and they talk much of horses and bows. You have relatives among the Medjay. Do you know their names?"

Alala nodded again.

"You wish to visit them and to introduce your husband to them. The Noble Qanju, who treats your husband as his son, may send him and you to them, with the soldiers of Parsa and me to protect you. They may know where Kames is, and if they do not they will surely know where he might be. Your husband will have gold for them, and smooth words. If many take the Great King's gold to guard Kemet, they cannot be hostile to Kemet or the Great King— no man pays those who hate him to guard him."

Qanju nodded and smiled. "Wisely spoken. You would go into the eastern desert as you say? You, Thotmaktef and his wife, and three soldiers? Only six in all?"

I shook my head. "Seven. I'll need to speak with this Medjay woman often. Myt-ser'eu must go with us so there will be a second woman."

Now she wishes to ask more questions. I will write here again soon.

WE BOUGHT HORSES today. The soldiers from Parsa were our advisors concerning their horses and our own; they are very happy now. Agathocles and Thotmaktef struck the bargains for us. If all goes well, Thotmaktef will sell these horses when we return to the ship and recover most of the money we spent.

Myt-ser'eu wanted my slave to come with us. So did he. Thotmaktef objected, saying truly that he had been given gold by Qanju for seven horses, not eight. Myt-ser'eu wanted me to buy a horse for the slave, whose name is Uraeus. I would not. She said, "If he had a horse—not bought with Qanju's gold—will you let him come?"

I saw no reason not to. Someone to serve us will save us work and time. Most significantly, a slave to serve us will maintain my standing with my men, which is always important. I urged this to Thotmaktef, saying Uraeus would serve him and his wife as well. He was persuaded.

Having no carts and no pack horses, we cannot carry much. Weapons, and a few clothes. Myt-ser'eu is bringing her jewelry, fearing it will be stolen if she leaves it on the *Gades*. No doubt she is right, though Neht-nefret might watch it for her. For me—two pairs of sandals, a spare tunic, Falcata, the leather case that carries this scroll, and two blankets. I have bought boots. I could not find the kind I wanted—the kind that seems proper to me for a horseman. These are near it, however. I will wear them tomorrow.

We have seen Medjay on horseback, and Alala has spoken with them, while Myt-ser'eu, Agathocles, and Thotmaktef stood by. Their feet were bare. They carried spears and knives, and were mounted on horses I envied. Alala says they would not speak much concerning the mines, but they have pointed the way to her father's clan.

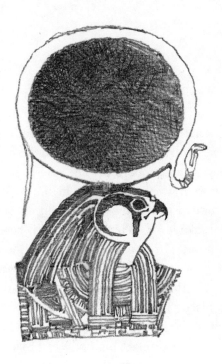

25

HOW LOVELY THIS IS!

WE ARE CAMPED among stones, sand, and grass, under the stars. We rode throughout a long day. When we made camp here, I did not know how I came to be here or who the others were. My wife had me read this. I have read, but found only confusion. I set down what I have learned from my wife, our servant, and the priest.

My bowmen are Baginu, Vayu, and Kakia. They are to obey me, and do. (I have tested this.)

The priest, Holy Thotmaktef, is our commander. I obey him. My servant says our commander often asks my advice. The tall young woman is Alala, our commander's wife.

My own wife is also young. I like both women, but like my own best. She sits close by, although she says she cannot read what I write. Our servant is the oldest man here and may be the wisest, too. He wears a hat like mine. My soldiers wear caps. The women cover their heads with shawls against the sun. I have a hat of striped cloth, like a bag without a bottom. The priest's head is shaved. He held a shade above it when the sun was high.

I wear a beetle of gold and enamel about my neck. Our servant says I must not take it off. Who would steal it here? Not he, or he would not warn me. The priest, who has already a bag of gold? His eyes say he does not steal. Kakia, perhaps. I must watch him.

The priest calls this desert the Red Land. He marvels to find it green in many places. I think it beautiful, though too dry for wheat or barley. With a pack of hounds and a few good horses, one might hunt here for years. There are high hills of broken rock, boulders, and—

A LION ROARED, not far off. It frightened our horses and the two women. I have set a watch, each to stand for a quarter of the night, taking the first myself. I to moonrise, Baginu until the moon is high, Vayu until it is behind the hills, and Kakia to sunup. Tomorrow each is to watch earlier, Baginu taking the first and I the last. If a horse breaks its tether, our sentry is to wake me.

We camped here at my urging because there is water, though not much. We have dug a little pool for our use, and another, catching the overflow from the first, for our horses. Both overflow now, but the water is soon lost in the sand of the dry watercourse. My servant found pictures on a rock. They are old, I would say, but sheltered by an overhang so that they have not weathered. The priest's wife said her people made them, and that defacing them offends the gods. I would not have defaced them anyway. Men cast their spears at a beast with a long nose and long fangs. If there are really such beasts in this land, I would like to see one.

I found another place and scratched my name there: LATRO. Also a picture of our camp: the fire, the people, and our horses. We are six men and two women. My wife sang and played for us. Now she sleeps, but the chill wind sings for me still, and the stars look down.

WE ARE SEVEN men and two women—no longer as I wrote. What happened this morning was—

I WILL WRITE and let the others talk. I listen to them, but write still. Myt-ser'eu says I forget what I do not write, and I feel she speaks truly.

When I woke I found I had slept with my head cradled in the hands of a black warrior who wore a plumed headdress. "You were not among us when I slept," I said. "Did Baginu welcome you to our camp?"

He laughed. I think I liked him already, but his laugh made me like him more, as I still do. It is rich and warm, a laugh that makes me want to laugh with him. "I go wherever I please," he told me, "and creep under the door."

"Then I must welcome you. We come in peace. Are these your hunting grounds?"

"Yes," he said, "but not mine alone."

At that moment one of the soldiers from Parsa came to me. "Who are you talking to, sir?"

I said, "I don't know his name. We have just met, but he comes as a friend."

"There's no one there!"

"What sort of sentry are you," I asked him, "if you can't see a man sitting before you?"

I found no name in me, but I remembered what my wife had called me; to the plumed stranger I said, "I am Latro," and offered my hand.

He clasped it as friends do. The bowman—his name is Kakia—gaped at that and backed away with his war ax in his hand.

Uraeus came and bowed very low to the stranger, who said, "Greetings, Uraeus of Sesostris. Well met!" At these words Uraeus backed away, still bowing.

By this time the sun had risen. I apologized to the plumed stranger, saying I must have rolled upon him while I slept.

"It was a small service," he said, "to give one from whom I hope so much help." Everything he says is said in my own tongue, not in the tongue these people speak nor as my soldiers speak to me. But I scarcely noticed it at the time.

Our talk woke my wife. "Who is this, Latro?"

"A friend," I said.

He smiled at her. "Your tribe calls me the Good Companion. You are fair to look upon, little cat of Hathor, but you must wear your gown or come to harm."

She did, putting it on quickly, though it was wrinkled from the washing she had given it before we slept.

"Does this man guard you well, little cat?"

"Oh, yes! He's loving, strong, very brave."

"It is well you spoke so. You have my blessing, little cat."

"Thank you, sir." Myt-ser'eu bowed. (There was no hint of mockery in that bow, though I think such mockery must often be found in her words and gestures.) "You should bless him, sir. Bless Latro."

"He is already blessed." The stranger spoke to me. "My name is Arensnuphis, Latro."

I said, "Well met!"

"So you must speak of me. I have other names in other places and for other men, just as you do. I require your help. Will you give it?"

"Certainly," I said, "if I can."

"Latro must do as Thotmaktef directs," Myt-ser'eu put in hastily. "Holy Thotmaktef is his commander."

Thotmaktef came to us at once. It may be that he came because he heard his name, but I felt that Arensnuphis had brought him; I cannot explain this.

"I am Thotmaktef," he said, and bowed.

"I am Onuris," Arensnuphis said, and rose. He is two heads taller than I, and his headdress of bright feathers makes him appear taller still. His weapons: a net, and a spear as tall as he.

Now he speaks with Thotmaktef, Alala, and Myt-ser'eu, and I no longer recall our making camp last night or which horse is mine, though I remember that I remembered both these things not long ago. Thotmaktef wishes everyone to help Arensnuphis, and suggests many ways in which it might be done. He wants only me, and tells the rest in many ways that their help is not needed. He does not say how he wishes me to help him, but I know he will tell me when the time is ripe.

HERE WE HALTED early because of the rain. It does not wet Arensnuphis, but he halted for my sake. I brought a little food, and there is water in plenty running from the rocks. I have drunk my fill.

Already the grass is greener.

He kindled a fire for me in the shelter of this great stone, a fire of dried dung, for there is no wood in this land—no wood at all. He bid me read all this before sunset. Now I have, beginning with Muslak, the ship, and the temple. I know now where I have been, though not who I am nor how I came to be as I am.

Arensnuphis stands upon one leg, on the hilltop in the rain. His plumes are not wet, and so bright that I can make out their colors from where I sit. He wears the sunrise.

We hunt his wife, Mehit, whom he must catch again and tame each year at this time. He wishes my help because I will see her among the hills though other men do not, a young lioness, shining and very great.

I have seen other gods, gods of whom I have read here. None could have been as fine as he, the Good Companion who kindled fire for me.

Set is god of the south. So I read not long ago. I am in the south, I think.

Twice today we saw black cattle. The herdsmen are dark, their horses of many colors, their dogs as black as the cattle they drive, sharp-eared as wolves, long-legged and very swift. They saw me and came toward me, then seemed to forget me and turn away. Arensnuphis did that, I feel sure. They do not see or wind him. He told me this. At his word they no longer saw me, and forgot me at once. So I believe.

WE CAPTURED HER. I saw her pug-marks in the mud, and we tracked her many miles.*

She was a lioness of gold, the most beautiful animal ever seen, and it was I who drove her into Arensnuphis's net, shouting and waving my sword. She could not understand how it was I saw her. I read it in her eyes.

This I will not believe when I read again. I know I will not, yet I write only the truth. When Arensnuphis had netted her, he drove his spear into her. She did not bleed, but rose and was a lovely woman as tall and dark as he, clad in a lion's skin. They embraced and were gone.

---

*A mile was one thousand double steps as marched by a Roman soldier: *miles militis.* Thus it is close kin to words like *military* and *militia,* and to the given name *Milo.* The narrator actually wrote "m."

Her lion's skin she left behind. At first, I feared to touch it. When I touched it at last, it vanished slowly as a morning mist of gold, leaving a single hair that shines very bright. I have rolled it into this scroll so that I may find it another day and remember.

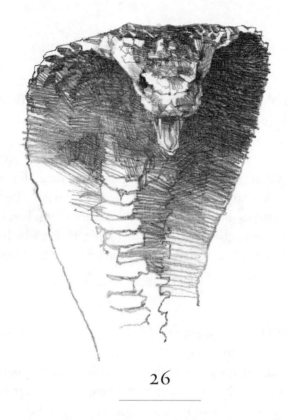

26

IN THE MINE

THERE IS LITTLE light and less comfort. Our friend Kames brought me this scroll, with the reed brushes and a block of ink, all in a leather case. I wet the brush with my drinking water, of which we have too little, and write so that he can watch me. He is rarely here, but Myt-ser'eu has told him I wrote so often, and wrote everything on this scroll. He tells me much of her and says this. So does the man who comes and goes, and Thotmaktef.

MYT-SER'EU CAME. SHE is my wife, Thotmaktef says. He had told me something of her before, but neither how beautiful she is nor how young. She kissed me, after which we spoke in whispers.

She is very frightened. She has been taken by force more than once, and talks of killing the men who did it. I told her she could not, that it was a man's work and I will do it.

As I will.

She brought more water. We thanked her, and asked for more. I asked for another lamp, too. It is dark here, save when they bring torches and make us dig. I am able to write these things because the man who comes and goes brought more oil for the lamp he brought us before. He wants me to read this. I have read of a plumed god and many other things.

KAMES CAME TO warn me. He says one of my men has told them about the bald man, saying he is my servant. He says they will question me about him. While he was with us in the mine, the priest's wife came. They forced her, she says, but fear her because she is of the Medjay. I asked about these Medjay, and they are the herdsmen I read of in this scroll. The prince said this, and that they were his forefathers' people, long ago. Now he digs like the rest of us.

Soon guards came and brought me to this hut by the smelter. They asked me about the case that holds this, and when I showed them what was in it they tried to take it. I killed them, striking them with my chain and strangling them afterward. I have their daggers now—two long blades. If someone else comes by day, I will kill him as well. When night comes I will go out, and we will see.

THE MAN WHO got away came. He is so silent that he stood before me before I knew he had come. They are looking for the two I killed, he said. Soon they will look here. I will fight until they kill me.

THERE WAS NOISE outside and much excited talk. I heard Kames's voice. He was speaking, first in one tongue and then in another. A woman spoke. Perhaps she was the Myt-ser'eu I have read about. She was not the priest's wife—I remember that voice. This woman spoke loudly, and her tones were less soft.

It is nearly dark. Someone plays a lute.

URAEUS AND I carried away the dead men and hid them among the rocks. These Nubians do not keep good watch. He wished to steal horses and go for help. I said I would not leave the others. I told him to steal a horse and bring whatever help he could. He did not wish to leave me, but I ordered him to go. He is my slave, he says. He said there would surely be a guard on the horses and asked whether he might kill him. I told him to kill anyone who tried to prevent him from carrying out my order.

URAEUS RETURNED. THERE are no horses. There is little grass here, he says, and they may have been taken where there is better grazing. Shortly before sundown he left me to look.

The sun set, and I went out. Four with spears came to this hut, and there was much loud talk. I wanted to go back into the mine, but there is a fire before it and guards with spears, shields, and swords. The new woman was talking at the big fire. I crept nearer to listen. She spoke the tongue of Kemet. Then Kames spoke as Nubians do. Another spoke, and Kames told her—and me—what had been said. So it went.

The woman: *"It is a great treasure, I tell you! A magical treasure. It is a woman of wax who will become a real woman at my command. You will have four women then instead of three."*

Another woman spoke as Nubians do, and they struck her.

Kames: *"Piy asks if you think they are to be lured away so easily? If they go, your friends will come to free Prince Nasakhma."*

The woman: *"Give me one man and three horses, and I will bring you this treasure in a day, a magical treasure for which your king will give a sack of gold. Then you will marry me, Piy, and we will be happy forever."*

Kames: *"He says you only wish food, rest, and a horse. Then you would escape from him. It would be easy to escape one man. He says, tell us where the treasure lies. I will send soldiers to get it. They will bring it here, and when they do, you must show me your magic. If you cannot, so much the worse for you."*

She told them where it was, and Uraeus and I left so as to be there before they came. We have found the box, and the dead horse that carried it. Now we three wait for them.

I hear voices.

PIY HAD SENT four of his dark soldiers with five horses. We waited to let them find the box and find it held no woman. Sabra went to them, showing by gestures that she was the one who had been in the box. They did not believe her. She lay down in the box, and when one bent over her to see, she stabbed him in the throat.

Uraeus bit one. He fell in convulsions, which I do not understand. I killed two with my daggers. We took the box, their horses, and their spears and rode to this place, where we have built a fire. I ate food from their saddlebags, but not Uraeus, who hunts among the rocks. Sabra says she does not eat, but needs a woman's blood. I did not believe it.

"Neht-nefret would have smeared me with her blood and uttered the spell to awaken me," Sabra explained. "That was what we planned. Love wakes me now."

"I do not love you," I told her. She is very beautiful, but I know that I could never love or trust her.

"No, you love your little singing girl. That silly lute player."

Now I know who played the lute I heard, and that I love her. I have written very much so that I will not forget. Uraeus insists that

I must do this. Sabra is a woman of wax, lying in her box; and I must sleep.

SABRA, URAEUS, AND I talked this morning of how we might free Myt-ser'eu and the others. I did not believe Uraeus could do as he said, but he called cobras from the rocks. He said I was to take up one and Sabra the other two. We did, and they were gentle in our hands. After that, Sabra and I rode here to the mine.

"This is a prisoner of yours," she told them. "I have recaptured him for you."

She spoke to me as she lay down in the box we had brought. "Go back to the mine, fellow!"

I did as she bid, still wearing the chain that had made it so difficult to ride.

The others welcomed me, having feared I was to be killed. "I escaped," I told them, "and we will all be free shortly. I've arranged it."

The prince—Nasakhma is his name—said, "But you have been retaken!"

"Only because I wished to be. I have these for you." I began taking the knives and daggers from under my tunic. There were six. Kames was above; thus I gave one to the prince, one to Thotmaktef, and one to each of my soldiers. One I kept for myself.

"Should we charge the guards?" asked Baginu.

I shook my head. "Charge when I give the order. If you fight bravely and skillfully, we'll be free. Now be silent a moment, all of you."

They were, until Thotmaktef whispered, "A lute . . ." His ears are better than mine.

"Then she has begun to dance," I said.

"My wife?"

I shook my head. "Sabra. She says you know her."

Thotmaktef stared.

"A woman called Neht-nefret brought her. Sabra says you know her, too."

"So do we," said Baginu. "She's the captain's woman."

"Sabra returned to wax when I left her," I explained to Thotmaktef. "Neht-nefret must have gashed her arm and smeared Sabra's face with blood, as they planned. When she stooped to whisper the spell, Sabra was to whisper to her, telling her what Kames and the women must do to be safe. She dances now to give Neht-nefret time to speak to them."

Vayu muttered, "I do not believe any of us understand you, Centurio."

"Soon the bracelets will fall from Sabra's wrists," I explained, "then it will be seen that they are not ornaments but living cobras. A great cobra has been coiled tightly about her waist, under her gown. It will fall to the ground and call others from the rocks. We hope—"

Baginu had snatched my arm. "That's a lion! Hear it?"

"We must fight too," I said. "Follow me!"

Our guards had left the entrance already. Fighting against men so disordered, many of whom had been bitten, was hardly fighting at all.

We have cleared the bodies from this place, loading them on horses and throwing them into the wadi. We will start back to the river tomorrow, but first it must grow dark, and Myt-ser'eu and I do many pleasant things. Thotmaktef and Alala, too, I suppose.

Myt-ser'eu had a hundred questions, but there is no need to give them all here.

"Where did the big cobra come from, Latro? I'd never seen one half as big as that."

"Uraeus produced it for us by magic. He left Sabra and me, after warning us that it would come and telling us what we must do."

"What did you and Sabra do when you were alone?"

"Talked," I said. "She told me everything she and Neht-nefret had planned, and we planned what we would do that day."

"Only talk?"

"Only talk," I said.

"I was hoping you had her then. No?"

I shook my head.

"Six of them had me," Myt-ser'eu said. "If I screamed or struggled, they struck me." She showed me the bruises on her face, and her eyes filled with tears. "Will you send me away?"

"Of course not."

"They had Alala, too. Eight or ten of them had her." Seeing that I did not credit her, she added, "They liked her better!"

I shrugged. "Perhaps Thotmaktef will send her back to her father. That's up to him."

"I don't think so. How did you get the lions?"

"I didn't." I shrugged again. "I didn't even know they were coming, and neither did Uraeus or Sabra. But I've been reading this, and I think a goddess must have sent them. Is there one called Mehit?"

"I've heard of her," Myt-ser'eu said, "but I don't know much about her. She's an Eye of Ra, and a moon goddess who lights the way for travelers." She paused, thoughtful. "Perhaps that's why Mehit favored you. You're from a faraway city called Sidon. That would make you a great traveler."

"I didn't know."

"Well, it's what Muslak says. Sidon's one of his people's towns."

I had forgotten who Muslak was, and made her explain.

Only a moment ago, Myt-ser'eu came with a new question. "Neht-nefret said we had to climb up on things and stay there, and if we did the cobras wouldn't bite us."

I nodded.

"So we did—Neht-nefret, Alala, and me. I stood on a stool, and they left me alone. Neht-nefret and Alala got up on the table, but we were afraid it would break if I got up there too. Neht-nefret couldn't find Kames to tell him, but he wasn't bitten anyway."

I shook my head.

"So how did they know? Why didn't they bite him when they were biting the other men?"

I said, "Why didn't they bite Baginu and me when we came up out of the mine?"

"Don't smile like that!"

"I'll smile any way I want to. Uraeus had seen that all of us were barefooted—Piy's soldiers had taken my boots and your sandals so we couldn't run away. Thotmaktef's wife says the Medjay never wear anything on their feet, but there are many sharp stones here. They will soon cut the feet of anyone accustomed to sandals. Piy's men wore sandals, so Uraeus told the cobras not to bite bare feet."

"He can do that?" Myt-ser'eu wanted to know.

"He did," I told her.

She is quiet now, and I must think back to the mine. I forget quickly, she says, and I know that it must be true. Before I forget the mine, I must be properly grateful to the gracious goddess who favored me there.

27

MYT-SER'EU IS GONE

THEY TOOK HER from me tonight, and left me here. I showed my guards this scroll and asked whether I might write. They said I might, but how long will they permit it? Other guards will come, and soon this will be taken too. I have read much, and will try to remember. Surely I can never forget the golden lioness!

Their horses were better than ours, but the men of Parsa plied the bow well and kept them off for a time, turning in the saddle and shooting behind them. They were fine bowmen and dropped man after man until their last arrow had been spent.

I told them to ride hard and save the women, that I would fight and delay our pursuers. They would not obey, but followed me with their war axes while the rest rode away.

How much blood Falcata drank then! It is a terrible thing to kill a woman's son, I know. Yet it does not feel terrible to me when he has come to kill me. Falcata caught the arm as the great sword went up, again and again until my horse fell.

They came with bows and Myt-ser'eu when their dead lay thick before me.

I cannot write the horse's name. That is the thought that returns and returns, no matter how often I send it away. It is all around me, like the flies. The horse could not tell me his name. I feel sure I must once have known it, but I have forgotten it. Poor horse, with no one but me to grieve for him!

I wet the reed in my blood, hoping it makes good ink. So I will write of him.

He fell, and I knew it meant he was dead. He was a fine horse, brown with a black mane, like many horses, but spirited and eager to obey. I had ridden him to his death, and I could not save him or save myself.

I killed a great, strong man with many scars. It was like killing the night, but a man. The look of surprise as Falcata caught his shoulder and bit to the heart. He had fought many times, no doubt sometimes in great battles. Twenty-to-one now against we four soldiers, yet it was his last. He had never thought to die so. I would rather have had those broad shoulders and mighty arms for me than against me, but he fell to my sword, and I was glad of it.

Then my horse fell beneath me. What was his name? As it was for him, so it is for me. I had thought that horse would never fail me. Nor had he thought to fail me, I know, nor any rider. We had taken him from someone, I feel sure. I wish I knew from whom, and how we came to take him.

I recall the little house, and the household god squatting by the hearth, ugly and good. My father bringing dried vine dressings to feed our fire, my mother stirring soup. How did the boy become the man who rode beside the lovely brown woman in the black wig?

When we turned to fight, she shouted, "Myt-ser'eu! I'm Kitten!" lingering too long before turning to flee as I had told her, turning to wave from the saddle, so slender and beautiful.

I told the soldiers from Parsa to protect her, but they would not obey me. Kakia was stirrup-to-stirrup with me when the arrow pierced his throat. Never did I trust his courage until the moment he died.

IF I WERE a god, my horse would live again, and speak to me. I would call him by name, and mount, and ride away. We would ride through the sky, far away to another, better land.

They held a knife to the kitten's throat, and I handed them Falcata.

Now my guard has cut my ropes, letting me write as I do. He could see I was too weak to stand. What danger am I to him now? To anyone? I thought to find no such kindness from his hard, dark face, no kindness from anyone. I do not believe I have ever been cruel, and wish I had been kinder.

If I had not surrendered Falcata, I would have been pierced by a score of arrows, long arrows with iron heads or stone ones. What harm in that? Am I better off as I tremble here, writing by firelight with a brush wet with my blood?

GEESE FLY OVERHEAD, flying by night, calling like new boots across the sky to their fellows. It may be the last sound I hear. Every man hears a last sound. For many it must be the clash of arms. That is a good last sound, but the shouts of geese in flight is a better one. We sink into the earth, down into the shadow lands of the dead, where I shall drink from Death's river to forget a life I cannot remember.

———

MY GUARD HAS been speaking to me. There is a tongue he speaks well that I barely understand. He can speak as I spoke to Myt-ser'eu, although less well, I think, than I. I asked him the name of my horse, but he did not know it. He said I must lie down and sleep so I may live. He tied my hand to his so he might sleep himself. The cord is long enough to let me spread this and write as I do. I would rather write than sleep tonight.

What if I die?

Soldiers fight, and kings take the spoil. What does a soldier get? A few coins, perhaps, a ring from a dead man's finger, and many scars. What does a horse get? Only death. We ride them, and they—our kings—ride us.

I remember the hot, bright sun, and others I hoped to save. These men have Myt-ser'eu. She was guarded when last I saw her.

This fire lights my scroll but does not warm me.

I told her to run. I wanted her to gallop away while I fought, wanted all of them to gallop away while I fought my last fight. How is it they have her? Are there two Kittens? I remember her smile and her eyes, so wide and so full of terror. The horse my legs held, his rippling muscles.

If a lion were to roar, I would be well, my wound healed. I told my guard this. There is no lion, only another flock of geese, geese flying by moonlight, tracing the distant river through the hot, still air. The Realm of Death is dark and cold—Mother told me. Death's name is Dis Pater, and he is the richest of all gods, with more subjects than any other, and still more arriving daily to people a dark, dank land so broad that it is never full.

Who will welcome me there? I have forgotten all the names, even the name of my horse. I sweat, and fear my sweat will make this ink run. Is it not my blood? Why should it not run now?

We saw them coming over the dry plain, riding hard behind us and faster than we. There was wind, a wind that stirred the dust and sent small white clouds scudding across the bright blue sky, hot clouds that never dimmed the sun. Can any sky be bluer than the sky here? Can any sun be harsher? More blinding? This sky never stretched above our little house. Ours is surely another sky, another sun.

"Ride!" I told the soldiers of Parsa. "Ride! Keep her safe. I'll kill the leaders and the rest will stop to kill me."

I drew Falcata. Oh, her bright blade flashing in the sun! Who is the man with the silver sword? If my foes did not speak so, I did.

I reined up and swung the mount, my strong, brown, black-maned stallion, to face them. How bravely he answered to the reins, galloping to his death!

He reared with flashing hooves when I pulled him up. I waved Falcata aloft and charged them all. If he impaled himself upon a lance, he lived long afterward. How long does it take to reap men like grain? A dozen breaths? A hundred?

But first, oh, first how we roared across the plain, Baginu to one side, Kakia to the other, and I saw Kakia die. Had I a shield? I remember none, or only Baginu's.

I took a shield from a dead man when my horse fell. I remember that, ducking, dodging, Falcata biting deep into the legs, red blood on black skin, Falcata biting through the blanket and wounding the mount.

They drew off, save for one crippled man, a cripple for life now, who dragged himself toward me. I struck his hand with the back of my blade, and his long dagger went flying.

Then they brought Myt-ser'eu with the knife at her throat.

I AM WEAK and sick, and cold. So cold. The fire came. I spoke to so many others, a crone, a cow with the body of a woman, an eagle on a staff. "Follow me," the eagle said. "Follow me!" But he has gone where I cannot follow. How I thirsted then, who shiver now in this cold!

There is no warmth in this fire. None. Only burning.

My wounds ache and bleed. Soon I will die. Tell Mother I fled no fight. Tell them in the Forum. I came and have gone. I am . . .

My name is . . .

PART II

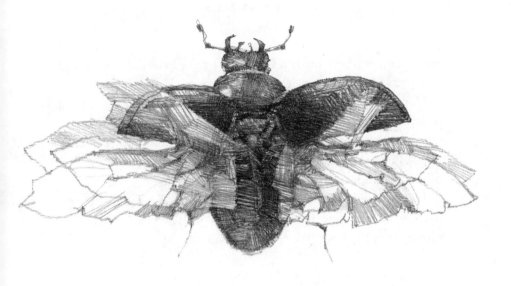

28

A STRANGE AWAKENING!

A WHISPER IN my ear woke me: *"Read this. . . ."* No doubt I woke too slowly; by the time I sat up, there was no one there. I looked for the speaker and saw this case, which lay close beside me. It is of well-tanned leather, stout but scarred and worn. Beginning to crack. I would oil it, had I oil. In it were this scroll, papyrus reeds for brushes, this block of ink, and a small dagger with an eye in its grip. No one was in sight, and the men to my left and right slept soundly, if men so ill can be said to sleep at all.

The man on my left will surely die. I thought at first he might be dead, but he is only sleeping. O you merciful gods, let him sleep and cough and sleep again, never to wake. That would be kindest.

The day brightened and I could read this. "L" forgets, it said. I cannot remember who I am. Am I this "L"? I write as he did, and in truth our letters are much alike. It may be the reason this was left with me.

Here everyone is ill. Some cannot sit up—I feel sure the man on my left could not. There is blood each time he coughs. There is an old scar on my head, above the ear. I can feel it under my hair, but it cannot be the reason I am here. I am very thin; even so it was hard for me to stand, and I sat again almost before I rose.

I wish I could look out the window. My chain is too short for it. There is an iron ring about my right ankle. The chain ends at another ring in the floor. We are all so chained.

I HAVE BEEN trying to talk with the man on my right. I could understand a few words of his speech, but only a few. He showed me his wound, which is far from healed. He rode (two fingers forking one). He fought (his hands drawing a bow). He was wounded below the ribs, I suppose by an arrow of his enemy's. I asked whether I had shot that arrow. He laughed and shook his head.

He showed me how I had lain on my pallet, babbling and thrashing about, standing sometimes and shouting—all this in pantomime. So I have been mad. I think I must be sane this morning. If I am sane, why can I not remember? I cannot have been mad all my life. I can read this, and write as it is written. No one could teach a madman to read and—

THE MAN TO my right took my arm and told me to hide this. I did, and in a few moments more the man with the spear and the woman had reached my pallet. She is small and young. Her back and arms show the marks of the stick, and I would like to beat the man who did it.

As I will when I can.

A chain smaller and lighter than mine joins her hands. It is long enough for her to hold her tablet and stylus, and write. The tall man with the spear grinned at us, finding us most amusing. She did not grin, but smiled at me. I watched to see whether she smiled at the others, but she did not, looking at each and writing. I wish she had spoken. I wish I could hear her voice.

The man on my right says we are to be sold, I think as rowers. He pointed to us, and counted coins that were not there. I tried to tell him I am no one's slave. He did not understand, or perhaps only did not believe me; but I know I spoke truth.

I HID THIS and brought it with me. Here is what I did. A smith came early this morning and chained us by the neck, not all of us—only eleven others and I. Each of us has a ring about his neck, closed with a bronze pin the smith crimped to hold it shut. He cut the rings about our ankles, putting each upon a little anvil and striking it with a chisel.

When we left we rolled up our pallets and carried them out of the city on our heads. I had hidden this brown case as well as I could, putting it in the angle of the wall behind my pallet and sprinkling it with brown dust I scratched from the floor. Before we left, I rolled it into my pallet. We marched all day, guarded by four men with spears and shields or shields and clubs. There are women with us. They are chained as we are, but are kept from us. One smiled at me, and my heart flew to her. With my eyes I tried to say that we would soon be free together. I hope she understood. Now everyone sleeps, and I watch the stars and write by firelight.

I DO NOT know how long it has been since I last wrote. Perhaps it was only last night. I hope so. She I love waved and shouted when a ship passed, at a place where the road runs near the river. A guard beat her for it. I killed him, dragging the others after me, knocking him down, and breaking his neck. The other three with spears and clubs wanted to kill me, but she stood between us shrieking. Our owner came. He spoke to her, and she to me. He showed me his sword. Here is what she said, the first quickly.

"I'm Kitten—you're Latro." More slowly now. "We belong to Master. He sees you're strong and brave. You must stand with him or against him. If you stand against him, he'll kill you. Will you stand with him?"

She nodded very slightly as she spoke, so I nodded as well.

He spoke and she said, "You are his. That does not change."

I nodded again because she had.

"He will take your chain off and give you the dead man's shield and club, but you must swear to guard the others and obey him in everything."

I swore, holding my left hand above the fire and pointing to the sun with the club he gave me. How am I to keep this oath if I forget all that I said? Will the gods by whom I swore condemn me for breaking an oath I will soon have forgotten?

Surely they will. That is the way of gods.

We have marched a long way since these things happened, leaving the dead man lying in the dust like a dead dog. The other guards hate me, but I am safe as long as they fear me.

NOW WE BELONG to the young priest who rides a white mule. He met us on the road this morning. I could understand some bits of the many things he said to our old master, though not everything. He wished to buy me. Our old master said he did not wish to sell me—that I was strong and brave and would fight for my owner. There is something he wants in the south. The people there will give him a piece as long as he is tall for me.

The priest said our old master offended his god in every way, that he was the stinking excrement of a depraved woman of no family. At last they agreed on a price, which the priest paid, and at once both began to smile. Only then did the priest speak to me, telling me to go with him.

I pretended not to understand, shaking my head and looking at the ground. Our old master spoke to the woman I love, and she to me, saying I must go. I told her truly that I would not go without her.

The priest struck me, and my eyes must have shown what I planned to do as soon as we were alone. I feel sure they did, because I saw the fear rush into his.

He spoke to the woman, saying he regretted striking me, and that he would be kind from this day forward. I pretended not to understand until the woman said it. I told her, "That's all very well, but I will not go without you."

She explained to the priest, at which our old master grinned widely and began to praise her. She is lovely and obedient, can read and write, can sing and play the lute in her wooden case.

At last everything was arranged between them. This woman is called Myt-ser'eu, and she is my wife. She explained these things later, as we walked. I think it fortunate—I love her and am glad indeed to learn that I have already won her. We were traveling south on a fine large ship, but left the ship to fight the people here and were taken and sold.

MYT-SER'EU SAYS I must write so I will not forget. We are going to a place called Meröe. We do not belong to the priest who guides us, but to his temple. It is the last temple—I overheard him telling her this. There are no more temples south of his. She wept to hear it. She is under the protection of a goddess and says her goddess cannot see her here. I tried to comfort her.

A strange thing happened just before midday. A beetle struck my chest and clung there. I could not brush it away. She said it was a sacred beetle and should not be touched or harmed. I promised not to pluck it off, believing it would soon fly again. It did not, but seized the string around my neck and held on to it, swinging and tapping my chest as I walked. I examined it quite carefully a moment ago, and it is enameled gold. She says it is another I wore before we were taken, a seal. I must surely have hidden it in the case in which we keep this scroll. If I had hidden it, there or anywhere, would I not remember finding it today?

The young priest rides a fine white mule. His name is Holy Kashta. My wife rides a donkey. She says she walked at first, as I do, but could not keep pace with us all day in this heat. My wife's donkey also carries a little food and other things. My wife keeps this scroll case for me when we travel, so that I do not have to carry it. I hang my club in the loops on the back of my shield and sling my shield behind me. When the sun is high I carry it on my head for shade.

Here the road leaves the river, which roars over rocks. The people of this village say a ship was taken apart here and carried south over the road, then launched again, which seems to me nearly as strange as the sacred beetle that has become my necklace. They were well paid to help carry the ship, and gave us food freely. My Myt-ser'eu says we had to threaten the people at the place where we stopped last night. I do not recall it. Fresh fish and flat barley cakes are our food, with the dates and raisins her donkey carries. Holy Kashta has blessed this place.

He tells us of his god, Seth, whom he says is very great. All gods are very great, I think, when their priests speak of them. Four temples remain in his city, that of Seth to which we belong, that of Isis, that of Apedemak, and that of the Sun. That of Seth is the southernmost, the last temple in his city and in all the world. My wife fears this god greatly.

"THE ROAD GOES south, always south." Myt-ser'eu says this, and weeps. Her home, she says, lies far to the north, near the Great

Sea—each step carries her farther from it. Mine too lies on a shore of that sea, she says. She does not know where. I said I would bind the priest, beat him, and steal a boat. In it we could follow the river north to her home. She said we would be pursued and retaken long before we reached Kemet, and that its southern border was still whole months of travel from her home. Our best chance, she said, was to follow the ship we had left, on which are many strong friends. Or else to win our freedom from the temple.

"The last temple," I said.

She agreed that it was the last—the priest says this—but wanted to know why I thought it important.

I did not know, nor do I know now. The answer may be in this scroll, as she says. But I could not find it tonight.

WE ARE IN Meröe, housed in the temple of Seth, the Great God of the South. Meröe is built on an island in the Great River. Our temple is at the southern end of this island, as is proper for Great Seth. Its door beholds the sun in winter—Holy Kashta says this.

There are three priests; Holy Alara is another, Most Holy Tobarqo the chief priest. He is old and forgetful, and wears a leopard skin. When Kashta presented us to him, he did not remember sending forth Kashta to buy us. We smiled much at him, bowed low, and promised to obey in all things, to do our work willingly, and not to steal. He smiled on us and gave us the blessing of his god. In truth, I would not wish to harm so old a man—it would be like fighting a child.

The priests have houses and families near the temple, but Mytser'eu and I live in it, she to sweep and scrub, cook, wash clothes, and gather flowers in season. I to guard it by night. There is much gold here, and the priests say thieves have robbed the city of the dead until there is nothing left.

"You must sleep by day so you will be awake by night," Kashta told me. "Do not unbar the doors unless one of us tells you to. They will throw a hook through the windows and climb a rope to enter, using the same rope to descend. Kill them."

I said I would. I will forget, I know, but I have told Myt-ser'eu, who will tell me each evening when I wake.

WE WENT TO the market today. Kashta wished to send Myt-ser'eu; but it is dangerous, he says, for a woman to go to the market alone. They woke me for this. I left my shield here, but took my club. Half the houses are in ruins, though men and women still live in many and their children play in the ruins. "This is too interesting not to look at," Myt-ser'eu declared. "Let's walk around the whole place and see everything we can. It's not large, and we can tell Holy Kashta we got lost."

I agreed and we set out, seeing many houses half fallen, and the broken doors of the houses of the dead. Voices called to me from the rifled tombs, but after the second I did not reply. "The ghosts are thirsty here," I told Myt-ser'eu; she told me of a woman of wax who thirsted for her blood and the blood of another woman. This woman fought for us in a terrible battle in which cobras and lions fought for us as well. I recall a great golden lioness, and told Myt-ser'eu of her. She said I could remember nothing, and so could not recall this lioness. Yet I do.

The palace that was the king's lies in ruins. We walked through parts of it, and saw the tank in which the king bathed. There is still a king, Myt-ser'eu says, but he rules from Napata and cares nothing for this ruinous city of Meröe. We were at Napata for a month or more, she says, but I was very ill. She had my scroll and could not return it to me because I was too ill to hide it.

The market seemed small, and there were more sellers than buyers. I saw the teeth of a great boar, curving tusks longer than a spear. This boar must have been very great. The meat was beef, pork, antelope, and river-horse. Myt-ser'eu says the priests eat pork, but it is an unclean meat. They will give her no meat at all. Of that she is glad, not wishing to eat pork.

Strange men from the south had come to the market to trade, tall scarred men who paint their bodies red and white. They have bows, spears, big shields, and long knives. One stall sold arrows and bows much like theirs. The bows seemed good, long and strong, but the arrows had heads of sharp stone. I inquired, and the one who kept the stall said iron is costly here. I must have seen arrows like his before, for something stirred in me when I examined them.

I wished to buy a little dish, but Myt-ser'eu would not buy it for me. There are many such small dishes in Kashta's house, she said, and when she brought my food she gave me one. I wished milk as well, and there was milk left from the dinner she made for his family. She went back to the priest's house and got it for me.

Thus I have filled my little dish, and set it near the crack from which the snake comes. He is my only company when I guard the temple by night, and I wish him to understand that I am his friend. Snakes like milk, I know.

Now I write by the light of my lamp, and read, too. The moon looks in at a window, a fair young woman with a round, pale face. The windows are high. From time to time I hear the god stir in his holiest place, but when I look in on him he has not moved. He is a god.

I AM AWAKE! I held my hand over the flame until the pain was too great. It was not yet gone. No man could sleep knowing such pain.

The god spoke to me. He came out, and his face was no longer the face of a wild dog but the face of a man as red as desert sand. He is taller than I, and stronger, too. "You have forgotten me," he said, and his voice was the wind among dry stones. "We are old comrades, you and I, and I thought you would never sleep."

I bowed and said that I must not sleep, that I must protect his temple.

"It will pass. The people will go, and not one stone will stand upon its brother. Do you not know you sleep?"

"I know I sleep by day," I said, "but never by night, Great Seth, for that is when I guard your house."

"Come to me," he said, and I came, though I trembled. He laid his hands upon my shoulders and made me turn about. "Look, and tell me what you see."

"Myself. My club lies beside me, the writing brush has fallen from my hand, and my scroll is spread across my knee."

"Do you sleep?"

"I do sleep," I acknowledged. "Spare me!"

"I will do more. I will see that you gain your dearest wish. Will you help me do it?"

"Gladly," I said.

"You have a small dagger. It was hidden in the case that holds your scroll when the woman returned it to you. It is there now."

"It is yours," I said, "if you wish it."

"I do not. This is what I wish. When you wake, you must carve two words in your club, carve them in the tongue in which you hear me now."

"I will, Great Seth. I will do whatever you ask. What are the words?"

"You act for yourself, not for me. Carve *lost temple.*"

I woke with the dagger in my hand. It is small but very sharp, with an eye in its grip like the eye of a needle. The wood is very hard, but I have incised the words spoken by the god deep into that wood.

Lost temple.

What a strange awakening!

29

WE ARE FREE

THE PAINTED KING of the south came to our temple today
with twenty painted warriors. He demanded to see me, and the
priest sent Myt-ser'eu to wake me. When the king had seen me, he
wished to buy me. He did not wish to buy Myt-ser'eu, but I swore I
would never obey him unless he did. We said these things by signs.
He sent a boy, and we waited until the boy returned.

When he did there were eunuchs with him, and a brown woman
richly robed. The painted king spoke with her in a tongue I did not
understand.

She looked carefully at me and made me stand in a place in
which the light was better. At length she nodded and spoke to him,
urging some course of action— or so it seemed to me.

He shook his head and turned away.

She returned to me. "You know me and I know you. I'm Queen Bittusilma. Confess that you know me!"

I knelt. "I do not know you, Great Queen. I do not remember as others do. The fault is mine." This was not in the tongue I speak to the priests and to Myt-ser'eu. Neither was it in the tongue in which I write it.

The king bought us both, though it was not said in that way. He made gifts of ivory and gold to the temple, and the priests gave us to him. Myt-ser'eu had to remove her gown then, and I my tunic. It was the queen who told us we must. Nakedness is the sign of slavery among the king's people. (She herself is of another nation, as she told me.) Boats rowed by warriors carried us and a score of others south until we halted here to make camp.

The country through which we passed was of great interest, and grew more so with each stroke of the paddles. Here the thatched houses of the poor are more numerous, larger, and cleaner, too. The land itself seems to me richer—yet more wild, its forests ever taller and its rolling grasslands dotted with more trees. It is a timeless land made for the chase, but there are wide swamps with many crocodiles. Myt-ser'eu says the biting flies are the worst we have seen. We rub ourselves with fat to keep them off, though ours is the fat used by eunuchs and women, not colored like the vermilion and white pastes worn by the king and his warriors.

When the king's tent was up he summoned us, sending away everyone save the queen and an old man who is his councillor.

"Seven Lions is my husband," the queen told us. "You do not remember him, but he remembers you very well. So do I. You and he were great friends long ago."

I said, "My heart warms to him, but I don't remember. As you say."

"I'm Babylonian. Seven Lions returned me to my home in Babylon, as I wished. He remained there with me for over a year. Then he wished to return to his own home and persuaded me to accompany him. He will not speak as you and I speak now, but he understands everything we say."

I nodded and explained what had been said to Myt-ser'eu.

"We came to the kingdom in the south that is now ours," the queen continued. "We found the throne vacant, and he took it for us. He is our king and our greatest warrior."

His size, his evident strength, and his eyes—his eyes most of all—told me she spoke the truth. "I do not wish to fight him," I told her.

She laughed, but at once grew serious. "No one does. I want him to come back to Babylon with me, Latro. He promised to do it. Then a god spoke to him in a dream, telling him you were in that temple in Meröe. I thought it nonsense, but we went, and there you were. The god had told him to take you to a certain ruin, where I have never been. It lies far to the south. We have to do it, and you have to go with us."

Recalling what I had promised when the king bought Myt-ser'eu, I said, "I am the king's slave. I'll go willingly wherever he may send me."

At this the king spoke vehemently, at first to the queen, then to his aged advisor, and then to queen again.

She said, "He will free you tonight, and your wife too. It is why he has summoned you. I was to tell you."

I thanked him, bowing.

"You understand that I wish to go to Babylon, not to this ruin."

The king spoke, this time to her alone.

"He says we will go to Babylon after we have done the will of the god. I might point out that we might as easily go to Babylon, and do the will of the god afterward."

The scarab I wore rose and fluttered on silver wings as she finished.

For the first time the old councilor spoke, pointing upstream—

the direction in which the scarab had sought to fly. The king nodded.

"That's a live beetle you wear," the queen said. "I thought it was an ornament."

"It is," I told her. I removed it and handed it to her. She examined it, stared at me, returned it suspended by the string, and turned her eyes to the ground.

The old councillor spoke again. It was in the tongue I use when I speak with Myt-ser'eu. "I am called Unguja," he said. "Our king is so kind as to hear me, though I am but a foolish grandfather. We cannot please the god unless we do his will, nor can we do his will unless we please him."

Myt-ser'eu said, "I'm under the protection of a goddess, wise one, and wish to return to my home in the north. The ship that will return me there is in the south. It may be that my goddess favors me, leading us to that ship."

He shrugged, but did not speak.

After that we were given new clothing. Slowly, with many invocations and great care, the old man painted me as King Seven Lions and his warriors are painted, as white as leprosy on one side and vermilion on the other. When it was finished, Myt-ser'eu and I dressed and thanked the king for our freedom. He embraced me, and I felt I knew him as well as he knew me. He is a good and brave man, I feel sure. His people call him Mfalme, and bend their heads when they speak the name.

Here I should stop and lie with Myt-ser'eu as she wishes. I will say one thing more, wisdom I took from the old man called Unguja. No one can be good unless he is brave; and any man who is brave is good in that, if in no other way. If he is brave enough, there must always be some good in him.

———

MYT-SER'EU IS DANCING with excitement. She wished
me to read this scroll while we were in the boat. I would not, knowing that the river water could destroy it very quickly. Thus she told
me instead—a great deal about the ship she seeks and the men and
women on board. There is a wonderful woman of wax who lives at
times (Myt-ser'eu says), which I do not believe. Myt-ser'eu also
says she was saved from this woman by a god, which I believe even
less than the first if that is possible. With this wax woman is a wizard who brings her to life, a priest, a wise man who once read her
future in the stars, and many others. I asked her future; but she
would not reveal it, saying that such prophecies only grow worse if
they are revealed. She appeared troubled. I asked whether this wise
man had read my future, too. She did not know.

All this was occasioned by our stopping at a village the night
before—the northernmost of those ruled by the king, Unguja says.
When we were about to leave it, Myt-ser'eu learned that the ship
she seeks had passed it yesterday.

She would have had us press on all night, if necessary, to over-
take it. Now she hopes that we may find it tomorrow. I asked
whether it was rowed or sailed. She said it was sailed, and only
rarely rowed. If that is so, her hope is well founded; there has been
but little wind.

AT THIS VILLAGE the river divides. Its forks are called the
Blue and the White. We will follow the White, the river on which
the ruin the king seeks lies. It was here that the king was born, the
queen says, though his capital lies far to the south. From here he
left to join the army of the Great King who rules her native city,
and Myt-ser'eu's as well. I spoke to him of that, and he listened
attentively. The queen translated his replies—I cannot say how
honestly. When he first knew me, I commanded a hundred sol-

diers from my own city; he commanded men from his village and others. They would have fought, but he and I prevented it. His eyes told me many other things had happened, but he would not speak of them. Perhaps he does not wish the queen to know certain things. Myt-ser'eu has told me how he freed us from slavery. We clasped hands, and I declared that because he had freed me I would fight for him whenever he required it.

In truth I have little to fight with. His warriors have big swords, shields, spears, and bows. I have a club carved with two words, and a dagger better suited to murder than to war. My club is heavy and well shaped, but it is only a club.

I HAVE BLOOD guilt, of which I shall tell the king in the morning. Myt-ser'eu says we often stop at villages like this. I hope the rest will be more fortunate than this one for me. The king and queen took the best hut, as is fitting. Myt-ser'eu and I were to be given another, but the woman and children who sleep in it now would have had to sleep outside. I saw how frightened the woman was, and said I would sleep outside if they would permit Myt-ser'eu to sleep in the hut, if the man slept outside with me. This was agreed.

Now I sit by the fire, read, and write. He is dead. I have blood guilt of which I must speak here and to the king, but first I must say that there is a barrier of thornbushes around the village. We are within it, and for that reason I felt there was nothing to fear. When the sun set, the gate was shut by dragging a mass of thornbushes into the opening. I asked how we were to leave in the morning, and the man who is dead now showed me the poles that would be used to push it aside.

As I sat reading by firelight, a ship glided past, some distance away, toward the middle of the channel. The current here is slow, although this scroll says it was swift in certain places to the north.

I felt that the ship was certainly the one of which Myt-ser'eu spoke. Since we had seen no such ship all day, there could not be many such ships here. I ran to the gate, but could not find the poles in the dark. Very eager to stop the ship if I could, I pushed the gate to one side with my club, moving it only a little and tearing the skin of both arms.

By the time I was through the gate, the ship was out of sight. I pursued it, running as fast as I could. There were crocodiles on the bank not far from this village; thus I could not run there. I turned inland but was soon stopped by thornbushes and trees. I turned aside, but found only a swamp in which were many crocodiles, and returned to the village.

An animal like a big dog—though a dog of no breed I know—stood over the man who had slept at our fire. Thinking it only a village dog, I kicked it. It bit my foot, and I struck it with my club—twice, though the second time its jaws were at my throat. It fled, and I found the ropes and pulled the thornbushes to close the gate.

Now I have washed my leg and foot, though I can clean nothing well and they still bleed, soaking the strips I tore from my tunic. The man who slept beside me is dead and his face torn away. Laid bare, his skull grins at me as I write this.

THE WOMEN SAW the dead man. They screamed, as was to be expected. I went to the king as soon as I could gain an audience with him and explained everything that had taken place. I spoke only the truth. He said that the man's family—in this case the whole village, for they are all related—would choose. If they wished, they might seek vengeance, choosing one of their number to fight me. Otherwise, I would be left to the king's judgment. I said of course that I would accept whatever punishment he chose to give me.

Now my wife (her name is Myt-ser'eu, as she has told me) and I are outside the village. She has washed my leg, and will salve it with medicines an old man (a friend of the king's) has given her. When it is salved, she will bandage it with clean cloths the queen provided. I have told her of the dog, and how I struck it to make it release its hold. She feels sure that it was the sacred beetle I wear that saved me. She once had an amulet that protected her always against crocodiles, but it was cast away. She laments its absence.

She asked whether she had been a good wife to me. She was weeping when she asked, so I swore that she had, and comforted her. The truth is that I do not remember. Yet I know I love her. Any wife who is loved has been good enough.

SOON I AM to fight a man of the village, a relative of the man who died. I will have my club, he whatever weapons he brings. I asked whether he would be permitted to shoot me with a bow. I was told that he might bring a bow, but we would stand close and he would not be allowed to take an arrow from his quiver until the signal was given.

He will have a spear and shield. Unguja says this.

My foot is still swollen, tender, and red.

WE STAYED HERE many days, Myt-ser'eu says, so I might fight about a death. Now the fight is over. This dead man's wife and children are mine now. So are his hut and boat. I have two wives, which the king says is common among his people. He himself has more than twenty, the queen being his chief wife. My old wife, the slender brown woman: Myt-ser'eu. My new one, the large black woman: Cheche. There are three children, two boys and a girl. I do not know their names.

Nor do I know the name of the man who fought me. I felt no enmity toward him, but he would have killed me if he could. We fought outside the village, in a pasture in which the villagers keep a few wild-looking cattle. The king called us before him and had us turn to face each other. We were five steps apart, perhaps. We were to fight, he said, when he clapped his hands. His warriors would keep the dead man's other relatives from interfering.

When he clapped I flung my club at my foe's face. He jerked his head away, and I think brought up his big shield. I cannot be certain of that, only that I dived at his legs and brought him down. He was a strong man, but not a good wrestler. I stabbed him with the knife he wore, and the fight was over very quickly.

I had my little dagger, too, but did not use it.

There was a small man in the crowd who seemed familiar, an older man than I. His face is brown, like Myt-ser'eu's. He says he is my slave, and she says this too. I offered to free him—am I not myself a free man, though she says I was the king's slave once? He would not take his freedom, saying that he wishes only to free me. He was on a ship, he says, but dove from it when he heard my voice. He swam to the wrong bank of the river, and thus it was some time before he found this village. I must ask Myt-ser'eu more about this man, and she must teach Cheche to remember for me as she does.

I have said I am free; but surely no man is free who does not know how he came to be so.

30

RICH IN GAME

DRY AND WET together. That is how I would describe this
beautiful country. There are steaming marshes near the river, vast
fields of reeds. Cheche says these are full of crocodiles, but that no
crocodile inflicted the wounds she has just re-wrapped for me.
There are river-horses in the river itself, some very large, black
where they are wet and gray where the sun has dried them. Our
king's warriors are eager to hunt them, and our king has promised
such a hunt when we halt tonight. The river-horses will come out of
the water to crop grass when the sun is low, and are best hunted at
that time. The king has lions trained for the hunt, but they are far
from us and we must do without them.

Beyond the marshes there are many trees. Most are not large, and lush grass sprouts between them. Antelope of many kinds are plentiful, some having long horns. (There are wild goats, too, some with horns of enormous length.) One of the smaller kinds seems to stay near the water. I see them running on the riverbank as I write, and wading in the river. No doubt many are killed by crocodiles; they may be the crocodiles' chief food. If a man so much as lifts his spear, they whistle and flee.

My wives are in this boat with me, Cheche's children in the one that follows ours, watched by my slave. Not long ago she pointed with her chin to show me a wild dog of the kind that killed their father. It was spotted and dotted with black and seemed crippled, its hind legs too short; but it trotted easily and swiftly, keeping pace with our boat until it took some scent and turned aside. I thought it ugly, but its shoulders seemed strong indeed. Few dogs, I think, would fight as well.

Such a wild dog bit Cheche's first husband while he slept, she says. This was said with her hands as well as her mouth, since neither Myt-ser'eu nor I understand much of her speech. We speak as the people of Kemet do, and she as the king speaks. Some words are the same, I think, but not many. In time, we will learn her speech, and she ours. I know a few words already.

There are many lions—*simba*—here, she says. Also many leopards—*chui*. With so much game that must surely be true.

WE HAVE STOPPED at a place that will be good for river-horses, building our fires some distance inland so as not to alarm them. While we waited for them to come out of the water, I spoke with my slave. His name is Uraeus. We have been together a long time, he says, but were separated when I went ashore to fight, taking Myt-ser'eu with me. I said I could not believe that I would take her if I were going to fight, but he swears I did. I have thought on this. Surely I did not trust her to be faithful, and here there are many strong men with whom she might betray me. The king has eunuchs to watch the queen; they are never far from her.

My sons wished to hunt with us, flourishing their spears. We made them stay with their mother. They are Vinjari and Utundu, and will be tall and strong soon.

We crept upwind with our spears, looking for a big bull. This kind of hunting is dangerous, as I had been told and soon learned for myself. One must keep the wind in one's face, stay down, and move quietly. I think I might have said that I could hunt as quietly as any other man, but it is not true. I know our king and the warriors with him stalked more quietly than I, though I did my best.

We had agreed that the king would stand first and throw his spear. As soon as he did, we would stand and throw too, at the same animal. We were very near a big bull. I waited for the king to throw, wondering what was wrong. When he stood, I saw he had crept very near. The river-horse roared, a terrible sound! We rose as one, and our spears rained upon it.

Then everyone was shouting and scattering. A second river-horse, one farther inland that we had failed to see, was charging toward us, not actually charging us but dashing back to the river. No one, seeing these huge creatures for the first time, would believe how swift they are. I think I might have been trampled if our king had not pulled me out of its path. Its side brushed me, and I felt that I had been struck; a bull river-horse must outweigh three or four ordinary horses.

The river-horse that so many spears had pierced reached water, but it soon died there and floated to the surface. By then we had gotten torches from the camp. My sons and I went out in a boat with a man of this place and tied a line to its foot. Now we have feasted. The skin has been awarded to men who wish to make shields of it. Myt-ser'eu says I had a shield; our king did not like it, so I left it behind when we left Cheche's village. I asked for a piece of hide with which to make myself a new shield. He would not give me one, saying I would have another soon, one chosen for me by a god. I wish I knew more of this, but he will not speak further.

WE ARE STAYING in the king's city, Mji Mkubwa. There are hundreds of huts, all on stout poles. I asked Unguja about this. He says that the river floods once a year, so that all this level land is under water. I said it must be inconvenient. He laughed. Everyone has a boat, the water sweeps the away all filth, and the people of the city can fish out of their doors.

Myt-ser'eu was with us when we spoke. She says that this flood occurs in Kemet, too. It is then that great blocks of stone are taken up from the quarries, set upon rafts of countless reeds, and floated to the sites at which tombs, temples, and fortresses are being built. The floodwater soaks their fields, too, and leaves a gift of rich black mud. There is a river god, a very great god. He is blue, and friendly to men. Each year the flood is decreed by a goddess. We asked Unguja whether these gods were worshipped here, but he would tell us nothing, only saying that we must speak of other things.

The king's people have no temples. They go to sacred places immemorially old and worship there. That seemed very strange to both Myt-ser'eu and me, but the more I think on it the wiser I think it. Temples are like the images they contain, things made by men. Gods shape trees and caves, and smile down on us when we stand upon the tops of hills.

Myt-ser'eu says that Alala's people worship as the king's people do. I asked her about this Alala and her people, but she would tell me only a little, saying I had written about them and should read what I wrote. After that, I read much in this scroll, finding it interesting indeed.

When my eyes were sore, I returned to Unguja to ask whether he knew of a cure for men like me, who forget very quickly. He said only that I had been blessed, and that he longs to forget all he knows and be a child again. He has been promised this, and expects it in a few years; still, I wish to be as other men.

I HAVE BEEN talking with Binti—talking with my hands as much as my mouth. She is my youngest, and a brave girl who will not permit her brothers to bully her. I applauded her, teaching her that it is better to fight and lose than not to fight. No one bullies anyone who fights and fights hard, although he is defeated. Such a person must be respected, and is. She said that women did not fight men—that they do not have to. If a man bullies a woman, all the women turn against him. Then the other men mock him because he sleeps alone. Women fight other women, however. She says that Cheche has fought others often, and won. I wondered then whether she would fight Myt-ser'eu. She is larger and stronger.

Binti said that Cheche would not, because Myt-ser'eu is my senior wife. I had known that, having read of her many times in this scroll; but I had not known Cheche would respect it. Two lesser wives may fight for precedence, Binti says, but more often it is the wives of different men who fight. Quarrels between lesser wives are judged by the senior wife.

Binti wanted to know which I would lie with tonight. I said I would lie with the wife who wished me to do so. She predicted that both would wish it. I told her I would never lie with her, but that I would protect her as well as I could. She sat close after that, and smiled so as to melt the hardest heart. Can a man who has no daughter be happy? It seems to me it must be difficult.

The king has many daughters and many sons, too. His palace is ten times larger than the other huts, a whole series of huts in which one opens into another. His children play everywhere in it, laughing and shouting.

ANOTHER DAY. NOW the sun is setting, and the wind grows cool. I do not know how many days have passed since the last on which I wrote, only that my ink was dry and hard.

Myt-ser'eu and I have been speaking with the queen. She told us how much she wishes to return to her native city, if only for half a year. She made us promise to help her in this. Myt-ser'eu sounded much the same. She is from a place called Sais, and begged me to return her there. She had jewelry and money, she says, and gained more on the voyage south; but she lost everything when we were enslaved. She does not understand how I kept the gold beetle. She wept, and embraced the queen, and swore that she would rather be penniless in Sais than a queen here. I had to translate all this for the queen, which I did badly.

Earlier I attended the king's court. I do not speak his tongue well, and I often found it hard to understand what was being said. Many of these cases concerned witchcraft. One accuses another of being a witch and laying a curse. The accused denies it. In each case the king asked again and again how the accuser knew that the person he had brought to court was the witch, but he seldom got a satisfactory answer.

A young girl came. She testified that she was oppressed by a demon, accusing no one of having cursed her, only asking that the king order the demon to quit her. He did, and the demon laughed and mocked him.

It angered me. I came forward and asked the king's permission to attack it. I speak the tongue these people use only a little, but I managed to make my meaning clear, and the king consented.

I struck at the demon, but it dodged the blow and closed with me, clawing me as it had clawed the girl. Many people screamed and ran. It was smooth and oily, but I jammed my thumb into the yellow flame that was its only eye and bent it across my knee. There was too much noise for me to hear its spine snap, but I felt it. At once it was gone.

The king had left his throne. There was fear in his face, but his spear was ready. Most of the others had fled, knocking down children and old people. We spoke as friends, the king and I, when we had helped the old to rise and comforted the children. There is a greater king here whom his people never see, a kind old man fond of music. I touched him once, the king said, then everyone saw him. So it was with the demon. When it closed with me, all could see it. This is very strange. I wish Myt-ser'eu had been with me. She might explain more.

The girl the demon clawed will not leave me. When I tell her she must go home to her mother, she insists she has none. She is afraid her demon will return to her, but that will pass. Myt-ser'eu calls it a xu, though Myt-ser'eu did not see it.

MY SENIOR WIFE says I must write on this scroll every day, and read it, too. Otherwise I forget. The light is fading, and I know it is not good to write by firelight. I will write first, telling all I know, and read much afterward while a little light remains.

There are five boats. The first is the king's, with twenty-six warriors, the queen, and others. The second is Unguja's, with fourteen warriors, some women, and many children. The third is mine, with twenty warriors, myself, my chief wife, my second wife, and our warriors' women. The fourth is my children's, with ten or twelve warriors, my servant, my chief wife's maidservant, and more women as well as many children. The fifth is the boat of the king's servants, with sixteen warriors and their women, the servants, and our supplies. It is larger than the king's, but is the slowest.

Our boats are hollowed from logs, which seems strange to me. The tree from which the king's was made must have been very large. Fires are laid on the log and carefully tended. When they go out, the charred wood beneath them is chipped away. Making a good boat takes great skill and many days of careful work. Boats are made of reeds as well. These can be built quickly and easily, but soon rot.

My chief wife's maidservant has brought me a gourd of good water. She is a girl older than my daughter. Some beast has clawed her, leaving scars like mine on her arms and back. These are heeling, I think. I asked what beast it was. She does not know its name, but says I killed it. Her own is Mtoto.

I WROTE THAT I would not write by firelight. So much for my wisdom! There is a madman laughing outside our camp. I asked Mvita whether we should not go out and drive him away. He said that there are many dangerous animals here and many demons. They will try all sorts of tricks to lure us away from the fires, and that we must not go.

THE WOMEN ARE breaking camp and will not let me help them. I will write of what I saw last night. A panther as large as a lion prowled around our camp. I woke and saw this. At times it came very near the fires. It was blacker than the night and very beautiful, seeming to flow from one place to another, but looked as dangerous as a chariot with blades. I held my spear, which I had driven into the ground near my head before I slept. Our sentries never turned their eyes toward it. If it was before a sentry, he looked to one side, or down, or up at the moon, or shut his eyes. This I saw more than once. It seems strange to me, and I wish to set it down. Perhaps it was a dream.

WE HAVE STOPPED at a village in which there is a man who is said to know where the temple we seek lies. He is hunting, and we wait his return. His name is Mzee.

Binti has been crying. I tried to comfort her. When I asked what was wrong, she said that when we find the holy place I will remember other people and go away. I said I would not, but she insisted. Perhaps she is right, I cannot say. I would have promised to stay, but what good is a promise from a man who cannot remember? I said that if I left she must come with me. It ended her tears, or nearly.

MZEE HAS RETURNED at last. He is older than I expected, the oldest man in this village, though he still hunts—and hunts well, for he brought a fine antelope. He warned us of the holy place, saying that there are many snakes. Uraeus says that we need not fear them as long as he is with us. My sons boast that they will kill them. I have warned them to leave them strictly alone. Snakes and boys are a bad combination at the best of times, and the snakes in a sacred place are surely sacred.

Myt-ser'eu talks of her home in Sais, of the kindness of the priests and of singing, playing, and dancing at parties where she drank good wine until she could scarcely stand. I said I was sorry that I had taken her so far away. She would not blame me, or anyone, saying it was the will of the gods—if she had stayed at home, something worse might have happened. She would implore the pity of her goddess, and her goddess would help her, if only she could find a temple. Hathor, she names her goddess. I said that the sacred place the king speaks of might be sacred to Hathor, and we would pray there. As I spoke those words the gold scarab on my chest stirred like a living thing.

Mzee has given his antelope to the king, and the king has contributed it to the feast Mzee's village is preparing for us tomorrow. I will hunt tomorrow morning with Vinjari and Utundu, and we will contribute any worthy game we take. If I can teach them nothing of hunting (which is what they say), it may be that they will teach me something.

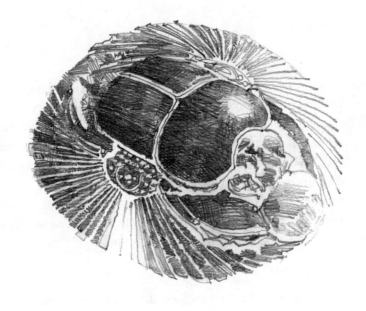

31

IN THE BUSH

WHERE WE ARE camped, there is no water. We have some in
gourds and in skin bags like wine skins, but not enough. Mzee says
we may find a spring tomorrow, before we reach the temple. There
is game here, though not much; the animals must get water somewhere.

We marched far from the river today, following a dry stream
through a deep gorge that may once have been a major tributary. I
no longer remember leaving the river, but I know we must have left
it at dawn from what Cheche and the children say.

My sandals are nearly worn out. I have been looking among the
things we brought for materials with which to make new ones.
Cheche asked what I was doing; when I told her, she said she would

make me new ones of braided grass. Perhaps I will cut up an empty water skin and give my new sandals a soft leather lining.

The temple is near. The scarab I wear sees it (or scents it, perhaps) and stirs as I write. The king does not wish to enter this temple after dark. No doubt this is wise; animals may den there—leopards or the skulking wild dogs we saw so often today.

The animal I saw outside our camp not long ago was a leopard, in form at least, although it was blacker than the night save for its burning eyes. Perhaps it resents our being so near.

I HAVE PROMISED my senior wife that she may leave me to return to her home. We may see a ship, she says, when we return to the river. This ship will carry her back there. Or so she hopes. It has been ahead of us for a long time, she says. I promised that if we found this ship we would board it. She said the king might not permit me to board it. She asked whether she might go alone. I said that she might, a pain that is never less. I had been looking forward to lying with her tonight, but how can I lie with her when I know she hopes to leave me? Perhaps I will lie with Cheche instead.

My senior wife swore that we have spoken like this many times.

WHILE I SAT here watching the fires and trying to choose, my slave came to tell me he had entered the temple. It is a good place, he says, though much decayed. There are snakes there, but only a few. I asked why the king wishes me to go there. The senior wife who wishes to leave me said it was because a god had ordered it in a dream. If nothing happens there, will the king blame me for it? I cannot say, and neither could they.

Certainly I put no trust in dreams. I would not like to meet the king singly; he is a skilled warrior, and his men say he is as bold as seven lions. If I took his life, his men would take mine, I feel sure.

————

I HAVE TRIED the sandals Cheche made. They need no lining, and are stronger than I would have thought possible. Now Myt-ser'eu and I will sleep.

VINJARI IS GONE. I have the shield the goddess gave. So much has happened that I despair of writing everything, though Myt-ser'eu and Cheche say I must. So does Myt-ser'eu's servant. I will write the first thing first.

We set out for the temple but had not gone far when a cry came from the back of the column. One of the king's warriors had trodden upon a snake, which bit him. The others killed it, a big brown snake with a head like a viper's. Unguja treated him, sucking the wound and dressing it with salve and the flesh of the dead snake; the bitten warrior soon died just the same. We buried him in the dry watercourse, heaping his grave with stones.

"I have promised you would be safe from us in the temple as long as I was with you, master," my slave whispered.

I said I had forgotten it.

"Of course, master. Yet I spoke as I said. I cannot promise that the others will be. Only you. Even you will not be safe unless I go ahead of you to tell the folk. May I go?"

I thought he merely wanted a respite from the work of piling stones, but I said he might. He left at once, and I did not see him again until the time I will write of.

The temple is stone, very old. Myt-ser'eu said that though she had seen many old things in her own land, it was older than any. Its roof has fallen in places. The king said that only he and I should enter. That was wise, I think, but Unguja pleaded with the king. When the king agreed to take him, he urged that Mzee come with us as well. That too was granted.

The king asked then whether there were any whom I would have with me. Myt-ser'eu wished to go, but I feared for her and took my sons instead. So we six entered the temple, bearing torches and un-aware that a seventh would slip away and follow us.

It seemed darker there than any night, for we stepped into dark-ness from sunlight bright enough to blind a lion. It seemed cool as well after the heat of the day, which had been very great. Bats stirred and squeaked on the false arches above us, and the floor was crusted with their droppings.

Soon I felt a stirring on my chest, as though the gold scarab I wore feared the bats. When I looked down, I saw that it was biting the string that held it. In a moment more the string had parted, and it flew some distance, still gleaming blue and gold in the light of our torches.

Behind me the king called, demanding to know what I was do-ing. I tried to explain that my scarab had come to life, and flown, and vanished into a crevice in the floor. This was difficult, because I do not speak his tongue well and could not lay hand to many words I required.

"The string broke," the king told me. His voice was kind. "Your scarab fell and rolled into the crevice. Forget it, as you forget so much. You will never see it again."

I asked him to help me lift the stone; he shook his head, backing away. "We must find the god," he said. "That is what is important, Latro—finding the god."

Lifting the stone was difficult, not only because of its weight, but because it was hard to grasp at first. My sons helped, but would not go down the worn steps with me. I went down, walking very slowly because my torch burned badly there. I thought that my scarab (I never found it) must have rolled down the long stair; when I motioned to my sons, they looked frightened and would not follow. So it was that they learned they were only boys, after all.

As I descended I saw that the temple had once been much

larger than the part that we had seen. Wind and time had heaped up soil around it; the part we had seen and entered had been an upper story once. There was a small god of black stone, in appearance a man as old as Unguja, in a niche at the landing. I held my torch close to see his face. He was bald, bearded, and smiling, round-bellied. He held a cup and a flute. I felt then as I do when I see the king, felt that he was a better friend than I knew. I touched him, and he moved at my touch. When I lifted him from the niche in which he stood, I saw that there was an opening behind him and a scroll smaller than this one in the opening.

I took it out; and as I replaced the image of the happy old god, I heard the voice of my senior wife, Myt-ser'eu, behind me. I turned at once, almost dropping the scroll he had given me.

She stood on the stair. Behind her was a man blacker than the king, not the small and friendly god whose image I had moved, but a tall man with the look of a warrior who kills the wounded. His hands were on her shoulders, and there was a thing in her face I cannot put into words. She might have been dreaming (though her eyes were very wide) and frightened by her dream. "You must give it to Sahuset," she told me. "Don't you remember? You promised to give it to Sahuset."

I did not remember, nor do I know who Sahuset may be.

"You promised him. Swore that you would give it to him."

I tried to untie the cords, for I wished to see whether I could read it. There was no knot.

"You must not open it," Myt-ser'eu told me.

I was afraid for her. I would have cast my spear at the black man behind her if he had stood alone; I felt I could not throw without killing her, for he would lift her to receive it. "I love you," I said; I knew it was true, and that she did not know it.

"If you open it," she told me, "you will never find your shield."

I saw it was important to her and said I would not. The truth is that I could not. The leather case that carries this scroll was slung on my back, as I would think it always must be on the march. I opened that instead, and put the scroll I had found into it. It is a smaller scroll than this, tightly wound.

I stopped just now to look at it again, but did not cut its cords. It is not mine to open, or so I feel.

When I had fastened the straps of my scroll case, the tall man who had held Myt-ser'eu was gone. I asked her who he had been; she said there had been no such man.

"A tall, hard-faced man," I said, "darker than your eyes. His own seemed to burn."

"I've seen many men like that here," Myt-ser'eu replied. "There are dozens like that with us. Did you mean it? What you said when I was on the steps above you?"

I nodded and she kissed me. I held her close, delighting in the breasts she pressed so tightly to me. How small she is! How sweet and good!

We descended the second stair to the bottom hand in hand, and searched for the inner room in which the god would stand. I knew it was what we must find, because the king had said it, and because Myt-ser'eu did not seem to understand me when I asked about the shield she had said only a moment before that I had lost. "I suppose I must have owned a shield once," I said, "but I don't recall it."

"You recall very little," she told me. "When you fought Cheche's brother-in-law you won his shield, but you did not like it. It was too big, you said, and not strong enough. The king did not want you to have it, either. You left it behind in Cheche's village."

If there were pictures on the walls of that temple once, the passing years had worn them away. We saw only bare stones, somewhat rough, somewhat soiled, and strangely fitted. Windows had spilled sand and shale onto the floor, and here and there a wall bulged and seemed about to fall. Once I heard a thrumming ahead of us, as if a beetle flew through the darkness there; and once I saw a faint gleam that might have been gold, though there was no gold there when I went to look where it had been.

The holiest place held the rude statue of a woman. From her left hand dangled such a cross as I know I have seen elsewhere, though I do not know where; her right held a long arrow. Her headdress was a disk, as of the sun or moon, held by curved supports.

Myt-ser'eu knelt to her, bent her head and prayed. Her whispers were too soft for me to make out the words, and I felt certain she was praying that she be returned to her city in the north.

The goddess stepped from her pedestal, becoming a living woman no larger than Myt-ser'eu herself—smaller, perhaps—but standing before a thing brighter than she. She held out her arrow to me; with the hand I freed by accepting it, she took the disk from her headdress and held it before Myt-ser'eu's eyes. "Your prayer for the man with you is granted," she told Myt-ser'eu. "You are to give him this. The wish you left unvoiced is granted as well. You shall return to your home as you desire, though you shall leave again by your desire."

Her arrow had melted into my hand the moment I grasped it. The disk she had shown Myt-ser'eu rang as it fell to the stones on which she stood, and at the sound there was no woman standing there, only the image of a woman standing upon its pedestal.

Myt-ser'eu straightened up and picked up a larger disk. "Look, Latro! A shield! We didn't see it because it lay flat on the floor, but here it is."

She held it out to me, and I took it. It is of bronze green with age. The handle on the back is bronze also. These small clipei have no strap for the arm. I have it before me as I write, and will polish it when I have written all I must.

When we returned to the upper level, I showed it to the king, who looked at it from every angle but would not touch it. When he had examined it in that fashion, he said that we must go, calling

Mzee and Unguja to him. I was about to call my sons, when they ran to me trembling. Vinjari had seen a big snake, the younger said, and cast his spear at it. When the spear struck, it was a man.

I ran to look, making them come with me, though they were badly frightened. The man was my slave. His mouth was wide as he coughed blood, and I saw that he had fangs. I do not believe I can ever have seen a man with fangs before. I do not think anyone else saw these fangs.

I gave my spear and shield to Utundu, and picked up my slave. He died in my arms. I told the king we must bury him. He had belonged to me, and I owed him that and more. The king agreed.

My wives, my sons, my daughter, and our servant girl went with me into the bush. In the bed of the dry stream, in a place of many stones, we dug a grave with spears; but when we would have laid him in it, he was gone. I said that some animal must have carried the body away while we worked. The women and girls said it could not be. They had been sitting beside it a moment before, talking quietly among themselves and waving off the flies.

Perhaps they slept.

Or it may be that Vinjari took it, and they would not tell me. However that may be, he has gone off into the bush. Utundu and I tracked him a long way, but lost the trail at last.

NOW I MUST write again. I have built up the fire, and there will be light enough for a time. I polished the new shield the goddess gave me while the others slept, rubbing it with fine sand to make it bright. Soon it was so clear in the place I rubbed that I could see the leaping flames behind me reflected there.

They vanished, and in their place I saw a self younger than I am whose head was wrapped in bloodstained bandages. This self threw his sword into the river, offering a prayer to the river god. The river god tempered it, heating it in flickering flames that rose from his waters and quenching it in them. At length he returned it, and nothing save my own shadow and the flickering flames showed in the bright metal over which I had labored.

But I remembered! I remember even now. Not just seeing it in the metal, but the whole event: How my head ached that day, and how weak I was. How I had prayed for the black man with me—he was the king, I know, for his face was the same.

He was my only friend, and the river god the only god I knew. I cast my sword into the river when I had asked the river god to bless him. The river god showed it to his daughters, beautiful young girls with skin as white as his, and his skin was as white as foam. When they had seen it and tried to take it from him, he returned it to me.

"Not wood, nor bronze, nor iron shall stand against her, and she will not fail you until you fail her."

I have failed her now, but I will redeem my failure. Or walk alone and sorrowing, as this says my son did, into the bush to die.

32

THE QUEEN IS OVERJOYED

TOMORROW WE WILL go down the Great River. Last night
I talked long with the king. I spoke as Hellenes do, he as his people
do. I understand that speech better than I speak it.

He told me many things that had taken place while we were together in Hellas. They are fading from my mind even as I write. It
may be well that they do, because there are many I cannot believe or
may have misunderstood.

I told him of casting Falcata into the river, and he said I had told
him of it before, long ago. I said that I must find her and hold her
again, or die in the attempt. I had spoken of Falcata to my senior
wife. (Myt-ser'eu is her name, and she is the smaller of the two.)

She told me how I had lost it when I fought the men of Nubia. It must surely be somewhere in Nubia now, I told the king, for no soldier would cast aside such a weapon. I was going there to find it, I said; and I asked in the light of our friendship that he see that my wives and children did not want while I was away. He said he would, but soon said that he himself would go with me. He will bring warriors and gold, for it may be that we will have to buy back Falcata from her new owner. He will bring the queen as well; and when I have regained Falcata, we will journey north into Riverland and from there to her city. Unguja will govern for the king in his absence. We spoke with him, and he swore that he would see that my wives and children are well treated and have good food.

AS SOON AS I could, I told Myt-ser'eu much of what the king and I had said. I do not recall it now—only the casting my sword into the river of Hellas—but when we spoke I did, and no doubt some are written here. She raged and wept and raged again. I swore, she said, that I would return her to her native city. She will have no gift from me, for I have become poor, her jewelry is gone, and now I intend to break my oath. She would take her own life—this she said again and again.

Then that she would take mine (though I do not fear her).

After that, that she would do both.

Weeping she spoke of all that we have been through together, of her faithful service and of the love she gave me without stinting.

I explained that I had sensed all those things, though I could not recall the events; and I told her what is very true—that she is first in my heart. Regaining Falcata may be dangerous indeed. The men she told me of, who had taken Falcata from me and enslaved us, were my foes. I might have to fight them again, and this time they might kill me.

She made me read the first part of this scroll, saying I would find my promise there. I read it. If I made such a promise, I did not record it. Yet her goddess had appeared to me, I had promised my protection, and the return of the singing girls was certainly implied in what the priest and the man with me had said. Further, it was implied that I would make Myt-ser'eu a suitable gift when we parted. As she said, I have none to give.

We spoke of this, and I read to her from this scroll, turning its speech into hers as I read. She asked again and again whether I had really spoken with her goddess. All that I could do was repeat that I did not know, that it was written as I had said.

"I have seen a god, however," I told her. "I saw the river god, and tried to give him my sword. He gave it back to me." I quoted his words to her again.

"Are you sure he didn't give me to you then?"

I shook my head. "Your own goddess gave you to me. That's what this says."

"You can't protect me if you're not here."

"I can leave you in good hands," I said, "instead of taking you into danger."

"That ugly old man's? Listen, I know women, which is more than you do. He and Cheche will have made a slave of me before you're out of sight."

"Have I ever beaten you?"

She shook her head. "I don't want to talk about that."

"Have I?"

"Yes!"

"Good. I'm glad to learn it. I can beat you whenever it's necessary. The priest said that. Not enough to put your life in danger, but a good beating. If you won't do as I say, I'll beat you."

"Is that the safety you want to provide for me? A beating? I'd rather have danger, with a chance of getting home."

There we left it, for we could not agree. I will go, and go without her. She may rage, but I will be far away. Perhaps I will leave the king and queen and return for her when I have regained Falcata, though I will have forgotten her long before that time, I know.

A SHIP HAS come, with many on board who say they are our friends. No doubt it is true of some. Myt-ser'eu's maidservant came to tell her of it, and she ran to the riverbank shouting. I ran after her, and the men on the ship, seeing us, anchored and came to shore in a boat. Myt-ser'eu has been talking ever since. I have heard everything with interest, but I cannot write all that here.

There is a woman on the ship who blows kisses to us, whom Myt-ser'eu says is her dearest friend. Of the men who came in the boat, I now know these: The small man, oldest of all, bearded, bald, and richly but simply dressed, is Noble Qanju. He commands the rests, and is of Parsa. The young man who helps him is of Kemet, like my wife. He is Holy Thotmaktef. The older man, not large but well muscled, is Captain Muslak. From what my wife had me read, I knew that it was he who went to the temple with me. We spoke of that. He says we are old friends, but I do not think I have known him as long as I have known the king.

The tall young man, Thotmaktef's friend, is Kames. He owes me much, he says, and will repay when he returns to his city.

The scholar Sahuset is tallest, lean, and older than I. The youngest is the prince. It is thought (Qanju says) that the priests will choose him if the Nubian king dies; thus the Nubian king hid him. We are not to speak of him.

Qanju has made gifts to King Seven Lions, and the king gifts to Qanju. There will be a feast.

When I learned that he, Thotmaktef, and Sahuset were all learned men, I asked them about the other scroll. All wished to see it, and Sahuset declared that I had promised long ago to give it to him.

I asked whether I had promised more than that, and he shook his head. I said that in that case I would give it to him gladly.

"You must show it to me first, Lucius," Qanju said. He says also that *Lucius* is my true name. The younger man agreed with him. Sahuset agreed to let Qanju look at the scroll, although with great reluctance.

I took it out, explaining that I could not find the knot to loose its cords.

Thotmaktef had a small knife, but dropped it each time he picked it up.

"The cords should not be cut," Qanju said. He took the scroll (not this one) from me, and at his touch the cords fell away. They were not cords at all, but snakes, small and slender black snakes that crawled away as swiftly as a deer might run, so that I did not see where they fled. Qanju opened the scroll, shook his head, and handed it to Sahuset.

Thotmaktef said, "Is it the character of my ancient nation? I will read it for you if you wish, Noble Qanju."

"It is not for you to read," Qanju told him.

Sahuset took black cords from the earth on which we sat and bound the scroll. "Neither is it for me to read at this time and in this place," he said, "but the scroll is mine. Do we agree upon that?"

Qanju nodded. Thotmaktef nodded too, though I saw that he did not wish to.

Sahuset said, "Latro?" (It is how my wife speaks to me.)

"You say I promised it to you," I said. "I give it to you now and am quit of my promise."

"Agreed." Sahuset put the scroll into his robe.

My wife says these people will take her home.

I HAVE SPOKEN again with Qanju. Our company was sent south by the satrap, and instructed to explore the river as far as possible. In Nubia, Qanju learned that Kames was held by the king. I and others freed him, but Myt-ser'eu and I were taken, and Qanju and the rest thought us dead.

There is a place where the river divides into streams called Blue and White. Our ship sailed the Blue as far as it could go, and Qanju and a certain woman questioned the men of the highlands as to its origin.

After that, our ship turned about, rowed back to the rivers' parting, and sailed up this river until it could sail no farther, seeing many strange sights and speaking with many strange peoples. Now it is returning to the satrap.

THE SHIP I wrote of has been pulled on shore. We have had a great feast, with much dancing and many good things to eat and drink. All sleep. I sit by the fire to think, knowing I ate too much, and that if I had drunk as much pombe as Myt-ser'eu I would not think at all.

She is very happy. Qanju will make a gift to her for my sake when we part, and he has much gold. The king will make her a gift, too, when he and I leave the ship. The ship will return her to her home, though the journey is long. I should be as happy as she, but am not. How can a man be happy, knowing he must part from his wives and children?

Nor can I be happy until I regain Falcata. She was at my side before Myt-ser'eu, I know. I cannot recall Myt-ser'eu beside the river. If we were together then, I would surely have thought of her.

I HAD BELIEVED myself the only person awake. There is another, a woman with a great cat. They do not come near me, but search among the sleepers. When I think they have gone for good, they return.

The queen came to me, walking badly. She wished to tell someone how happy she was, talked much of it, and lifted her skirt to show what I might have if I wished it. I did not wish it, and returned her to the palace, making her lie beside the king. No good can come of such things.

Is it she the tall woman and her cat seek? They came near while we spoke. Her cat is black, not spotted, though I believed such cats spotted. I must ask someone about this.

I WOKE EARLY on this ship. Only my sentry and one woman were awake. The sentry saluted me, and I told him he might sleep if he could; I would take the rest of his watch.

The woman is Sahuset's wife. He is a wise man of Riverland. I explained that I had been trying to recall how I came here. She said I forget more quickly than most men, though all forget in time, and in time everything is forgotten. She showed me the leather case that holds this, and said it held my memory. I have read enough now to know that she spoke the truth.

I told her all that I remember—my mother and father, our house and our fields, and casting my sword Falcata into a river whose god restored it to me.

She told me who she was, and offered to point out all the persons of importance who slept on the ship. Most, she said, were the king's warriors (men she does not know), sailors of no importance, and my soldiers, whom she said were of still less importance. I protested that since they were mine, as I knew they were, they were important to me; but she does not know their names.

She showed me the queen, who slept in a little tent on deck with the king. She must have the queen's blood to live, she said. The queen stirred at our words, and we went away. She showed me her husband, too, and my wife.

"I will be your wife when she has gone," she said, "and a better wife than she."

I asked whether my wife would leave me, and she said she would, very soon.

"It is nearly sunrise," she said, "and I must go to bed. Will you do me a service, Latro? A small favor for someone who fought the Nubians with you?"

I said I would if I could.

"You can, and very easily. Did you see the amulet your wife wears? The bull's head? I want you to cut the cord and drop the amulet into the water. Great good will come to you if you do this."

I said I would never do such a thing without my wife's permission.

"Then gain it, and do it."

I nodded, but promised nothing. She went below—her bed is in the hold.

My weapons lie where I slept. I have a spear, a club, and a small shield in need of polishing. I must tell one of my soldiers to do that when they wake.

The sun is above the trees. A few stir, but most still sleep. The trees near the river are tall and thick, the home of many bright birds who call among the topmost branches. Beautiful white wading birds are everywhere, and small birds hop in and out of the mouths of crocodiles. This is a lovely land and a terrible land, but it is not my land.

THE QUEEN CAME to sit with me while I wrote. We are old friends, she says. She is a handsome woman, somewhat heavier than either of us might like. Her name is Bittusilma. I asked how she had injured her arm. She said she fell on the night of the feast and cut it. I did not remember this feast, yet I was there, and danced—badly, she said—and drank and feasted with the others. She told me a great deal about it.

After that, as the others were waking and rising, she talked of her native city. It is walled, and its walls are the highest in all the world. She told me much of it, and its conquest by the Great King—too much to write. We are going there soon, which makes Bittusilma very happy.

33

OUR WHOLE COMPANY

THE SAILORS AND my soldiers, as well as the persons of greater importance, gathered in the ship's waist this morning as we lay at anchor in the middle of the river. I told them of the river god I remember so well and how he had returned Falcata to me. I told them also that I was determined to find her again and reclaim her. I said that if need be I would leave the ship and remain behind in Nubia. That I will find her or die in the attempt.

Qanju said he could not stay or order the ship to, but he would give me all the help he could. We would stop at every town and village so I might search. The captain explained that he was under Qanju's orders and could not do as he might wish. Furthermore, he has been chartered by the king; when he has reported to the satrap, he will bear the king and queen to the Great Sea, and over it to the cities of the Crimson Men, from which they can proceed by an easy road to the queen's city. He would return to Nubia, however, when this voyage had ended, find me there, assist me if he could, and take me home or to Sidon, as I preferred.

Through his queen, the king expressed his great friendship. He and his four warriors will help me search in every place we pass, and help me regain Falcata if we find her. He has given me gold.

Kames spoke of his fear at reentering Nubia. He will not dare to show his face as long as our ship is there; but if I must remain behind—as I have sworn I will if I do not find Falcata—he will send me aid from his father's house in Wast.

Prince Nasakhma promised to assist me in every possible way, should the gods choose him to wear the crown; and Sahuset said that he would help me as long as I remained with the ship, searching for my sword by magic and telling me everything that he discovered.

At this Qanju said he would sift the wisdom of the stars this very night. He too will tell me all he learns.

Thotmaktef promised to speak with the priests at the temple of Thoth in Napata (where the Nubian king's house is), describing me and my search, and ask them to help me. When he has prepared, he will bestow upon me the great blessing of his god, which he says will prompt me to write my scroll. Thus I will record much that I would otherwise forget and so lose. He will do this after the noon meal.

At his words his tame baboon stirred and gave me a look so long and piercing that in the end it was I who turned my eyes away. I had believed that no mere animal could look me in the eye for long. I know better now.

(It puzzles me that no one ever speaks of this baboon or pays the slightest heed to it, although it is large and would surely be very dangerous if aroused. The sailors do not tease it, Thotmaktef does not stroke it, and the women do not show the least fear of it. Having nothing to feed it, I have ignored it like the rest.)

Thotmaktef's wife promised that she would speak with the men of her tribe on my behalf. They often come into the towns to trade in the markets, she said. She will tell them about me and ask their help in finding Falcata.

Neht-nefret said that I must understand that she and Myt-ser'eu mean to return to the temple of Hathor in Sais. The captain agreed with this. They have been away for many months—far longer than most voyages up the Great River require. At this, Myt-ser'eu squeezed my hand and wept; but I know she feels as Neht-nefret does—she told me so before we met with the rest. Both promised to help as long as they were with me, and both hoped (Myt-ser'eu very fervently) that I would find my sword before the ship reached the border of their nation, which lies (our captain said) north of the first cataract.

My soldiers offered to help me search for my sword as long as we are with the ship. They are familiar with her, they said, and will know her at once if they so much as glimpse her. Baginu spoke for himself as the only soldier from Parsa, Aahmes for all five of Myt-ser'eu's nation.

In the same way, Azibaal spoke for the sailors. They will search too, and are (as he said) the most numerous group on the ship. I have more faith in my six soldiers, but hope the sailors will prove me wrong.

I HAVE RECEIVED the great blessing of his god from Thotmaktef. We sang, and offered too many prayers to count—prayers I could not set down here even if I were minded to commit an act so foolhardy.

When our ship had anchored, he and I went deep into the reeds in the boat. These marshes are very dangerous, the haunts of river-horses, snakes, and crocodiles. I thought we would remain in the boat, but we did not, leaving it to wade through the reeds in water up to our knees. It is from reeds like these that my scroll is made, as Thotmaktef explained, and it is one of those very reeds I hold to write. My ink is black with their ashes, and it clings to the papyrus because it holds their blood. Those whom the gods of Kemet find without fault at death are sent into the Field of Reeds to await new life.

As Thotmaktef spoke of this, I saw that his baboon had followed us, or perhaps had been brought after us by the fair-haired huntress who held its paw as they walked over the tops of the thronging reeds. She smiled at me and was gone, though my heart ached for her. Now that the ceremony is over, I recall her better than any part of it, her graceful figure, high cheekbones, and smiling blue eyes. One breast was bare. Her gown* covered the other, if there was another breast there. From her side she drew the arrow that had dyed her gown with her own blood. After rinsing its head in the water, she wiped it and put it into her quiver.

TWICE I WAS awakened in the night. I longed to write of those awakenings but could not, for I had no lamp. Now I have seen a boat bring the sun. The baboon (who brought the woman I wrote of when I last unrolled this scroll) rode in its prow.

Qanju awakened me first. He told me his name, fearing I had forgotten it while I slept. "I have scanned the stars for you," he said, "and they speak of wars and long and hazardous journeys. For years you will walk in a circle, following the path left by your own feet."

I asked whether I would find Falcata, and when and where I would find her if I did.

"You will find her," he said. "I could tell you more if I knew the day of your birth, and the position of the stars at that time."

---

*The narrator uses the word *stola* here, in place of his usual *vestis*. The stola was a woman's garment fastened at a shoulder that left the other shoulder bare.

I could not tell him those things.

He sighed. "In which case nothing is sure. You will find your sword, but from what I saw you will not find it in the place in which you look for it, since the Sky-Hunter has his back to you. As for when you will find it, the stars declare that you have never lost it."

I shook my head. "I don't understand."

"Neither do I, Lucius. When you have your sword again, I hope you will tell me how you regained it."

The second person to interrupt my sleep was a lovely woman; she touched me in a place in which I would hesitate to touch any woman save my wife. "You have waked me," she whispered, "thus I wake you. Whom do you trust?"

"No one," I whispered in reply, "not even myself—though I would trust my sword, if I had her. That's one reason I'm trying to find her."

"The lying woman beside you does not trust you. Too many men have played her false. She expects it from you each time you speak to her."

"Nor do I trust myself," I repeated.

"So you say. But you do. I trust you also. Do me a small favor, and I will tell you much that is to your advantage to know."

"Tell me now," I whispered, "if you trust me. Tell me, and if what you say is to my advantage, I'll do the small favor you ask."

"Will you?"

I rose as quietly as I could. "You have my word on it."

"Have you forgotten Sahuset?"

"The wise man of Myt-ser'eu's nation? I have forgotten his appearance, but before I slept I read that he would search for my sword by magic."

"He is doing that as we speak, but you must believe nothing he tells you. He lies to enlarge himself in his own sight; and if he finds your sword, you will never regain it."

"You seem to know him well. Are you Neht-nefret?" I had read that name in this scroll before I slept, and I knew that the woman beside me was Myt-ser'eu.

"I am Sabra, his wife." Sabra laughed very softly, but her laugh made me wish my spear were in my hand. "I know him better than any. I am he, in a way that you will never understand. I am also the woman who aided you against King Siaspiqa's soldiers. You have forgotten it, but they would have killed all of you if it had not been for me. Now you are returning to Siaspiqa's realm to seek the sword you left there. You may have need of me again."

"I hope not." I forget quickly, I know; but I had not forgotten her laugh as quickly as that.

"I said that I would tell you something of value. I have warned you against my husband, which may save your life if you will heed it. Now I will tell you something more, and claim the small favor you promised. I am Sahuset's wife, but I would prefer to be yours."

I shook my head. "That is of no value to me. I would never take another man's wife." A step or two away, Myt-ser'eu stirred at the sound of our voices.

"Am I nothing?" Sabra stroked my cheek as she spoke, and her hand was smooth and cold.

"You are beautiful," I whispered, "and have no need of the jewels you wear to tempt any man. If you were mine, I would rejoice in you. You aren't, and if your husband found us together he might kill you."

"He will not. He has spells, but I have his and my own."

A beast snarled as she spoke, and I turned to see burning eyes behind me.

"Beteshu will not harm you, but you need not fear Sahuset as long as Beteshu is with us. Listen to me. You say you do not trust that woman, and you are wise not to. But you love her. Deny it if you like—it will remain true through you deny it with every oath."

I shrugged. "Go on."

"She wears an amulet my husband gave her, a bull's head.

Sahuset is the bull—it will draw her to him. That is the last coin in my hand. If it is of no value to you, you owe me no favor."

I was kneeling next to Myt-ser'eu before Sabra finished speaking. The cord that held her amulet snapped between my fingers and I threw both over the side. "You deserve whatever favor you ask," I told Sabra. "What is it you want?"

I could see the gleam of her teeth in the dark. "You have given the favor I intended to ask. May I have another?"

I rose again. "What is it?"

"A kiss."

When our lips met, it seemed I held a score of women in my arms. Myt-ser'eu was one, the queen another. The rest—and there were many more—I did not know.

When we parted, I whispered, "You are—are not as other women."

She laughed as before, chilling all my ardor. "I was a crocodile once. Perhaps you tasted it."

I watched her go toward the stern and vanish into the darkness. It may be that the panther went with her. I do not know.

SOMEONE ATTACKED THE queen last night, cutting her thigh without waking her. Qanju—our leader, Myt-ser'eu says, and the oldest man on the ship—is trying to discover the culprit. The tall man Myt-ser'eu swears is a warlock was talking to the carpenter when I began writing this. He wanted the carpenter to lend him his hammer and give him seven nails. The carpenter would not lend his hammer, but offered to nail down the lid of the box the tall man wishes to close. They have gone into the hold, and I hear the blows of the carpenter's hammer.

The warlock told the king he knew the queen's attacker and would see that she was not troubled again. The king raged, wishing to kill the guilty man with his own hand; but the warlock said he could not speak the guilty name. The king would have broken his arm, and Qanju ordered me to prevent it, which I did.

This has made the king my enemy, though I know he was once my friend. I am to paint myself as his warriors do no longer.

WE ARE AT Naqa, and thus in Nubia. So says my friend the captain. My men and I went through the market and the shops in search of the sword the river god tempered for me. Myt-ser'eu came too, but did not search on her own because she has forgotten my sword, to which she says she paid little heed when I had it. (She thought it large and heavy.) More signally, this is not a place in which women alone are safe.

We will sleep ashore tonight, and everyone is delighted. There is a big public building here in which travelers may stable their horses and store their goods. It has small rooms to which we must bring our own bedding. Nights on the ship were cold, I know, in spite of the day's heat; and with so many on board we slept in each other's armpits, as the captain says. Here each couple will have a room. The walls are thick mud brick, and there is a little fireplace in each. We will buy charcoal in the market, and be private, snug, and warm.

Myt-ser'eu says these people are barbarians, and that everyone not of Kemet is a barbarian. Thus I am a barbarian myself, which explains why I like the people here so much. Some are of Alala's tribe, some of another; but the men are as large as the king, and from their scars, brave. The women smile, laugh long, and flirt without shame. They seem a good people to me.

34

I AM ALONE

NOTHING COULD BE more useless than continuing this scroll, though I have been reading it ever since the baboon untied its cords. I sprang for it, catching it as the baboon dropped it. Its cords were tied again, and I felt the baboon had been a dream. Untying them, I began to read and saw that I had seen him before, and learned much else.

The man with my sword was Sabra's husband. I feel sure of it after reading what I just did.

We did not find Falcata in Naqa. Myt-ser'eu and I ate fried fish at a cookshop (very good) and tried the local beer. I thought it too sweet. She said it was like that we got in the south. When she had drunk all she could hold, we returned to the room we had rented earlier, I built a fire while she dozed, and we made love. I lay awake long after she was asleep, thinking how miserable I would be if I remained behind to search when she went north with the others. I do not know how I knew she would leave me and go with them, but I did, and found it bitter. Perhaps some god had revealed it to me. I resolved to reclaim Falcata before we reached the first cataract. No excuses would do. Falcata was here, her new owner had no reason to hide her, and I would find her. At last I slept.

The ringing of her blade woke me. I rose and unbarred the door. A tall man, older than I, stood outside holding Falcata. I gaped at him. He rang her blade again, striking it with something in his hand, perhaps a coin. I tried to explain that I wished to buy her from him, speaking as Myt-ser'eu did. He vanished, but I caught sight of his head and shoulders over the stalled horses.

I ought to have followed him naked into the street, but I did not. I went back to get the burse I had been given on the ship, putting on the tunic I had bought earlier and taking up this case that holds my scroll, too, when the baboon signed that I must. I might have killed the baboon with my club, but it was easier and quicker to do as he wished.

Outside I searched the dark streets. Once, when I was about to give up, I saw him. I ran after him shouting and he vanished. I have not seen him since.

The sun rose. I set out for the place where Myt-ser'eu and I had stayed but became lost. I asked several people where it was. Perhaps they misdirected me or I misunderstood them. Certainly the streets were crooked, and I did not know what many of the places they spoke of were.

When I found the building in which we had slept at last, Myt-ser'eu was gone. I asked the old man who rented rooms, and he said she had left some time ago when another man came for her. I did not recognize this man from his description—a young foreigner, smaller than I.

The old man had my shield and spear, which he handed over readily to me. Myt-ser'eu had them, he said, and he had made her surrender them because he thought she might be stealing them. She had told him I was already on the ship, but he had said that I must come back and claim them myself if I wanted them. He told me all this at length, speaking in the tongue used here. How angry she was, and how eager to be gone the man with her seemed.

I went to the docks. There was no ship, and Myt-ser'eu was not there. I asked a man fishing from a pier, and he said that the big foreign ship had sailed not long after sunrise. It was the *Gades,* he said. I cannot remember the name of our ship, but I believe the one he described must have been ours.

It will stop for the night at some city or town, I think, as it did at Naqa. With luck it may be delayed, and I have seen that ships going downriver move but slowly—the current carries them, but the wind is against them. They may be rowed, but rowing tires the crew; they row only enough to give the steering oar bite. If our ship ties up at a place on the other side of the river, I can pay someone to row me across.

I have walked and even run today, but that was foolish. Tomorrow I will buy a small boat. Let it carry my spear and shield, and my club. I will row hard, and not tire.

I FEEL WEAK and ill, hot at times and chilled at others, so that I huddle near this fire, which does not warm me. He makes me write this.

IT IS NEARLY noon. I am stronger, but not strong. Last night I was terribly sick, shaking when I was not burning with fever. Perhaps I only dreamed of the woman who burned, yet I hope not. Is there any use in writing of such things? The baboon would say there was, I know. He would make his meaning clear by signs.

Which is what I do here with my slip of frayed reed.

I feel I may die. If I do, the rain will come, my scroll will fall to bits, and no one will ever read the record of so many days of my life, days of interest to no one but myself in any event. If I do not die, I will find a way to protect it from the weather and deposit it in a safe place. There is only a single sheet left. Then the stick. The Hellenes have a name for that final sheet, I know. I wish I could recall it.

My fire is dying amid greasy ashes, but I no longer require it. The sun is high and the land is warm. I will rise and walk until I find a place where they will feed me. Then I may write more.

THESE PEOPLE FOUND me on the road. They had many questions, of which I could answer only a few. They are the Medjay, they say, the Lion People. We talked of horses, I thinking that I might buy a horse if the price was not too high. They asked whether I could ride. Feeling it to be true, I said I could, which surprised them. They think me a man of Kemet, and say few of us can ride. They invited me to their camp, where I am now, to see more horses. I agreed, and walked beside them as they rode. None had been to Kemet, but they talked of going there, where the satrap might hire them as he has others of their nation.

They warned me of the Nehasyu, the Men of Kush, with tales of their dishonesty and cruelty. Kush is the nation I call Nubia, it seems.

Here we looked at horses, and they shared their food with me. They had fresh beef and cheese. It has been a long time, I think, since I have eaten either. They measure their wealth in cattle and horses.

THEIR CHIEF HAS come. He is older than my new friends, and has been to Kemet and many other places. He fought, he says, for the Great King. When I could not answer his questions, I explained that I forget and showed him this. He said I had been touched by a god, and that I am a holy man.

I said, "If I have been touched by a god, it was only to curse me."

He nodded. "All who are touched by gods are holy."

"I would rather remember, as other men do."

"There are many things it is better to forget." He laughed. "Women!"

"There is a woman I must write of here before I forget her," I told him.

"Tell me," he said, "if you forget I will tell you."

I agreed. "Last night I camped alone. I have no cloak to sleep in, but I made a little fire and lay down."

He nodded. "I have often done the same."

"A woman came to my fire, a lovely woman with bracelets, a fine necklace, many rings. She said she was my wife, that she loved me and would always care for me and serve me. I was cold and asked her to warm me, but she said she could not do that."

"She was a ghost," the Medjay chief declared. "I have met many, and there is no warmth in them."

I shrugged. "She begged me to accept her, to love and cherish her. I said I would, and we kissed. When we parted, there was a man behind her, tall and angry."

The chief laughed aloud. "Her husband. I have been caught like that too."

"I agree, but he did not say he was. He did not speak at all. He only advanced toward her, scowling. She argued with him, retreating step by step, and at last drew a crooked knife. By then she stood very near the fire, and I saw that her back was melting as ice does, running like water into my fire, which leaped in triumph."

"This is a good story. Go on!"

"They spoke more, and he pushed her into the fire. For a moment nothing happened. I tried to stand, steadying myself with my spear. It was hard because I was so ill. As I stood, my little fire burst into a ball of flame that blinded me and singed my hair. When I could see again, both were gone."

The Medjay chief nodded. "Your face has been burned on one side, I see. Your hair is singed, as you say."

"I thought it was a dream," I told him. "Was it?"

He sighed. "You have been touched by a god."

"I looked in the ashes," I told him, "and found these." I showed him two of her bracelets. "Do you like them? I'll give both to you for a good horse. Not just any horse, a good one."

He returned them to me. "I will show you a wonderful horse to-morrow," he promised, "a horse you may have as my gift, if you can ride him."

I HAVE NOT yet caught the stallion the Medjay chief showed me as the sun rose; but I have come to know the marks of his hooves, and will track him again in the morning. He is bigger than most, and as brown as a chestnut. There is a light in his eyes. If some god were to transform one of the Medjay warriors, he would be as this stallion is, I think.

He looks at me in fear, and I at him in desire. If he were to seek to master me, I would look at him as he does at me, and he at me as I do at him. Or so I believe. What is the life of a horse but slavery? I would treat him well—if I could. As I am, I cannot even treat my-self well.

There is gold in the bag at my belt, but it buys no food here. He crops the fresh green grass. Which of us will tire first?

WHEN I UNROLLED this to read what I had written last night, there was a curved pin of bright gold in it. It melted as I held it in my hand, and was gone. Then I thought the sun had brought a waking dream. It seemed to me that a great lioness paced beside me, and afterward that a tree-tall woman walked there. When I turned to look, there was no one.

Now I write, though there is so little space left. She led me to her temple. There was an antelope there, dead upon her altar, a large one and very fine.

I drank from her spring, cut flesh from the antelope's flank, and cooked it over a fire of brown grass and dried dung. She is Mehit; she sat with me and shared my food. She laughed at me, and her laugh was forgotten gold shaken in a cup. "Can you who caught me not catch a stallion?" She told me that I would never catch him, but that he would catch me.

I RODE TODAY, north because I did not know in which way to go and it seemed best. A lively boy driving cattle said that in the city men would fill my hands with gold for my horse. I told him about the lions, and how my horse Ater had come to me for protection.

"Does that name mean something?" he asked.

"Darkness, gloom, ill luck."

"He's not! He's beautiful!"

"He is," I said, "and I am his ill luck."

The city, the boy said, is on a river island. If my own luck is as bad as Ater's, the ship will have passed it already. But where there is a city there are many men, and one may have the blade the river god returned to me.

I WONDER WHERE I got the bridle I have taken from Ater? Did I write of that here? I tied him by the reins, but a moment ago I set him free. Beasts prowl the night—lions and worse. I would rather he escape me than that he fall to such a beast.

There are horses too bad to be ridden. It may be that there are horses too good to be ridden as well.

For a time I heard him not far off. I no longer do. I sit before my little fire, my own protection from the beasts we both fear, with only the baboon for company. He prompts me to write again and again—to write smaller and smaller. There is little fuel for the fire, and so small a fire cannot be a great protection. The lions roar. I have heard them twice. A madman laughs, not far from my fire.

THE BABOON LEFT while I read. Who was Mehit, who sat at meat with me? Surely she was a friend, and I wish she were here with me. I am alone with the night, and shivering in a wind that will soon be cold.

35

TWO

ATER AND I came to the river. He was no longer afraid, but thought only of mares and of fighting the stallions who held them, of coupling with them, and of protecting them and the foals they would bear. It cannot be right for a man to know every thought of the horse he straddles, yet I knew his.

While I was polishing my shield last night, I remembered a white stallion—the armor I wore, and the lions that roared on either side as I spurred toward my enemy. But most of all the stallion, the swift white stallion of the sun. How fine he was! How strong and beautiful and brave! I did not keep him, and I resolved that I would not keep Ater.

When we reached the river, I dismounted, took away his bridle, and threw it into the water. "You have repaid me for saving you from the lions," I told him. (I had read of it here.) "We're quit, and I will not keep you as a slave. Go in peace."

He watched me with one eye, afraid to believe in freedom.

"Go! Good luck to you!" I slapped his flank. "Find her!"

He trotted for a hundred paces or so before he turned to look back at me. *Are we enemies, Latro?*

"No!" I shouted. "Friends! Friends forever!"

He stared for a moment, again through the left eye, turned, and trotted away.

A boatman who had been watching me said, "You must be mad to free that animal. I'm going to catch it."

"I am." The point of my spear stopped him before he had taken a step. "Mad indeed! My whole family will tell you when you meet them in the Deadland." Leaning toward him I whispered, "I killed them. Killed them all. My wife. Our children. My own parents, her parents, and our children's parents. All dead! Dead! But I've forgotten it." I laughed, not to impress him but because it had struck me that it might be true. "You must row me to the city on an island. Take me this instant! A great fish means to swallow it. The crocodile told me, and I must warn the people."

I untied the painter and got into his boat. "We go. Or I go. Wouldn't this sail better if it were turned over?"

He hurried to jump in with me. "It's mine. My boat. I'd starve without it."

"Make sail," I told him. When he landed me on this island I gave him a coin, which surprised him no end.

I found a cookshop and ate, not because I was hungry but because I knew it had been long since I had eaten, and I felt weak. I ate bread hot from the pan, steaming, strengthening, and greasy, and a big bowl of fish soup that was at least tolerable. In the market I bought a few fresh dates. These left my hands sticky but were as good, I believe, as any food any man has ever put into his mouth.

When I had finished the last and let a starving cur lick my hands, it occurred to me that I might go to a temple, make some small offering, and pray that I again remember as other men do. Then that I might so visit all the temples in the city, telling the priests about Falcata and asking the help of the gods in reclaiming her.

A man I spoke with recommended the Sun Temple, but it is on the mainland. I resolved to visit it when I left, and returned to the quay, eventually walking all around the island. Several people told me that a large foreign ship had passed that way three days before. One said it had docked for a time, pointing to the place. All agreed that there was no such ship in the docks now. When I inquired about a lofty building not far from the water, I was told it was the temple of Isis. I had already passed one such temple on the southern end of the island without entering, and resolved that I would not thus pass this one.

A priest waited at the entrance to collect the offerings of those who had come to petition the goddess. Watching him for a time, I observed that he accepted any offering, no matter how small.

I gave him a silver shekel, and asked the best way of gaining her gracious attention.

"Leave those weapons with me," he said, "I will watch over them and return them when you leave. Prostrate yourself before the goddess, swearing to do anything she may command, make your petition, and listen in silence, waiting for her to speak in your heart."

I thanked him and did as he suggested. The doors of the holiest place were half open, so we might glimpse the goddess within. I prostrated myself. "I am a strong man, O great Isis, well able to work and fight. I have lost my sword Falcata, which I beg you to restore to me. Any order you give me I will forget in a day or less, I know. But I will write it where I will see it again, and obey you without fail. Have I murdered my parents? My wife? Our children? I ask these things because the words came to my lips today, and I cannot remember. Grant, please, that I may remember as others do!"

She motioned to me, and I rose and entered the holiest place.

"I am the daughter of Ra," she told me, "the mother of many kings, the mistress of magic, and the friend of women." Her voice was slow and warm, the voice of a loving woman speaking to a child. Stooping, she laid her hand on my head. "I cannot heal you. Walk toward the north star until you find your sword. Turn your steps then toward the rising sun. I would teach you magic, but you would soon lose all my teaching, for you are but a broken vessel. Receive my blessing."

Her murmured blessing was spoken too quickly for me to understand it, and was perhaps in a tongue I do not have. Yet it filled me with warmth and light.

"Look behind you," she said, "and you will see a big man in a dirty tunic, prostrate on my floor. You must return to him."

I was leaving the holiest place when her voice stopped me. "I found no blood guilt in you," she called after me. "You have murdered no one."

When I reclaimed my spear, my shield, and my "lost temple" club, I spoke of Falcata with the priest. He had never seen such a sword. The swords of this land are long and straight, two-edged. I saw such swords in the market.

Now I sit upon a floating pier to write, wetting my pen in the river.

I WAS A slave once in this temple. The priest Kashta tells me this. "You were our watchman," he said, "and we haven't had such a good watchman since. Directed by the god, we gave you and your wife to a king from the south."

I said that I would make an offering to the god—he is the God of the south—if he would help me remember.

Holy Kashta shook his head. "We were blessed with rich gifts for you. I won't tax that burse you wear. Your means must be slender."

I protested, but he interrupted me. "You served Seth faithfully while you were here. If he will not oblige you for your service, he will not oblige you for a coin. Come in and make your petition."

He let me keep my weapons. When I had offered my prayer, he asked where I would sleep that night.

"I haven't found a place yet," I said, "but there must be those in this city who'll rent a bed to an honest man."

"You will be robbed. Sleep here. We will make a bed for you in the alcove. Six laymen are coming to guard the temple tonight. I'll tell them about you, and suggest they wake you if they need another man."

I write in this temple by the last light of the declining sun.

THIS MORNING I talked to the leader of the men who guarded the temple. "No trouble," he said. "None at all. They know we're here. Did the woman wake you?"

No one had awakened me and I said so.

"She was looking for her husband. In a temple! At night! Drunk, if you ask me, and she must beat that little maid of hers unmercifully. But the thing is, a dog ran in when I opened the door for her. The priests won't like that, so we've got to find him and give him the boot before they get here. Will you help us?"

I said I would, but when we found him, he was hiding under a big table on which royal gifts were displayed. One man crawled under it to lay hold of him, but he came out quickly to beg a rag for his bleeding hand.

"We'll have to kill him," the one who had spoken to me said. "It'll be a mess."

Already, street vendors were crying their wares outside the temple. I told him he knew nothing of dogs, cautioned him to wait, and for one copper got ground meat of who knows what kind rolled in a broad green leaf. By offering it to the dog and speaking kindly to him, I had him in less time than it has taken me to write of it.

My difficulty is that this dog followed me when I left Set's temple, swam after the boat I hired, and followed me again when I left the temple of the sun.

He is with me still. He obeys at times, but will not obey when I order him to leave. Am I to stone a dog who loves me? This afternoon I was able to spear fish enough to feed us both, but what am I to do with a dog?

CAUTUS'S BARKING WOKE me. The women wish me to read this when day returns; but I will write now as the baboon directs, though I know the beautiful one waits for my embrace. There is but a small strip of papyrus left to fill.

"They said you were on the ship, all of them, even Neht-nefret. But you weren't! You weren't! Qanju didn't want us to go, but Mtoto and I stole away the next night and went back to Naqa to find you. I'm your wife, Latro. You're my husband. I've been asking about your sword wherever it was safe to talk to people. I didn't find it, but I'll help you look for it for as long as you want to search. Only . . . Only you must never leave me again."

Tomorrow we two (we four) will go in search of Falcata—the scarred child, Cautus, the beautiful woman, and I.

I think her dishonest, but she is young and willing, and who is not?

[THESE ARE THE final words on the scroll from Lake Nasser.]

GLOSSARY

THE PRINCIPAL PROPER names in the third scroll are identified here. A few whose identity should be obvious have been omitted. I have ventured to translate a few names that the reader is unlikely to translate for himself; all such translations are merely tentative. A few other terms that may pose difficulties are defined.

Aahmes. The leader of the Egyptian soldiers aboard the *Gades.*

Abu. At the time of this scroll, the southernmost city in Egypt.

Achaemenes. The satrap of Egypt. His Persian name was Hakhdmanish "Friend."

Agathocles. "Of Good Fame." A trader from Athens.

Ahura Mazda. In ancient Persia, the god of good.

Alala. Thotmaktef's wife.

Amamu. One of the Egyptian soldiers on the *Gades.*

Ammut. The Eater of the Dead.

Angra Manyu. In ancient Persia, the god of evil.

ankh. A cross with a loop top, the hieroglyph for life. Gods are often shown holding an ankh, their fingers through the loop. The *crux ansata.*

Anubis. The jackal-headed god of death.

Apedemak. The lion-headed war god of Nubia.

Ap-uat. The wolf-headed war god of Egypt, often difficult to distinguish from Anubis in art. (When "Anubis" holds a weapon, Ap-uat is intended.) Also called Wepwawet "Opener of the Way."

Arensnuphis. Called Onuris in Egypt. He was the god of hunting and a protector of travelers.

Asyut. A city roughly midway between the sea and the first cataract.

Ater. The stallion given the narrator by the Medjay.

Azibaal. The first mate of the *Gades.*

Baginu. Probably "Fortunate." The leader of the Persian soldiers aboard the *Gades.*

Beteshu. A demon.

Binti. "Daughter." The girl the narrator inherits when his carelessness results in her father's death. Cheche's daughter.

Bittusilma. "House of Perfection." Seven Lions' queen, a Babylonian.

Black Land. The fertile land of the Nile Valley, Egypt.

Byblos. A Phoenician city, the home port of the *Gades.*

Cautus. "Watchful." A stray dog. This name may be a pun on *canis,* "dog."

Charthi. A wealthy and aristocratic Egyptian, the father of Kames.

Cheche. "Small One." A woman of Nysa who becomes a new wife of the narrator's.

Crimson Men. Phoenicians, from the color of their clothing.

daric. A gold coin of ancient Persia, on which King Darius appeared bow in hand. This coin was vulgarly called an archer.

Dis. The Roman King of the Dead. As lord of the underground realm he was immensely rich, since all unmined metals and gems were his. He symbolized the benevolent aspect of death, as opposed to Orcus, the demon-god of violent death.

Egypt. At the time of the scroll, a province of the Persian Empire. Visualize a flower with one leaf (the Faiyum) and a long, straggling stem. The blossom is the delta, and the stem is the Nile Valley. The stem ends at the first cataract.

Falcata. The narrator's sword. Much used in the ancient world, falcatas varied in size between hunting knives and full-fledged swords. Blades were wide and slightly curved, sharp on the concave side. They may have originated in Iberia.

Field of Reeds. The dwelling-place of the blessed dead. Paradise.

firman. A letter or document entitling the bearer to protection or stated privileges.

Gades. The Phoenician trading vessel that brought the narrator to Egypt.

Great King. We know him as Xerxes. His name was actually Khshayarsha, "King."

Great River. The Nile; it stretches more than four thousand miles from Central Africa to the Mediterranean Sea, is the longest river on earth, and is the only major river to flow north.

Hathor. The goddess of joy, perfumes, cows, and much else, she was one of the kindest and most important Egyptian deities.

Hemuset. The goddess of fate. She was one of several invisible presences who attended the birth of an Egyptian child.

Horus. The hawk-headed pilot of the Sun Boat. He was the son of Osiris and Isis, the god of the day sky and of light, and a brave and chivalrous fighter for good.

House of Life. There is no modern equivalent for this term.

315

Houses of Life were attached to temples. (A Pharaonic palace was a temple as well as a residence.) A House of Life might be a school, a college, a library, a hospital, or a combination of these.

Isis. The most important Egyptian goddess, whose cult soon spread to Nubia. When she was held captive following the murder of her husband, Osiris, Thoth helped her escape. She was the mother of Horus and commanded seven magical scorpions. She was also called Ast and Eset.

Kakia. One of the narrator's Persian soldiers.

Kames. A young Egyptian of good family.

Kashta. A Nubian priest of Set.

Kemet. Literally, "Black"—the Egyptians' name for their country.

Kush. The Nile Valley south of the third cataract and north of the confluence of the White and Blue Niles. The Nubian kings had originally been kings of Kush.

Latro. It seems clear that the narrator bore one name among the Egyptians and another among the Phoenician crew of the *Gades,* while his Persian soldiers and Median commander employed a third. For the most part, he represents all three by "L"; I have used *Latro, Lewqys,* and *Lucius* respectively.

Luhitu. This appears to be the Phoenician name for the narrator's nation or area.

Magi. One of the six Median tribes. Our word *magic* is derived from the name of this tribe.

Medjay. Nomads who roved the eastern and western edges of Kush and Wawat. The Lion People.

Mehit. One of several lion-headed goddesses, she seems to have been the actual lion goddess, as opposed to the better-known Sekhmet, who was fundamentally a war goddess. Note that Mehit was the wife of a hunting god, and that tame lions were used in the hunt.

Mennufer. The city the narrator designates by this name is certainly Memphis, a metropolis south of the delta. It was the capital of Egypt under the Persians.

Meröe. A principal city of southern Nubia (Kush).

Mfalme. That is, "king." Seven Lions.

Miam. A city of Wawat founded by Egyptians.

Mtoto. Probably "Child." The demon-scarred girl who becomes Myt-ser'eu's maidservant.

Muslak. The captain of the *Gades.*

Myt-ser'eu. "Kitten." The singing girl employed by the narrator.

Mzee. Probably "Elder." The man who guided Seven Lions' party.

Nehasyu. The dominant tribe in Nubia, whom the narrator often calls the Crocodile People.

Nasakhma. A young Nubian of royal blood.

Neht-nefret. "Tall Sycamore." The singing girl employed by Muslak.

Nekhen. One of the centers of the cult of Horus.

Nine Bows. Egypt's foreign enemies, a traditional phrase.

Nubia. Egypt's principal rival in Africa. At the time of the scroll, Nubia appears to have extended from the first cataract to the sixth. Earlier, its northern border had been at the third, and its rule had extended south into the valley of the Blue Nile.

Nysa. The original Nysa is said to have been a man killed by Dionysus. Some authorities list ten places in Europe, Asia, and Africa called Nysa. See the Foreword.

Osiris. One of the most important Egyptian gods. He was the god of resurrection and the patron of the dead. Isis was his wife, Set his wicked brother. The popular faith of Egypt hinged upon the cult of Osiris.

Parsa. Persia, or the Persian Empire.

Piy. The supervisor at a Nubian gold mine.

Pre. One of the divisions of the Nile, which split as it flowed through the delta.

Punt. A remote part of Africa, probably the coast of Somalia.

Qanju. A Mede dispatched by Prince Achaemenes to explore the Nile south of Egypt.

Ra. One of the most important Egyptian gods, the god of the sun and commander of the sun boat. Each pharaoh was fathered by Ra. He was also called Re and Phra.

Ra'hotep. "Ra Is Content." An Egyptian physician.

Red God. Set, q.v.

Red Land. The desert east and west of Egypt.

Riverland. Egypt. Our word comes from the Latin name for this country, which was taken from Greek; the Greek word originally designated the Nile, not the nation.

Sabra. The wax woman animated by Sahuset and the narrator.

sagan. The lieutenant of a governor.

Sahuset. A magician of Mennufer.

Sais. A major city of the delta.

satrap. The governor of a province of the Persian Empire.

scarab. A sacred beetle. An amulet in the shape of this beetle; these were used as seals.

Seven Lions. A king of Nysa.

Sesostris. A pharaoh of the Twelfth Dynasty, better known as Senusret.

Set. Osiris's brother, the god of the south and the desert. Also Seth, Sethi, Sit, et cetera.

Sidon. A Phoenician city at the eastern end of the Mediterranean, north of Tyre.

Tepu. The hippopotamus.

Thoth. The god of wisdom, learning, and the moon. He is most often depicted as an ibis-headed man. Also *Thot.*

Thotmaktef. Qanju's Egyptian scribe.

Tin Isles. The Scillys and the Cornish coast.

Unguja. Perhaps "Burned." Seven Lions' chief advisor.

Uraeus. The narrator's slave. The sacred cobra.

Uro. One of the narrator's Egyptian soldiers.

Utundu. "Mischief." Cheche's younger son.

Vayu. One of the narrator's Persian soldiers.

Vinjari. "Roamer." Cheche's older son.

wadi. A dry watercourse.

Wast. The Egyptian Thebes.

Wawat. Northern Nubia. The Nile Valley between the first and third cataracts.

White Wall. The strongest fortress in Egypt.

xu. An evil spirit, a demon. (I have so translated the scroll's *daemonium.*)

Yam. The Nile Valley between the second and third cataracts, once independent.

Yeb. The Persian name for Abu.